Books by Laurien Berenson

A PEDIGREE TO DIE FOR

UNDERDOG

DOG EAT DOG

HAIR OF THE DOG

WATCHDOG

HUSH PUPPY

UNLEASHED

ONCE BITTEN

HOT DOG

BEST IN SHOW

JINGLE BELL BARK

RAINING CATS AND DOGS

CHOW DOWN

HOUNDED TO DEATH

DOGGIE DAY CARE MURDER

GONE WITH THE WOOF

DEATH OF A DOG WHISPERER

hed by Kensington Publishing Corporation

Deat
Dog W

Publi

A Melanie Travis Mystery

Death of a Dog Whisperer

Laurien Berenson

KENSINGTON BOOKS
http://www.kensingtonbooks.com

KENSINGTON BOOKS are published by

Kensington Publishing Corp.
119 West 40th Street
New York, NY 10018

All Kensington titles, imprints, and distributed lines are available at special quantity discounts for bulk purchases for sales promotion, premiums, fund-raising, educational, or institutional use. Special book excerpts or customized printings can also be created to fit specific needs. For details, write or phone the office of the Kensington Special Sales Manager: Attn. Special Sales Department. Kensington Publishing Corp., 119 West 40th Street, New York, NY 10018. Phone: 1-800-221-2647.

Kensington and the K logo Reg. U.S. Pat. & TM Off.

Library of Congress Card Catalogue Number: 2014934277

ISBN-13: 978-0-7582-8455-6
ISBN-10: 0-7582-8455-1
First Kensington Hardcover Edition: September 2014

eISBN-13: 978-0-7582-8457-0
eISBN-10: 0-7582-8457-8
First Kensington Electronic Edition: September 2014

10 9 8 7 6 5 4 3 2 1

Printed in the United States of America

This book is dedicated to all the readers who missed Melanie's adventures and who welcomed her back with open arms. Your support means everything to me.

And to my good friends Dee and Tim. Be careful what you wish for!

Death of a Dog Whisperer

Chapter 1

"Do you believe in ghosts?" asked Bob.

I stared at my ex-husband, eyes widening in surprise. Sadly I was also tempted to laugh. When Bob had asked me over to his house to talk, the last thing I'd expected was a question like that.

On the plus side, that meant that our son, Davey, eleven years old and often on the edge of mayhem, hadn't gotten into any new trouble that I didn't know about. On the minus side . . . ghosts? *Really?*

"I don't know," I said carefully. "I grew up Catholic. So I was raised to believe in things I can't see."

"Not the Holy Ghost." Bob snorted. "You know, regular, garden-variety ghosts. Like Casper."

Casper was a cartoon. So the chances of my believing in his existence were slim. I really hoped I didn't need to point that out.

Before I could come up with a suitable reply—which at this point seemed to be just about anything that didn't involve rolling my eyes—Bob pushed back his chair and stood. We were sitting in his kitchen, a room I was intimately familiar with as my ex-husband's house had formerly belonged to me.

After the small clapboard home had changed hands several years earlier, Bob had started renovating. He'd worked room by room, doing most of the work himself. The faded kitchen wallpaper and worn linoleum that Davey and I had lived with were now gone, replaced by sunny yellow paint and a polished hardwood floor. Even the appliances were new, although I couldn't remember ever seeing Bob do any cooking.

He walked around the table, stepping carefully over Faith, my Standard Poodle, who was snoozing on the floor beside my chair. Bob isn't a dog person, but he likes Faith. Not that he's ever had any choice in the matter.

Love me, love my dog. That's my mantra.

Big, black, and beautiful, Faith embodies all the best attributes of her breed. She's intelligent, empathetic, and has a great sense of humor. She was the first dog I'd ever owned and our connection, swift and all-encompassing, had taken me by surprise. Faith had entered my life and immediately filled a void I hadn't even known existed. She'd stolen my heart and held it still.

The Poodle opened her eyes and followed Bob's progress across the room. I saw her gaze lift and realized that she was looking at Bob's chocolate point Siamese, Bosco. The cat was sitting on top of the refrigerator, gazing down at us mere mortals with an expression of disdain. Feigning similar indifference, Faith sighed softly and closed her eyes again.

"Want something to drink?" asked Bob.

"I'll take a Coke, if you have it. Or green tea?"

It turned out that my ex-husband had both on hand. That was a bad sign. Bob wanted something from me, I just knew it.

He and I had been married for two years and divorced for more than a decade. We were better friends now than we'd ever been, but that didn't make me blind to his faults.

"Ghosts," I said, steering him back on topic. "Why do you ask?"

Bob flicked the cap off his soda and took a long swallow. Then he poured mine into a glass over ice, just the way I like it. Yet another bad sign.

"I think this place is haunted," he said.

Oh man. He was really going to go there.

"You've got to be kidding," I told him.

Bob shrugged disarmingly. He half smiled and quirked a brow. His sandy hair was too long and beginning to curl at the ends. He reached up and brushed it back. Once upon a time I'd fallen in love with that boyish charm.

Back when I was very, very young.

Now on the other side of thirty, I was immune to Bob's artless appeal. And experience had made me more of a skeptic than I'd been in my youth.

"Why not?" he said. "It happens."

"Not here." I shook my head. "Not in my house."

"My house," he corrected gently, retaking his seat.

"But I lived here for ten years. Surely if this place was haunted, I'd have noticed."

"Maybe the ghost is new."

I sputtered a laugh. "I don't think that's the way it works, Bob."

"You see?" he said. "You know these things. I knew I'd come to the right person."

"For what?" I stared at him suspiciously.

This isn't the first time a family member has wanted something from me. I'm working on learning to say no, but unfortunately I'm not nearly as good at it as I ought to be.

"I've been hearing things," said Bob. "Sounds in the middle of the night."

"Ghostly noises?" I asked in a hushed voice. "Woo . . . wooo . . . like that?"

He frowned at my response but didn't back down. "More like creaking and groaning. And maybe a thump or two."

"This is an old house, Bob. It's probably settling. Was the wind blowing when you heard these ghostly noises?"

"I'm not talking about shutters banging. It sounds like the noises are inside the house, and it's pretty creepy."

I'd be creeped out too. If I thought my ex wasn't letting his imagination run away with him.

"So here's the thing," Bob said.

The thing. Somehow, with my family, there was always *a thing*.

"I was thinking you might lend me a guard dog."

I sat up straight in my seat. "A what?"

"You know. A big black dog that could live here for a while and patrol the house at night. I figured you must have a spare." Bob was alluding to the fact that my second husband, Sam, and I have a houseful of Standard Poodles. Six to be exact, including Davey's new puppy, Augie. Bob flicked a hand toward the floor and said brightly, "Maybe that one."

That one? I thought with a grimace. As if Faith was just some random Poodle. Perhaps one that didn't even have a name.

Faith didn't lift her head from her paws, but she did flap her tail up and down on the floor to acknowledge the fact that we were talking about her. It's a sad thing when your dog is paying more attention to details than the other human in the room.

On the other hand, Bob could probably be forgiven for not being able to tell my dogs apart. All six were black Standard Poodles. Faith and Eve, the two that had originally been mine, were mother and daughter. Casey, Tar, and Raven—the three Poodles Sam had brought with him to the marriage—were also related. So they all shared a familial similarity.

Not only that, but Augie the puppy was the only one in show trim. The five adult Poodles were all retired champions, now maintained in practical kennel clips. Each sported a blanket of short dense curls covering her entire body. Faces and feet were shaved and there was a pom-pon on the end of the tail. Even Davey had to sometimes look twice to see who was who.

"That's Faith," I told Bob.

He managed a wounded look. "I know that."

"She's six years old."

Bob peered under the table. "She doesn't look old."

"She's not." I reached down and ruffled my fingers through the big Poodle's topknot. The bond I shared with Faith was deeper than the one I had with most people. It was certainly stronger than my feelings for my ex-husband.

"But she's no youngster either," I added. "There's no way I'm leaving her here with you to hunt ghosts."

I heard Faith blow out a fractured breath from beneath the table. Either she was snoring or she was laughing at Bob. I was betting on the latter.

"Fine," he said quickly. "It doesn't have to be that one. How about the big male? The scary-looking one."

Only Bob, whose idea of wildlife was his kitty Bosco, would think that Tar was scary. The rest of the world knew him for the playful, not-too-bright, cream puff that he really was.

"I'm not lending you a dog," I said firmly. "You don't even know how to take care of one."

"Come on, how hard can it be? Buy a couple cans of food, put water in a bowl on the floor, let the dog outside when it needs to go. Done."

Done indeed.

"I rest my case," I said. Bracing my hands on the edge of the table, I stood up to go. "No way. It's not going to happen."

I was rather proud of that declaration. It sounded strong and definitive. Like I was a woman in charge for once.

"If you say so," Bob said easily, shrugging off my refusal. "But listen, sit down for another minute, would you? I got you over here today to ask you something."

"You just did ask me something," I pointed out. "That wasn't it?"

"Oh heck, no. That was just a spur-of-the-moment idea."

I'd known that Bob was buttering me up for something. I should have realized that sidestepping his first request had been entirely too easy. So much for being in charge. I sank back down into my seat and prepared myself for round two.

"Now what?"

"I met a guy," said Bob.

I looked at him, deadpan. "I'm very happy for you. Is it serious?"

"What? No! Wait a minute . . . what are you talking about?"

"Just kidding," I said with a smirk. "Go on."

"I'm talking about a guy who's a friend of mine," Bob began again. "His name is Nick Walden. I met him a few months ago, through James. You know, from next door?"

That got my attention. During my tenure in the house, I'd lived beside Amber Fine for more than a year. In all that time I had never even seen her husband, much less met him. My friend Alice Brickman and I had even engaged in a running debate about whether or not the man actually existed.

"*You've met James?*" I said.

Bob looked at me like I was daft. "Sure. He's my neighbor. He lives right there."

He was pointing toward the kitchen wall, but I knew what he meant. Just a dozen feet beyond that wall was the Fines' house.

Flower Estates was a subdivision built in the late 1940s to provide affordable housing for returning WWII veterans and their families. The homes were small, snug, and designed for practicality: row upon row of clapboard cottages situated on lots whose dimensions were measured in feet rather than acres.

The neighborhood had sidewalks, quiet roads, and plenty of charm. And compared to the rest of lower Fairfield County, the houses were reasonably affordable. Young families bought starter homes there. Retirees traded down.

The layout of the neighborhood, with houses sitting side by side and back to back, provided homeowners with a welcome feeling of security. But privacy? Not so much. Which made it all the more unusual that I'd never met my neighbor's husband.

"I know Amber," I said. "But I never met James. When I lived here he was always away. Amber said he was traveling all the time for his job. Importing, or maybe exporting. She was a little vague on the subject of what he did. To tell the truth, I wondered if she'd made him up."

"No, James is real, all right. And he's not traveling now. He lost his job when the economy tanked."

"That's too bad."

Bob nodded. "I guess he doesn't have much to do because he's around all the time now. He comes over here to hang out."

"Maybe he's trying to get away from all the cats," I said mildly.

Amber's large, unsupervised, feline population had been a niggling source of annoyance when I had lived beside her. Sam and Davey liked the cats. The Poodles found them interesting. But I was the one left with an itchy nose and claw marks down my drapes.

"Could be. Anyway, he brought Nick by one day. Nick is a dog guy." Bob beamed at me happily. Like he thought the fact that his buddy Nick liked dogs should make my day. "He's *the* dog guy."

"*The* dog guy?" I repeated. "What does that mean? He has dogs? He trains dogs? What?"

"Get this," said Bob. "Nick is a dog whisperer."

Okeydoke. I processed that. And still came up blank.

"And?" I prompted.

"He helps people who have problems with their pets. He has interventions and stuff to fix their issues. Nick talks to dogs and they talk back. It's like a real conversation."

I lifted a brow. Not that I wasn't a believer in such things. I'd been known to hold conversations with my Poodles on more than one occasion. But the words sounded strange coming out of my ex-husband's mouth.

Bear in mind that Bob thought Goofy was the best dog *ever*.

So when it came to judging someone's ability to communicate with canines, Bob had no frame of reference. Nick Walden might be an animal savant. Or he might be a total charlatan. There was no way to know.

"He sounds like an interesting man," I said politely. "Is there a lot of call for dog whispering?"

"More than you'd think. It's a whole business."

"And what does that have to do with me?"

"I thought you might like to meet him."

"Sure, why not?" I agreed. I was always happy to meet a fellow dog lover.

"And I thought you might want to introduce him to Aunt Peg."

And with a deafening thud, the other shoe dropped.

"What?"

"Aunt Peg. You know. She likes dogs too."

Saying that Aunt Peg liked dogs was like saying that Madame Curie had been slightly interested in science. The depth of understatement was staggering.

My aunt was Margaret Turnbull, longtime breeder of the Cedar Crest Standard Poodles, past president of the Poodle Club of America, acclaimed dog show judge, and one of only very few exhibitors in the century-plus history of the Westminster dog show to win the Non-Sporting

Group as a breeder/owner/handler. Her devotion to the Poodle breed was second only to her love of dogs in general.

When it came to the care of the canines she adored, Aunt Peg's standards were impossibly high. She had little patience for those who fell below them and suffered fools not at all. Unfortunately she had long since delegated my ex-husband to the latter category. A recommendation from him about someone she ought to meet sounded like just the sort of thing that would set Aunt Peg's teeth on edge.

"You want *me* to introduce *your* friend to Aunt Peg," I said slowly.

"Right. I'm sure they'll get along great. And then Peg can introduce him to all her friends. An entrée to the dog community from Margaret Turnbull would really help Nick drum up new clients."

A pulse began to pound in my forehead. That was *so* not something I could see happening.

"I'd do it myself," said Bob. "But you know . . . Peg likes you better than she likes me."

I stared at him across the table. I couldn't believe I even had to say this.

"Of course Aunt Peg likes me better. I'm a member of her family. As far as she's concerned, you're just the guy who ran off one day and left me on my own with a ten-month-old baby and a high interest mortgage."

Bob winced. "You had a job."

"A teacher's salary doesn't stretch very far. Especially not for a single parent."

"Yeah, I know. But that all happened more than a decade ago. I was a lot younger and dumber then."

"Well, Aunt Peg has a long memory."

"Which is why *you* ought to be the one to introduce her to Nick."

If nothing else, you had to give the guy points for perseverance. Still I shook my head.

"I've never even met Nick Walden," I said. "The only thing I know about him is that you like him. Which frankly, when it comes to dogs and dog people, doesn't count for much. Not only that, but I doubt that Aunt Peg would be happy to meet someone who apparently thinks it's a good idea to make use of her and her connections."

"That was my idea," Bob corrected. "So don't hold it against Nick. Look, he likes dogs. And you and Peg like dogs. Symbiosis, you know what I mean? It's like fate is pushing you guys together."

"More like you're the one who's pushing us together," I grumbled.

It didn't matter what I said. Bob wasn't listening to me. Along with a host of other good reasons, this was why we weren't married anymore.

"As for you two not knowing each other," Bob said brightly, "I can fix that."

As if on cue, the doorbell rang.

I looked at Bob. He smiled back.

"What did I tell you?" he said. "It's fate. Nick's here."

Oh joy.

Chapter 2

"I hope I'm not interrupting anything," Nick Walden said.

I had remained seated at the table in the kitchen when Bob went to answer the door. The way things had gone thus far, I was half-afraid that if I showed any enthusiasm for Bob's visitor, I might immediately find the two of us strapped into my car and on our way to Aunt Peg's house. So instead, Faith and I waited for him to come to us.

Now as he followed Bob into the room, I got my first look at the dog whisperer. Nick was slightly taller than Bob. He had a wiry build and dark, curly hair. There was a mischievous glint in his deep brown eyes and his smile lit up the room.

Well. If nothing else, he was pleasant to look at.

"Not at all," I said. "I was just getting ready to leave."

I glared at Bob behind Nick's back, then realized that the reason his back was facing me was because Nick had walked around my chair and squatted down to say hello to Faith.

"May I?" he asked before touching her.

"Sure." It was hard not to like Nick's quiet, respectful, approach. "She's very friendly. Her name is Faith."

The Poodle lifted her head and Nick cupped her muzzle

in his palm. Slowly he rubbed his thumb back and forth along her cheek.

"Hello, Faith," he said. "What a good girl you are."

Faith thumped her tail up and down in response. Clearly Nick had merited her approval too.

"See?" Bob crowed. "What did I tell you? Dogs love Nick."

"Faith likes everybody," I said dryly.

"Of course she does." Nick pulled out a chair and sat down. "She's a Poodle. It's a wonderful breed. I see a lot of Toys and Minis when I'm working, not too many Standards. She looks like a good one. Did you ever think about showing her?"

"Faith's a champion," I told him. "And a champion producer."

"I knew she looked like quality," Nick said with a nod. "Where did you get her?"

Out of the corner of my eye, I saw Bob smile. It wasn't hard to figure out where this conversation was being directed.

"My aunt breeds Standard Poodles. Her name is Margaret Turnbull. Maybe you've heard of her?"

"I'm sorry, I haven't," Nick replied. "But I don't really follow the show scene much. People who have that kind of commitment to their dogs usually understand the canine dynamic. They're not likely to have the kinds of problems I get called upon to solve."

That was unexpected. Maybe Bob had been telling the truth and getting Nick together with Aunt Peg really *had* been his idea.

"Tell Melanie about some of your clients," Bob prompted.

"I'd really rather not," Nick said affably. "It wouldn't be fair. Just because someone's having a problem handling their dog doesn't mean that they're not entitled to privacy."

I'd been prepared to find Nick Walden pushy and irritating. Instead he was turning out to be one surprise after another. Maybe I wasn't in as big a hurry to leave as I had thought.

"So listen," said Nick, turning from me to Bob. "Here's why I came. You need a dog."

My ex-husband's expression froze. In the space of an instant, our roles reversed. He went from thinking that he was the one managing the meeting to feeling just as I had a few minutes earlier: like he was being set up. The irony was delicious. I folded my arms over my chest and sat back to watch.

"No," Bob said quickly. "I don't think so."

"Really, you do. You'd be great with a dog."

I had rather serious doubts on that score but I wasn't about to intervene. I was having too much fun watching my ex squirm.

"I already have a cat. And I did have a pony once . . ." Bob stopped and shook his head. "That didn't work out."

"Dogs and cats do just fine together as long as you get them started the right way," said Nick. "There's a puppy at the shelter that really needs a home. Ten weeks old, part Lab, maybe part Chow? He's cute, he's smart, a little golden ball of fluff. He'd be perfect for you."

"In what way?" Bob's voice had a strangled quality. His eyes darted around the room. He looked like he was thinking about making a run for it.

If so, I thought snidely, it wouldn't be the first time.

Nick's response was interesting. He shifted slightly in his chair and angled his body away, treating Bob the way he would have treated an agitated dog—by giving him some extra space. Breathing room, so to speak.

"The truth is," Nick admitted, "that you'd be perfect for him. The little guy needs a home. He's a great puppy and I'd love to see him end up in the right situation. So I'm talking to everyone I know to see if I can make that happen."

"Funny thing about that," I said. "Before you got here, Bob was just asking if he could borrow a dog from me."

"Really?" Nick was interested. "Do you have extras?"

"Not extras, just multiples."

"Eight," said Bob, taking a shot in the dark.

"Six," I corrected. "Blended family."

"And everyone gets along?"

"They're Standard Poodles." Enough said.

"Right," Nick agreed. He shifted back to Bob. "So then you *do* want a dog."

"Not a puppy," Bob said firmly. "An adult dog that already knows stuff. I was looking for something temporary. A dog that could live here for a little while and then go home again."

"That seems like an odd request," Nick mused.

He was probably hoping for enlightenment. But if Bob wasn't going to bring up his ghost problem, I certainly wasn't about to either. My relatives may have their crazy moments, but they're family. I didn't see any reason to advertise the insanity to outsiders.

"Yeah, well, Melanie already talked me out of it."

"That's what ex-wives are for," I said.

"To remind us that we're usually wrong," Bob translated for Nick in case he'd missed the point.

"I wouldn't know," Nick replied. "I've never been married."

"He's having too good a time being single," Bob said to me. "Most of Nick's clients are rich, bored, Fairfield County matrons. If you know what I mean."

Only an idiot wouldn't have grasped Bob's meaning. All that was missing from his arch delivery were a couple of broad winks and a lecherous thumbs-up. I had no desire to take the bait, however, and Nick was clearly disinterested in the topic as well.

Instead he stood up and held out his hand. "I guess I'd better be going then. Nice to meet you, Melanie. Bob, think about that puppy. I'd like to get him placed as soon as possible."

This time, Bob and I both walked to the door. Faith came along too. Nick patted the Poodle's head and said good-bye to her too before he left.

"Nice guy," I said as Nick drove away.

"I told you so. So will you introduce him to Aunt Peg?"

Half an hour earlier I'd have been shocked to hear my reply, but now I found myself nodding. "Sure. Aunt Peg will like him. Probably better than she likes you." I thought for a few seconds, then added, "Probably even better than she likes me."

Nick was Aunt Peg's very favorite kind of human, a true dog person—someone whose instinctive response was to treat canines as fellow sentient beings whose feelings and opinions were as worthy of consideration as his own. I was betting that Aunt Peg and Nick Walden would attract like a pair of magnets. They'd sync on sight and get along like crazy.

My own relationship with my aunt is a constantly shifting work in progress. Most days, it consists of equal parts adulation and exasperation, with a small dose of healthy terror thrown in. Unfortunately I often fail to live up to her lofty expectations.

There are few enough opportunities in my life to score brownie points with Aunt Peg. I wasn't about to pass this one up.

"Whatever works," said Bob.

The drive home took less than ten minutes. Bob and I both live in North Stamford, a city in southwest Connecticut. Like its neighbors in Fairfield County, Stamford once served primarily as a bedroom community for New York. The city has grown exponentially in the last several decades, however, and now its thriving business district serves as a corporate destination all its own.

Stamford's residential areas are comprised of an assortment of varied neighborhoods ranging from small villages, to upscale country cottages, to the sheltered coastal enclave of Shippan Point. Sam's and my house is located north of the Merritt Parkway, an area that has so far been spared the rush of development that characterizes much of the southern portion of the town. It's a great place to raise a family.

Sam and I have been married for three years. The blending of our two households, both humane and canine, had necessitated a move to a more spacious residence. Long story short, that was how Bob had ended up in Davey's and my old house and why my family now occupied the lovely Colonial my ex-husband had purchased as an investment several years earlier.

The house was of classic New England design, painted cream with black shutters, and situated on a wooded two-acre lot. Its backyard, perimeter securely fenced, afforded us plenty of room to in which to entertain two growing boys and six large dogs. Best of all, for most of the year that big yard enabled us to channel much of the mayhem to outside the house. Speaking as the person most likely to be picking things up off the floor, I appreciated that enormously.

Connecticut is at its best in the spring. By mid-June, the sky is a clear, cerulean blue and the season's bright foliage is in full bloom. Days are warm, but not yet hot. The air is redolent with the aroma of new blossoms and freshly mowed grass. Faith and I made the drive between the two houses with the car windows open so we could enjoy the warm, fragrant, breeze. The Poodle was riding shotgun and when I made the turn onto our street, she stood up and began to wag her tail.

Sam was outside in the driveway with Kevin, our two-and-a-half–year-old son. Father and son—blond-haired, blue-eyed, mirror images of one another—were engaged in a rollicking game of peewee basketball. The soft rubber basket was affixed to a plastic stand that barely reached Sam's waist. The ball was small enough to fit snugly in a toddler's hand. Every score was a slam dunk. With the windows open, I could hear Kevin's shrieks of laughter before the Volvo had even coasted to a stop.

In the last six months, Kevin had morphed from a baby into his own small person. Walking now, and talking when it suited him, he was a bundle of boundless energy and contradiction. When something interesting caught his eye, the only gear he had was full speed ahead. Conversely when something annoyed him, he had no compunction about announcing his dissatisfaction to the world.

Our other son, Davey, was nowhere in sight. School had let out for the year only a few days earlier and having just finished sixth grade, Davey was still giddy with the prospect of nearly three months of freedom. In a few weeks he would start soccer camp, but other than that we'd kept his organized activities to a minimum so that he could spend time with Kevin and his new puppy, Augie. Which was why I was surprised not to see him outside playing along.

Then Faith gave a small woof. I turned to see what had caught her attention and realized that a maroon minivan was parked on the side of the house near the garage. I opened the car door and Faith scrambled past me. She hopped out and ran to check out the van.

"Peg's here," said Sam.

He paused the game long enough to stride across the driveway and give me a quick hug. Kevin trotted along behind and got a hug too. Davey's old enough to object to our displays of affection but Kevin doesn't mind a bit.

"Aunt Peg!" he cried, just in case I'd missed the news the first time.

"So I see," I said.

I took the ball from Sam and bounced it gently back to Kevin. The toddler's hands came up and flailed in the air.

He almost caught the pass but at the last second the rubber ball slipped through his fingers. It ricocheted off his foot and rolled away. Kevin spun around and gave chase.

"Is something the matter?" I asked Sam, watching as Kevin caught up with the ball. He picked it up and carried it back to the basket. Dribbling is a skill he has yet to attempt.

"No, everything's fine. Why do you ask?"

"Because Aunt Peg always seems to show up when there's a problem." I paused and considered. "Or maybe she brings the problems with her."

Sometimes it's hard to tell about these things.

"Not this time," said Sam. "She said she just dropped by to give Davey a handling lesson with Augie. You know, for the Rhinebeck show?"

That explained why my older son was missing.

"Did Davey *want* a handling lesson?" I asked.

Sam grinned. "Let's just say he's acquiescing gracefully. The two of them are in the backyard."

I called Faith over and Sam picked up Kevin. The four of us headed around the side of the house to see how Davey and Aunt Peg were doing.

Augie was a relatively new addition to our pack of Poodles. Though sired by Sam's stud dog, Tar, Augie had been bred and initially owned by friends of ours who had gotten divorced over the winter. When their marriage broke apart, Augie became available.

It had been Sam's idea that Augie should be Davey's dog and I had concurred wholeheartedly. Despite having spent much of his childhood surrounded by Poodles, Davey had never had a dog of his very own. He was old enough now to handle the responsibility of caring for a pet—even one that required some rather intensive grooming in addition to the usual duties.

At eleven months of age, Augie was in full show trim.

Since he was technically still a puppy, that meant that his entire body was covered by a plush coat of dense black hair. The hair was longest on his head, his ears, and the back of his neck. The shaping on his body and legs provided a more tapered look, and there was a jaunty pompon on the end of his tail.

It had been a condition of Augie's purchase that his championship be completed and Sam and Davey were working on the process together. So far, with Sam showing and Davey cheering from the sidelines, Augie had compiled six of the fifteen points he would need to finish his championship. The upcoming Rhinebeck show was to be Davey's first foray into the ring since he'd taken a brief fling at Junior Showmanship two years earlier.

With an event like that in the offing, I should have guessed that Aunt Peg wouldn't be able to leave well enough alone.

"She does remember that she drilled him pretty thoroughly when he first tried it, doesn't she?" I asked as we walked through the gate.

"I imagine so," Sam said under his breath.

Out in the middle of the yard, I saw Davey standing with Augie beside him. His fingers cupped the puppy's muzzle, a slender show leash was balled up in his hand. Aunt Peg appeared to be lecturing the two of them.

She was good at that.

"And that maybe that's why he stopped competing in the first place?" I added.

Sam nodded. "I believe I mentioned that to her earlier."

"It doesn't seem to have made an impression," I grumbled.

The other Poodles must have been locked inside the house because no one came running to greet us. Augie, stacked in the stance that would be required for examination in the ring, was the first to sense our presence. His head whipped around and his body began to wiggle. Uncoiling like a spring, he gave a four-footed leap in the air. Quite the athlete, that puppy.

Davey started to laugh, while Aunt Peg glowered at the interruption. My lovely child, the only person I knew who wasn't even slightly intimidated by his imposing aunt, slipped the collar off over Augie's head and turned the puppy loose.

Immediately Augie darted in our direction. Faith left my side and began to run. The two Poodles met in the middle between us, feinting and bobbing, and dancing around each other happily.

"In the show ring, behavior like that would have the makings of a disaster," Aunt Peg said sternly.

She stands nearly six feet tall and is not above using her height advantage to glare down her nose at me or anyone else she finds lacking. Now in her mid-sixties, Peg has been a fixture in the dog show world since before I was born. The sheer breadth of her experience was as daunting as it was hard to live up to.

"Luckily for us, we're only in the backyard," I said cheerfully. "That will look totally different on Saturday."

I slipped Davey a wink. He checked to see whether his aunt was watching, then returned the gesture in kind.

My older son had shot up three inches over the winter and the growth spurt was playing havoc with his coordination so I was happy to cut him some slack. Davey would be twelve in three months and his body was already beginning losing its youthful roundness, reshaping itself along leaner, more adolescent lines. Just as Kevin resembled his father, Davey had Bob's brown eyes and sandy hair. He shared Bob's thoughtful demeanor as well, tempered by an innate sense of kindness that I liked to think he'd gotten from me.

"It will only look better this weekend if we practice now," Aunt Peg warned with a frown.

She retrieved the crumpled leash from Davey's hand and snapped her fingers at Augie. At once the puppy stopped playing and ran back to her side. Aunt Peg has that effect on humans and canines alike.

"Or," said Sam before she could slip the collar back into place, "I could light the grill and we could cook up some burgers and corn. You'll join us for dinner, won't you, Peg?"

"I suppose I might—"

"Great!" Walking past her, he skimmed the leash out of her hands and kept going. "Davey, come and help me in the kitchen."

By the time I reached the deck, Sam had opened the back door. The rest of the Poodles came spilling out into the yard. Lesson time was officially over.

"I owe you one," I told him.

"You know it," Sam agreed.

Chapter 3

Over dinner I told Aunt Peg about Nick Walden.

"He's a friend of Bob's?" She arched one brow, signaling her disapproval. "And I would need to make this young man's acquaintance *why?*"

"Because you'll like him anyway."

"I wouldn't be so sure of that." Peg sniffed.

"Where did Bob meet him?" Sam asked, trying to be helpful.

"His neighbor, James, introduced them."

"James Fine?" Sam swiveled around and stared.

"Precisely."

I wasn't surprised that Sam would be interested. Like me, he had never met Amber's husband. Unlike me, he had tended to treat our former neighbor with an attitude of bemused forbearance. And no wonder.

Amber Fine was a pert blonde with a killer body and a penchant for running outside in the morning to pick her newspaper wearing little more than a diaphanous negligee. She had a houseful of cats and an irrational fear of dogs that was most likely to manifest itself when there happened to be a big, strong, man in the vicinity into whose protective arms she could flee. Like for example, my husband.

"So the ever elusive James has finally shown up," said Sam.

"Not only shown up. He's apparently around all the time now. He lost his job."

"I've met James," Davey piped up. He had been helping Kevin with his mini-burger, and slipping Eve bits of food under the table when he thought I wouldn't notice. Now we all stopped and looked at him.

"You have?" said Sam.

"Sure. James stops by Dad's house sometimes when I'm there. He walks in the back door, opens up the fridge, and gets himself a beer. Then he just kind of hangs around."

"How very unusual," said Aunt Peg. She picked up her ear of corn and nibbled a dainty row along its length.

"What's he like?" I asked Davey. "Aside from his obvious lack of manners."

"Dunno." Davey shrugged. My disdain for James's etiquette was lost on him. "Just a guy. He's not cool like Amber."

In Davey's eyes Amber qualified for cool status because she had seven cats, HBO, and a tendency to dole out candy like every day was Halloween. Considering the criteria, a little less cool would have suited me just fine.

"So what's the matter with this James character?" Aunt Peg asked. "Why have we never met him before? Was he missing? Was he in jail?"

"When we lived next door to the Fines, he was always away traveling," I explained. "Apparently he had a job that kept him constantly on the move. And now he doesn't."

"Perhaps he was detained somewhere," Peg said with interest. There's nothing she likes more than a puzzle to solve.

"Could be," I said with a shrug. It was time to get the conversation back on track. "But what's important here is what Nick does."

"And what would that be, pray tell?"

"He's a dog whisperer."

Sam laughed out loud. Quickly he lifted his napkin and covered his mouth. "Sorry about that," he muttered.

"Don't be," I said. "That was my first reaction too. But he turned out to be an interesting guy."

"Whispering is overrated," Aunt Peg said firmly. "What dogs really need is a sympathetic owner and quality training time."

"I only met Nick briefly," I said, "but I'm pretty sure that he would agree with you. Just watching the way he related to Faith impressed me. I think there's a lot more to him than the pop-psychology label might indicate."

"If Faith liked him, I suppose I might reconsider," Peg mused.

Abruptly I jumped in my seat. Sam had kicked me under the table. He knew I was about to say something we'd both regret. But seriously? My opinion of the man was open to question, but Faith's sealed the deal?

"Bob wants you to meet Nick," I said. "He asked me to arrange an introduction."

"He thinks I'll take him under my wing," Peg said shrewdly.

"Your approval would mean a lot," Sam pointed out. "And if I know Bob, he's thinking about the bottom line."

My ex was an accountant. He was always running numbers in his head.

I nodded. "Bob thinks your support will attract new customers to Nick's business."

"For once, your ex-husband is right." False modesty had never been one of Aunt Peg's faults. "But let's not get ahead of ourselves. I haven't even met the man yet."

"I'll see if Bob can bring him to the dog show this weekend," I said. "That way the two of you can meet on neutral ground. If you like Nick, you can spend some time with him. If not, you can simply tell him you're busy and walk away."

"Tell him I'm busy?" Peg said archly. "I plan to *be* busy."

"Really?" Sam managed an innocent look. "Doing what?"

"This is Davey's first dog show in two years! I'm sure he'll need help grooming Augie and preparing for the ring. Not to mention handicapping the competition."

Davey was still occupied with Kevin, but I heard him suck in a breath. Grateful as I had always been for Aunt Peg's assistance when I was showing my own dogs, it was time to tamp down her ambitions on my son's behalf before they got wildly out of hand.

My initial experiences as a dog show exhibitor had been those of a wide-eyed neophyte confronted by an alien, and often capricious, world. With much to learn, I'd willingly absorbed every nugget of knowledge and advice that Aunt Peg had provided. From wrapping ears and setting topknots, to scissoring just the right lines, she had taught me everything I knew about showing a Standard Poodle.

But that education had come at a cost. Acquiring the skills necessary to present a Poodle well enough to compete with the pros was a rare and difficult achievement. The fact that Aunt Peg had been doing so for many years and that such expertise was now second nature to her, didn't make her the most sympathetic of teachers.

It was one thing for me to choose to immolate myself on Aunt Peg's rather steep learning curve. It was quite another for me to allow Davey to do the same. Besides, hadn't we already been here once before?

But before I had a chance to argue, Sam had already stepped in smoothly. "You don't need to worry about a thing, Peg. Between us, Davey and I will have things well in hand. Your only job will be to stake out a good place at ringside to sit down and watch."

Aunt Peg looked around the table, gazing at each of us in turn. "If you're quite sure . . ." she said dubiously.

"We are," Sam replied. Beside him, Davey nodded.

"This isn't Augie's first show. And Davey knows his way around the ring. The two of them will have a great time together."

"And that's what it's all about," I said firmly.

Kevin, who had been largely ignored by the adults at the table for at least five minutes, began to squirm in his seat. "Get down," he demanded.

Belatedly paying attention, I was pleased to see that his plate was nearly empty. How much food had ended up in Kevin's mouth, and how much might have gone to the Poodles lying innocently on the floor beneath his chair, was probably open for debate. At least he only had one smear of ketchup across his shirt.

"Come on, kiddo," I said. "You're with me." I plucked the toddler out of his booster seat and balanced him on my hip. "We have ice cream for dessert. Want to help me dish it out?"

"Ice cream," cried Kevin. "Yay!"

I couldn't have said it better myself.

Saturday's dog show, sponsored by the Hudson Valley Kennel Club was held at a county fairground near Rhinebeck, New York. Not only was the location spacious and easy to navigate, it was only an hour's drive from home—a perk that any dog show exhibitor knows better than to take for granted.

Even better, the weather chose to cooperate beautifully. The morning was cool, but with a promise of afternoon warmth. A light breeze ruffled the tent's raveled flap as Sam pulled the SUV up beside the grooming area and we began to unload our gear.

It came as no surprise to any of us that Aunt Peg was already there. With Standard Poodles scheduled to be judged at noon, Sam and I had decided on a midmorning arrival. We'd calculated that would give us plenty of time to groom

Augie and let Davey become comfortable with his surroundings, but not so much that the two youngsters would begin to grow bored and lose interest in the whole idea.

Aunt Peg had probably gotten there shortly after dawn. By the time we arrived, she was holding court under the handlers' tent. In the grooming area, exhibitors tend to group together by breed. Half the fun of going to a dog show is catching up with friends and sharing all the latest gossip. Win or lose, the time spent under the handlers' tent is often the best part of the day.

Aunt Peg had saved us room to set up in the middle of a sea of Poodles. Sam and I placed the grooming table and Augie's wire crate side by side. The wooden grooming box—holding everything from brushes and combs to tiny colored rubber bands and hairspray—went on top of the crate for easy access. Space was at a premium so I shoved Kevin's diaper bag under the grooming table and wedged a small cooler containing snacks for the boys under a table from the setup next door.

"Oh excellent, goodies!"

Terry Denunzio, assistant to top Poodle handler Crawford Langley and one of my best friends, leaned around the Mini he was line brushing on top of that table, and aimed a pair of air kisses in my direction. His hair—currently golden blond and styled in waves—was impeccably coiffed. His skin was smoother than my own. Sadly his outfit was more stylish as well. In my own defense, I try not to make comparisons when Terry's around, but sometimes it just happens.

"It's about time you people arrived!" he trilled.

"I believe that's supposed to be my line," said Aunt Peg. "*Where* have you been?"

"Sleeping," I told her. "Then eating breakfast, then packing the car, then driving."

"But we're here now," Sam said cheerfully. "Morning,

Peg." He sketched a wave in her direction, left me with puppy and children, and went to park the car.

I put Kevin down for a minute so that I could hoist Augie up onto the rubber matted grooming table. The puppy knew the drill. When I lifted his front paws and placed them on the table's edge, he leapt up in the air then landed lightly on the rubber surface.

Kevin, meanwhile, ran across the aisle and wrapped his chubby arms around Aunt Peg's knees. "Pick up!"

Peg gazed downward uncertainly. Dogs were her specialty. Children, not so much.

"Go ahead," I invited. "Make yourself useful."

Behind me, Terry snorted under his breath. Useful people were Aunt Peg's favorite kind. Over the years, we had both been the object of similar commands at her behest.

While she considered that, I began to unpack the grooming box. One by one, I laid out the tools of the trade on top of the table. Several seconds passed.

Finally Aunt Peg bent down and looked Kevin in the eye. "I will pick you up, young man," she said. "But only if you promise not to wiggle."

"Wiggle," Kevin agreed happily. He held up his arms.

"Just pretend he's a puppy and hold him firmly," I told her. "Trust me, it's easier than you think."

Ready to begin brushing, Davey looped his arms around Augie's legs and gently laid the puppy down on his left side. The right side—the one that faced away from the judge while the dog was in the ring—was always worked on first since it would inevitably be flattened while the show side was attended to. Davey picked up a pin brush and spray bottle of water and began to carefully work his way through Augie's thick coat. Later he would need help setting the puppy's topknot, doing the final scissoring, and spraying up Augie's neck hair, but Sam and I were both determined that he should do as much of the prep work as possible on his own.

"Good morning, all!" Crawford Langley came striding back into his setup.

Tall, tan, and Whippet-thin, he moved with the assurance of a man who was at the very top of his game. Like Aunt Peg, Crawford had been in dogs for decades, and even on his bad days, he was a force to be reckoned with. Having come from the ring, the handler had a Silky Terrier tucked snugly beneath his arm, and a purple and gold Best of Breed ribbon clutched in his hand.

Crawford paused to glance down at Augie, then addressed himself to Davey. "I see you've brought the tough competition today. I'll be showing against you in the Puppy class. I'm going to have to be on my toes."

Davey beamed beneath the handler's regard. "I'll do my best to beat you," he said seriously.

"And you may well succeed." Crawford laughed. "How many points does that puppy have now?"

"Six," Davey told him. "But no majors."

In order to complete its championship, a dog must earn a total of fifteen points. The number of points awarded at each show is determined by the size of the entry. Included within the fifteen points, a dog must accrue at least two major wins—awards of three or more points, indicating that he has defeated a significant number of dogs on the day.

So far, Augie had amassed only "singles." But today, with more than forty Standard Poodles entered in the various classes, the competition would be topnotch. Presiding over the Poodle ring was Vivian Hadley, a popular judge admired by professionals and owner-handlers alike. She had drawn major entries in dogs and bitches both.

In an entry that size there was every possibility that Davey and Augie would be in over their heads. But Sam and I had both exhibited under Mrs. Hadley in the past.

She was known to have a gentle touch on a puppy and to treat all of her exhibitors with kindness. While it was unlikely that Augie would take home any points, he and Davey were almost assured of having a good experience in the show ring.

"Don't you worry about that," Crawford said to Davey. "That puppy's only going to get better as he matures. There'll be plenty of time for you to look for majors when he's an adult."

Davey nodded. He'd heard much the same thing from Sam and me.

Crawford removed the Silky's leash, opened a wooden crate in the middle of his stacks, and slipped the small dog inside. As soon as his hands were free, Terry handed him a Pomeranian that was ready to go.

Deftly the assistant slid the Silky's numbered armband out from beneath the rubber band looped at the top of Crawford's arm, and replaced it with the Pom's number. Then the handler spun around and headed back to the ring. Judging by the size of his setup, Crawford had brought a full complement of dogs to the show. He and Terry would be running all day just to keep up.

"Look who I found on my way back from the parking lot," said Sam. He was threading his way toward us through the packed tent. Following along behind were Bob and Nick Walden.

"Dad, you came!" Davey cried happily.

"Of course I came," Bob replied. "Your first show with your puppy? You didn't think I'd miss that, did you?"

He reached over to give Augie a careless pat, his hand heading straight for the hair that Davey had been working on for the last ten minutes. Without missing a beat, Davey intercepted his father's hand before it could make contact and guided it gently away.

"You can play with Augie afterward," he told Bob. "But right now, he and I have to get ready."

I bit back a smile. Aunt Peg harrumphed her approval. Only Bob was happily oblivious.

He ushered Nick forward and introductions were made. I stood back and watched with interest as Aunt Peg and Nick Walden sized each other up. I was guessing it wouldn't be long before the two of them were trading war stories.

Terry sidled up behind me. "Who's the hunk?" he whispered in my ear.

Terry is the gayest man I know. He cuts my hair, he critiques my clothes, and even though he and Crawford have been in a committed relationship for years, he's not above keeping tabs on any new talent that wanders into his vicinity.

"Nick's a dog whisperer," I told him. "He fixes peoples' problem dogs."

"Yeah, right. Peg will cut him off at the knees," Terry predicted.

"No, she'll be charmed. Just watch."

"Five bucks says you're wrong."

"You're on," I said.

Chapter 4

I won the bet. It didn't even take five minutes.

In less than half that amount of time, Nick and Aunt Peg were already chatting like old friends. Terry sighed and conceded defeat. He dug in his pocket and pulled out a crumpled five-dollar bill.

"Keep it," I said. "The thrill of victory is compensation enough."

Terry stuck out his tongue and went back to work.

Sam took over helping Davey so I walked across the setup to join Nick and Aunt Peg. As soon as I approached she extended her arms, offering my child back to me. Kevin dangled between us with a goofy grin on his face. I lifted the toddler out of her hands and put him down in the grass.

"If you were tired of holding him, you could have done that," I told her.

Aunt Peg frowned. "How was I supposed to know? He's not wearing a leash. What if he wandered off?"

I grabbed a pair of Matchbox cars out of the diaper bag and handed them to Kevin. He immediately sat down and turned the ground beside him into an impromptu roadway.

"He won't," I said. "See? It's like magic."

"I take it he's yours?" asked Nick.

"They both are." I nodded toward Davey too.

"And the Standard Poodle?"

"That's Augie. He belongs to Davey. But in a roundabout way, he comes from Peg's breeding. Which is also partly why we ended up with him."

"In order for that to truly make sense," Nick said, shaking his head, "I think I'm going to require further explanation."

"Several years ago I bred a litter of puppies, intending to keep a bitch," Aunt Peg told him. "But there was a male in the group that was an absolute standout. Even though he wasn't what I wanted, I couldn't take my eyes off him. I knew he had to go to just the right person."

"Fortunately," I said, taking up the story, "Sam saw the puppy and fell in love with him."

"And you and Sam were married then?" asked Nick.

"No, we were dating . . . sort of."

"Sort of?"

"Let's just say, we had our ups and downs."

Sam, who was listening in, leaned over and said to Nick, "Melanie had her ups and downs. I was a model of consistency."

"Except for when he got back together with his ex-wife," I muttered.

"I did *not* get back together with Sheila."

"She thought you had. And so did everybody else. You were the only person who didn't see what was going on."

"Aren't you glad you asked?" said Terry.

Everyone in the vicinity was listening now. Pretty soon, exhibitors from nearby setups were going to be weighing in with opinions.

"Ask me again in five minutes," said Nick. "I want to hear how this turns out. Then what happened?"

"I'll skip ahead," I told him. "So Tar grew up to be a really handsome Poodle."

"No surprise there," Aunt Peg interjected.

"With Sam handling, he won twenty-five groups and eight Best in Shows. Then he retired to stud."

"At the rate this story is going," Terry said, "Davey will be in the ring before you're finished."

"Do you think you can do better?" I asked.

"Of course." Terry fluttered his lashes. "I can *always* do better."

The sad thing was, he was probably right.

Terry elbowed me aside. He pointed to the puppy with a flourish. "Peg is Tar's breeder. Tar is Augie's sire. Augie's breeders got divorced. Davey needed a puppy. He ended up with custody. And six months later, here we all are. Now seriously? Was that so hard?"

"Apparently not," Bob said with a laugh. "Nick, I hope you were paying attention. There will be a quiz later."

"Bring it on," Nick said. "I'm pretty sure I caught most of that."

"Good," said Terry. "Because I have scissoring to do."

Davey had turned Augie over and was now using a slicker brush on the puppy's legs. Next door at Crawford's setup, four Standard Poodles were out on their tables in varying stages of ring-readiness. The clock was counting down. Terry stood up the Poodle nearest him and began to shape its back bracelets.

"Now that we have Melanie's life sorted out," Aunt Peg said to Nick, "tell me about your business."

"I'd be happy to," Nick replied.

"That's my cue to hit up the concession stand," said Bob. Unlike the rest of us, he hadn't been to enough dog shows to realize how vile the food offerings were likely to be. "Anyone want to join me?"

We all shook out heads, and Bob headed out.

"Ring three at noon!" I called after him.

He held his thumb up in the air and kept walking.

"Mostly I get calls from families who purchased a cute puppy without ever stopping to think about how much time and effort would be involved in raising it to become a solid, upstanding citizen," Nick said. "Some of the dogs I see never even got housebroken. Others might have nipped a child and been banished outside, chained to a tree. Some are running loose around their neighborhoods, creating havoc.

"By the time they get around to calling me, dog owners are usually feeling pretty desperate. Their husbands and sometimes their neighbors are complaining. There may have even been a run-in with Animal Control. Their dogs are driving them crazy."

"So the majority of your clients are women?" I asked.

Nick nodded. "It almost always seems to work out that way. Their husbands go off to work, their kids are in school. They're the ones left to handle the problem. A lot of these women have time on their hands. Maybe they're a little bored. So they call me to come and train their dog and maybe provide a little entertainment at the same time."

"And *do* you provide entertainment?" Aunt Peg inquired archly.

"Not in the way you're implying." Nick laughed. "Not that it hasn't been offered. But I'm trying to build a business and I want to be taken seriously. Which is already hard enough when your title is The Dog Whisperer."

Davey had finished brushing Augie's show side. Now he stepped back as Sam encouraged the puppy to get to his feet and give a hearty shake. Augie's hair straightened and fluffed, then settled into place. Davey raised his hand and propped it under the puppy's muzzle, supporting his head in the position it would assume in the show ring. Sam picked up a pair of long Japanese scissors and went to work. The three of them made a great team.

"What's your success rate?" asked Aunt Peg. She'd never been one to beat around the bush.

"So far, no complaints. Ever since I was a little kid, I've always had a connection with dogs. I just understand what they're thinking. I have yet to meet a dog I didn't click with on one level or another."

Warming to his subject, Nick's eyes lit with enthusiasm. "Even the tough guys respond when they realize that you're trying to help them. And once I went into business I figured out pretty quickly that the dogs are the easy part. It's people who are hard. I'll let you in on a secret. Most times, I'm not really training the dogs. I'm training their owners."

Aunt Peg was nodding her head as Nick spoke. I wasn't surprised. Anyone could see that the two of them were on the same wavelength.

"Bob seems to think I might be useful to you," she said.

"He told me that as well," Nick replied. "Bob said you know just about everyone in the dog world."

"It's one of the very few perks of being old. If you've lived an interesting life, eventually you've run across everybody that matters."

"Let me tell you why I need your help," Nick said earnestly. "I know I can do more than I'm doing now. There are a lot of dogs out there whose lives could be improved immeasurably if only their owners had the right tools to turn things around. And I'm the guy who can make that happen. Truthfully? The clients I have now are great. But ultimately, I want to be more than a distraction for bored housewives."

"It sounds like a very worthwhile goal," Aunt Peg agreed. "Perhaps you'd like to stop by my house one day this week so that we can sit down and continue our discussion further?"

"I'd be happy to," said Nick. "It's been a pleasure meeting you. Thanks for taking the time to talk to me."

"I've enjoyed it," Aunt Peg said honestly.

"He seemed like a nice guy," Sam commented, when Nick had left the tent.

"He did," Peg agreed. "Of course, before I decide whether or not I want to help him, I'll need to see him actually interact with a dog. Or five, as the case may be."

So the dog whisperer was going to meet the Cedar Crest Poodles en masse. That should prove interesting. I wondered if I ought to try to wrangle an invitation for the occasion.

"How's everything coming? Just about ready?" Crawford came hurrying back to the setup.

His Standard Poodles' topknots were in and all four dogs had been scissored. When he wasn't busy gossiping, Terry was a whiz at prep. Now he was just beginning to spray up. Crawford stashed the Pom in a crate, tossed its red ribbon into the tack box, picked up a can of spray, and went to work too. It was almost show time.

Augie, meanwhile, was lying upright on his table. Davey, who had been practicing at home, was about to put in his first official topknot. Aunt Peg and I both sidled closer for a better look.

I watched as Davey used a knitting needle to part the puppy's silky topknot from side to side across his head. The section of hair gathered into the front ponytail would be used to make the all-important bubble over Augie's eyes. Too small a bubble would make the puppy's expression appear severe. Too large, and it would flop and separate.

On Davey's first attempt, he didn't gather enough hair into the tiny colored rubber band. On his second, the band snapped just as he was twisting it tight. Davey muttered something under his breath that we all pretended not to hear.

"Don't worry," Sam said calmly. "You have plenty of time to get this right. Just try again."

Then he lifted his gaze to Peg and me. Considering that we weren't involved in the process, both of us were standing needlessly close to the table. All right, we were hovering.

"Everything's under control here," Sam pointed out. "Maybe the two of you would like to go pick up Davey's number?"

Armbands can be retrieved at any point prior to entering the ring. Sending someone to pick up a number was the equivalent of telling them to get lost. I should know; Aunt Peg does it to me all the time.

"I'm quite happy right here," Peg said.

I leaned over and dug an elbow into her ribs.

Thankfully she reconsidered. "On the other hand, I'm sure Kevin could use a walk. Melanie and I will each take a hand. We'll check and see how fast the ring is moving as well."

"Perfect," Sam replied. His left hand was cupping Augie's muzzle to hold it steady. With his right, he shooed us on our way.

"I could have made myself useful back there," Aunt Peg grumbled as we left the tent.

"I know." I extended my arm outward as Kevin kicked up his feet and swung between us. "But Augie is Davey's dog. And finishing his championship is a goal for him and Sam to work toward together. You can't always manipulate people's behavior to suit yourself."

"Why on earth not?" Peg wanted to know. "It's what I'm good at."

"Nick Walden," I said succinctly. "Leave Augie's career alone and make Nick your next project."

"I might just do that," Aunt Peg agreed.

As expected, Mrs. Hadley had her assignment well in hand and her ring was running on time. Kevin and I watched a Mini Poodle class while Aunt Peg conferred with the steward and picked up Davey's armband.

Since Augie was entered in Puppy Dogs, his class would be first in the ring for the Standard variety. There were four other male puppies entered in the class. Of those, three would be handled by professionals. Davey was definitely going to have his work cut out for him.

Despite Aunt Peg's impatience, I managed to use up a little more time by taking the scenic route back to the grooming tent. Once there, we discovered that in the ten minutes we'd been gone, a transformation had taken place. Augie's collar was on, his topknot was in, and his neck hair had been sprayed into place. He was ready to impress even the most discerning judge.

And to think, it had all come to pass without Aunt Peg's interference. It was almost a miracle.

"Doesn't he look great?" Davey asked proudly.

"Terrific," I agreed. As Aunt Peg slipped his armband into place, I smoothed my fingers through my son's hair. "And you look great, too."

Not unexpectedly, Davey rolled his eyes. Sam only laughed.

"Everybody ready?" he asked. "Let's get moving."

Sam carried a can of hairspray and the long slender comb that Davey would use to make touch-ups in the ring. I had Kevin. Aunt Peg led the way imperiously, slicing through the crowd and running interference, so that no one we passed on the way to the ring could brush up against Davey's carefully coiffed entry.

We only had a brief wait before the Puppy Dog class was called. Sam tucked the comb into the top of Davey's armband and wished him luck. Aunt Peg and I hurried around the side of the ring to find an optimal viewing spot. Davey followed Crawford in through the gate and found himself standing third in the line of five.

Augie knew what was expected of him. And if Davey was feeling any nerves, they weren't visible from where I stood. He walked the puppy into a stacked pose and waited for the judge to take her first look down the line. As she did so, I saw him slip his right hand into his pocket in preparation for the initial gait around the ring.

Abruptly his face fell.

"Crap," I muttered heartily.

"What?" Sam had just come to join us.

"I don't think Davey has any bait. Did you give him some?"

Sam shook his head. "I forgot all about it. You?" He looked at Peg.

"I was assured that my assistance wasn't needed," she snapped.

Back in the tack box we had a baggie filled with dried liver that I'd prepared the night before. Davey should have had it with him, but in the rush to get to ringside nobody had thought to dig it out.

Augie didn't *have* to have bait. He would show well enough without it. But the incentive of being rewarded with his favorite treat would have added sparkle to his performance. Not only that, but Davey would be the only handler in the ring who wasn't carrying treats, which would leave Augie at a disadvantage.

There was nothing we could do about that now, however. In the time it would take me to return to the grooming tent, find the liver, and get back to the ring, the class would already be over.

Then Sam touched my shoulder and directed my attention back to the ring. Apparently we weren't the only ones who had noticed Davey's dilemma. As the first handler in line straightened his puppy and prepared to move out,

Crawford held back for a moment. He brushed past Davey and dropped a handful of liver into his palm.

"Great," Davey said with a broad grin. "Thanks!"

"Don't mention it," I heard Crawford tell him. "Now see if you can beat me fair and square."

Davey didn't quite manage to do that, but he did come close. Crawford's big white puppy was beautifully made and a natural showman. No one was surprised when Mrs. Hadley quickly moved him to the head of the line. But just as quickly she pulled Augie out and placed him second. For their first time out together as a team, it was a very creditable performance.

Davey was beaming as he left the ring with the red ribbon clutched in his hand. Since he had beaten two other professional handlers, both of whom had shown nice puppies, I could well understand his delight.

"Careful," Aunt Peg admonished, when we'd all gone around to meet the pair at the gate. Augie, pleased with his performance, was leaping and twirling in place. "Don't let him get messed up. You might have to go back in."

She was right, of course. Once all the dog classes had been judged, the winners of those classes would return to the ring to compete for the Winners Dog award and the all-important points that came with it. In our excitement, the rest of us had overlooked that fact that if Crawford's puppy went Winners, Augie, who had been second to him, would be eligible to compete for Reserve.

And that was exactly what happened. Crawford's pretty puppy beat the Open class winner handily. Then Davey hustled Augie back into line and proceeded to do the same. Mrs. Hadley smiled as she handed him the purple and white striped ribbon signifying that Augie had taken Reserve Winners Dog in the major entry.

"Well done, young man," she said. "That's a very nice puppy. You're going to have a lot of fun with him."

"Thank you." Davey blushed and ducked his head. "I already am."

It was the perfect conclusion to their first dog show venture. Davey smiled for the rest of the day. Even Aunt Peg looked pleased.

I love it when a plan comes together.

Chapter 5

"*Now* what?" I said to Bob. I had read his name on caller ID as I picked up the phone. "I introduced Nick to Aunt Peg just like you wanted. Trust me, they're halfway to being best friends already."

"Good afternoon to you too," my ex-husband replied. "I would ask how you're doing on this fine day but judging by your greeting, I guess I already know."

Let's be clear on something. Bob and I have worked on maintaining our friendship in the years since we got divorced. Davey will always be a bond between us. Not only that, but now Bob is also partners with my brother, Frank, in his North Stamford coffee bar, The Bean Counter. So it's inevitable that there are areas where our lives will overlap.

But I never lose sight of the fact that there are a number of good reasons why Bob and I are no longer married. Among them, his propensity to act first and think about consequences afterward. Just because I had allowed myself to be drawn into my ex-husband's most recent scheme didn't mean that I was willing to become involved in whatever brilliant new idea he had come up with now.

"I'm having a perfectly wonderful day," I told him.

At least I had been until the phone rang. The Poodles

and I had just come in from a long walk. Casey, Raven, and Faith trotted back to the kitchen for a drink of water. Tar picked up a knotted rope and dangled it under Augie's nose. The puppy snatched the other end of the toy and the two of them began to pull.

I carried the phone over to the living room couch and sat down. Eve hopped up and draped herself across my lap. My fingers tangled idly through her hair.

"Sam took the kids to the Maritime Aquarium in Norwalk to see the penguin exhibit," I said to Bob.

"I know. He called this morning and asked if I wanted to go with them. I told him I was too busy working on the house."

A decade earlier when Bob and I were married, he'd been employed by a major accounting firm in White Plains. Post-separation he had wandered for a while, eventually ending up in Texas. There he'd taken a job doing the books for a small, struggling, oil company engaged in wildcat drilling.

When the company had been unable to make payroll, Bob had accepted a share in several wells in lieu of salary. Six months later, nobody had been more shocked than he was when his new partners had struck oil. Now, aside from his accounting duties at The Bean Counter, Bob was free to devote the rest of his time to his many do-it-yourself projects.

"How's that coming?" I asked. "You're working on something upstairs now, right?"

"Yeah, I'm expanding the bathroom. That's what I wanted to talk to you about."

That made me laugh. "Sorry, you've called the wrong person. I don't know a thing about plumbing. And even less about construction."

"That doesn't matter. What I care about is that you lived in this house a lot longer than I have."

Eve tipped her face up to mine. I blew softly into her nose and rubbed a hand along her muzzle. "So?"

"So I found something interesting. Something you're really going to want to see."

"What is it?"

"Come over and I'll show you."

Of course he couldn't tell me over the phone. That would be too easy.

I lifted Eve off my lap and stood up. "If it's Davey's retainer that he lost in fifth grade, we don't want it back. In fact, I don't even want to see it."

"You'll want to see *this*," Bob said. "I promise."

He hung up the phone before I could ask any more questions.

Faith and Raven came trotting down the hallway. Casey followed close behind. While I'd been talking, Tar had managed to tangle the rope toy around both the leg of the coffee table and his ear. Now he was stuck.

Augie backed away, then sat down and stared, his head tipped comically to one side. Faith took in the situation in a glance. She looked as though she was rolling her eyes.

While I considered whether or not I wanted to humor Bob, I lifted the table and unwound the rope, then teased it free from the big dog's ear. Liberated, Tar jumped up and shook his head. He was probably trying to figure out how the table had gotten the better of him.

The phone rang again. I lifted it to my ear.

"Don't sit there and think about it," said Bob. "Just come."

Maybe he knew me better than I realized.

"Does this have anything to do with your ghost problem?" I asked.

"Mel, just get in your car."

"This had better be good," I told him.

"It's better than good. It's amazing." Bob hung up again.

I guessed that meant I was going.

I popped Augie—whose show coat needed to be protected—into a crate and left the rest of the Poodles loose to guard the house while I was gone. They didn't look very fierce to me, but sheer numbers probably made them deterrent enough. Ten minutes later, I pulled into Bob's driveway and parked the Volvo in front of his garage.

The small, cape-style home was freshly painted in a soft shade of dove gray, accented by white shutters. Bob had redone the walkway that led to the front door; and a month earlier he'd planted a colorful assortment of spring flowers in the beds that skirted the home's foundation. I had to admit, the place looked great.

I paused on my way to the house and glanced at the neighboring home that belonged to James and Amber Fine. The front door was closed. The shades were drawn against the summer sun. A black and white cat lay on the warm stoop, one hind leg lifted straight up in the air as it arched around nimbly and licked its stomach. Nothing new to see there.

Bob didn't wait for me to knock. Before I could even climb the steps, he already had the front door open. "Finally!" he cried. "Come on in."

I hurried inside and Bob shut the door behind me.

"What's this all about?" I said. "What could you possibly have, that I would need to see so desperately?"

Instead of answering, Bob dug his hand deep into the pocket of his cargo shorts. When he pulled it out a moment later, his fingers were curled protectively around something. He held out his hand and opened it slowly. Nestled in his palm was a diamond ring.

"This," he said.

"Holy moley." I expelled a sharp breath. No wonder he'd been excited.

I bent down for a closer inspection. Bob's find was an ornate, Art Deco-style cocktail ring. In the center was a round cut diamond that was at least a carat in size. Surrounding its high setting were several rows of smaller diamonds. The band appeared to be made of platinum.

"Where did you get that?"

"It was here in the house," said Bob. "I found it upstairs."

"May I?" I reached forward tentatively.

He nodded and I skimmed the piece of jewelry up off his palm. It was heavier than I'd expected. Grasping the band, I held the ring up into a shaft of sunlight coming in through a front window. The stones sparkled and a prism of colors shifted and danced on the wall behind us.

"Is it real?" I asked.

"Apparently so. I took it to a jeweler in Greenwich this morning and had it appraised. Judging by the design, they figured it was probably made sometime in the early twentieth century."

I couldn't resist. I slipped the band onto the tip of my ring finger. It wouldn't slide past the first knuckle.

"It's tiny," I said.

"People had smaller hands then."

I tugged the ring off and handed it back. "I want to hear the whole story," I told him. "I think you'd better start at the beginning."

"I don't know the whole story," Bob replied. "That's why I wanted you to see it. I thought maybe you'd have a story for me. I was wondering if the ring was yours."

"No way." I laughed. "Where would I have gotten a ring like that? I've never seen it before in my life."

"Too bad," said Bob. "That would have made things easy."

The dining room was just to the right of the front hall.

Bob walked that way. We each took a seat and he set the ring down on the table between us.

I'm not usually drawn to sparkly things, but I couldn't seem to take my eyes off the jewel-encrusted bauble. I scooped it up, cradled it in my palm for a moment, then tried sliding the band onto my pinkie. This time, with a little effort, the ring pushed down to the base of my finger.

“”It's beautiful,” I said, holding out my hand to admire the effect. “You'd think that whoever lost this ring would have moved heaven and earth to get it back. Where did you find it?”

“I've been working on the bathroom. I'd imagine you remember how small it was?”

“Oh yeah,” I said with a laugh.

Bathrooms constructed sixty years earlier had been designed for function not luxury. This one contained just a sink, a toilet, and a bathtub, all wedged into the smallest possible amount of space. The only towel rack was on the back of the door and there was barely enough room for a hamper. I could well understand why Bob might want to do some updating.

“I decided to make it bigger. I started last week.”

I pictured the home's compact second storey. There were just two bedrooms, the bathroom, and a couple of small closets. “Where?”

“I took out the linen closet and expanded in that direction. I broke through the wall in between, and that's where I found the ring. When the dust settled, it was just sitting there on the floor. At first I thought it was a piece of broken glass. Then I took a closer look, and here we are.”

“What did the appraiser tell you? Is it worth a lot of money?”

“Probably somewhere between four and five thousand dollars. To get a better estimate, the jeweler said he'd have to remove the center stone from its setting but I told him that wasn't necessary. Aside from the big diamond in the middle, the others are mostly just chips. Apparently the workmanship is pretty special though and that added to its value too."

"So it's valuable, but not worth a fortune." I wriggled it off my finger and placed it back on the table. "Even so, a ring that was made nearly a hundred years ago probably has sentimental value too . . . for somebody."

"I agree," Bob said with a nod. "Now that I know it isn't yours, it seems to me that we ought to try and figure out who it *does* belong to. I've been thinking about this since I found it. Probably the best place to start is with the people we bought the house from. Do you remember their name?"

He didn't ask for much, did he? That was thirteen years ago.

I frowned, thinking back. "It was Morris, wasn't it? Dan and Emily Morris? I'm pretty sure he worked in New York. They'd just had their second child and needed more room; that was why they were moving. At the closing, Emily Morris told me she hoped that you and I would be as happy in this house as she and Dan had been."

Abruptly I stopped speaking as the remembered sentiment hit home.

Bob looked at me and sighed. "Well, that didn't happen. But at least we're both in a good place now."

"Absolutely," I agreed. I was as eager to put that topic to rest as my ex-husband was. "Why don't you look around online and see if you can find the Morrises? Maybe they still live around here. If that doesn't work, we can go down to the Town Clerk's office and have a look at the property records—"

"Hey, Bob! Are you home?" The question was punctuated by the sound of the back door slamming shut. Footsteps headed in our direction.

James, Bob mouthed silently to me. *From next door.*

"In the dining room," he called back.

"Phil and I came by to see if you wanted to come with us to Home Depot . . . whoa!"

Two men appeared in the door. Seeing Bob and me sitting together at the table, the man in front came to an abrupt halt. The one behind bumped into him, then stepped back and righted himself.

The speaker, James, looked nothing like I'd imagined in all those months that he'd remained out of sight. He was older than Amber by at least a decade, with pleasant features and hair that was thinning on the top and sides. His body was sturdy and more than a bit overweight. James's rumpled polo shirt was tucked into an equally creased pair of khakis.

Somehow I'd pictured Amber's world-traveling husband as someone who'd appear more dashing. Or at the very least, less wrinkled.

Compared to his tall, skinny, companion, however, James looked positively dapper. Phil sported a faded T-shirt worn over baggy jeans that drooped at the waist. Round tortoiseshell glasses, frames too big for his face, magnified his watery brown eyes. His wide, friendly, smile revealed a pair of dimples bracketing his slightly uneven teeth.

"Sorry," said James. "I didn't realize you had company."

"Not company exactly," Bob told them. "Melanie is my ex-wife."

"I think there's a joke in there somewhere." I stood up and shook hands with the new arrivals. "I used to live here," I said to James. "Amber and I were neighbors for a while."

"Is that so? Then that makes you the . . ." James stopped and gulped.

"The what?" I asked.

"Poodle lady." A flush rose over the man's neck. "Sorry, I shouldn't have blurted that out. Amber used to call you that sometimes. I don't think she meant anything by it."

"No problem," I said. "I've been called worse."

And considering that I'd been known to refer to Amber as the cat lady, I really didn't have room to complain. Not that I intended to tell James that.

"Anyway," James continued, turning back to Bob, "Phil and I are going out to pick up supplies. Phil has a greenhouse that needs some repairs. I know how renovations go, I figured you might need something too."

"No, thanks, I'm all set." Bob slid his hand across the table and cupped it quietly around the ring. Unfortunately the movement had the opposite effect than the one he'd intended.

"Nice jewelry," Phil said, eyeing the prize. He stepped closer to the table to get a better look.

"Yours?" James asked me. Now he'd noticed the ring too.

"No. It's Bob's. At least for now."

Damn. I gave myself a mental kick. I was just as guilty of blurting out something dumb as James had been. I knew right away that answer wouldn't satisfy him, and it didn't.

"For now?" James repeated.

"I found it earlier today when I was knocking down a wall," Bob said.

"Sharp!" said Phil. "Can I see?"

Bob handed the ring over. He and I both kept an eye on it.

"So it's like buried treasure," said James. "You're rich."

"Not exactly," I said drily. "For one thing, it's not worth enough to make anyone rich. And for another, it doesn't belong to us."

"Finders, keepers," James intoned.

Phil nodded. "That's the law."

"Not around here," I told them. "Bob and I are going to figure out who the ring belongs to and return it."

"That's no fun." James plucked the jewel out of Phil's hand and held it up to the light. "You ought to do some more digging around up there. Where there's one piece of loot, there's bound to be more. Let me know if you want my help."

"No, thanks," said Bob. "There's no need to get carried away. It's not like pirates stopped by and buried a treasure here. It's just one old ring, that's all."

He held out his hand. James dropped the jewelry into it.

"Pretty, though," Phil commented. "I wouldn't mind finding something like that around my house."

"And you'd know better than to give it back," James pointed out.

"I sure would," Phil agreed.

"Nice to meet you, Melanie," James said. He and Phil headed for the back door. "Do me a favor? If you don't mention that Poodle lady thing to Amber, my life will go a little smoother. If you know what I mean."

"Consider it forgotten," I said.

I watched the two men walk through the kitchen and let themselves out. "Don't you ever lock your doors?" I asked.

"Not when I'm here." Bob shrugged. "It's not like this is New York. Or even downtown Stamford. Isn't that why people move to the suburbs? So that they can feel safe without having a million locks on everything?"

"I don't know about you," I said. "But I'd feel safer without neighbors who felt free to wander through my house whenever they felt like it."

"Don't mind James. He means well. The poor guy is just

bored. As soon as the economy picks up and somebody gives him a job, things will go back to normal around here."

"Or maybe you should just think about locking your doors," I said.

Chapter 6

Kevin and I were out running errands when Aunt Peg called.

"Melanie!" she sang out cheerfully. "You're a genius."

There's nothing that pleases my aunt more than having one of her relatives succeed at something she considers important. She doesn't hand out accolades lightly—and almost never to me. So even though I had no idea what had occasioned that unexpected burst of praise, it seemed safer not to question my good fortune in case she might be tempted to change her mind.

"Thank you," I replied. "I'm happy to be of service."

"I'm not sure I'd go that far," Peg retorted.

Of course not. I shouldn't have presumed.

"But you did introduce me to Nick Walden and that was well done. He's quite an interesting young man."

"So I take it his visit to meet your Poodles went well?"

"I should say so. . . . Melanie, what is that noise? Where are you?"

We were on the Merritt Parkway approaching North Street exit in Greenwich. A driver in the left lane ahead of us must have seen the exit sign too late because he swerved to the right, heedless of oncoming traffic. Horns blared. He flipped the other drivers the bird and shot up the ramp.

"Kevin and I are running errands," I told her. "But as it

happens we're not too far from you. Should we stop by for a few minutes?"

Perhaps it was immodest of me to want to prolong the conversation. But seriously? I'm not in Aunt Peg's good graces often and I wanted to bask a little.

Besides, Peg's sweet tooth is legendary. And she *always* has cake.

My aunt lives in back country Greenwich. Her house, once the hub of a working farm, is situated on five acres of private, rolling land. The kennel building behind the house—which over the years had housed dozens of Cedar Crest champion Poodles—now sits empty. Due to the time and travel demands of her busy judging schedule, Peg has had to greatly curtail her own showing and breeding.

Her five remaining Standard Poodles are all house dogs. Among them are Faith's litter sister Hope, Eve's litter brother Zeke, and Beau, an older, neutered, male who is the love of her life. Since Aunt Peg is the one who got me started in Poodles, it's not surprising that our canine connection is as interwoven as our human one.

As always, Aunt Peg's Poodles alerted her to our arrival. She opened the front door and the pack came spilling out onto the porch. Together they galloped down the steps and raced across the driveway. I had unsnapped Kevin from his car seat and placed him on the ground but as the Poodles quickly surrounded us I reached down and hoisted the toddler up so that he wouldn't get bowled over by their enthusiastic greeting.

"Put down," Kevin said firmly. Just like his older brother; if something interesting was happening, he wanted to be right in the middle of it.

With caution, I complied. Now that the race to welcome us was over, the Poodles' tempo slowed. They swarmed around our legs and sniffed our clothes. No doubt they were comparing notes on where Kevin and I had been before our arrival in their world.

"Zeke," Kevin announced, pointing. The male dog wagged his tail.

"Hope." He pointed again. And was right for the second time.

"Amazing," I said.

Even at his young age Kevin was clearly a dog lover, but I'd never seen him do that before. There were plenty of adults who couldn't separate out a group of similarly bred, similarly groomed, black dogs with just a single glance.

"Bobo!" Kevin finished with a triumphant giggle. The Poodle in question sidled over and pressed his nose against Kevin's chest.

"Just Beau," Aunt Peg corrected sternly. She had come down the steps to join us.

"Bobo!" Kevin repeated just as forcefully.

I could see this wasn't going to end well.

Aunt Peg hunkered down so that she and Kevin were eye to eye. "His name is Beau," she said again. "Bobo sounds like the name of a clown. It's much too undignified for a Poodle of Beau's stature."

"You're trying to reason with a two-year-old," I told her. "That doesn't work."

"Nonsense! There's no reason a child shouldn't respond to training just as a puppy would."

Aunt Peg never had children of her own, can you tell?

"Bobo!" Kevin crowed happily. Now that he'd discovered that the name got a reaction from his aunt, it was his new favorite word.

Aunt Peg waggled a finger in his direction. "I said *no*."

Wonderful. Two of the most stubborn people I'd ever met were facing off. Left to their own devices, they'd probably be happy to stand there and argue all afternoon. I swooped down and picked Kevin up.

"He's two, Aunt Peg. He thinks the word *no* is a challenge."

"Indeed." Peg snorted.

She made a swishing motion with her hand. Immediately the Poodles stopped what they were doing and preceded us into the house. Aunt Peg closed the door behind us, then cocked a critical eye at Kevin.

"Maybe you're not as good a parent as you used to be," she said. "As I recall, Davey was better behaved at that age."

"You didn't know Davey when he was two," I pointed out.

I could see that Aunt Peg wanted to disagree. But then she thought for a moment, and nodded. When Davey was a toddler, she and I had been virtual strangers. Back then, the Turnbull clan had been hopelessly fractured due to a longstanding rift between my father and his brother, Peg's husband, Max. Ironically it had been Max's death that had brought Aunt Peg and me together. We'd worked as a team to find his killer and unexpectedly become friends in the process.

"Tell me all about Nick's visit," I said ten minutes later. Peg and I were settled out back on the wraparound porch with iced tea and thick slices of shadow cake. "Did it go well?"

Below us, Kevin had followed the dogs down into the yard. He was holding his piece of cake cupped in his hands. The Poodles were too polite to steal it from him but all five were keeping a hopeful eye on the proceedings. The moment anything slipped through his fingers, it would be snatched up before it could hit the ground.

"It went very well," Aunt Peg replied. "Despite that silly Dog Whisperer title, Nick is quite serious about what he does. I enjoyed watching him interact with my Poodles, and trust me, that's not something I say often. Many people think they understand dogs but unfortunately a good number of them are simply flattering themselves."

I knew better than to inquire into which camp she thought I fell.

"Nick gets it," said Aunt Peg. That was high praise in her book. "Maybe it's empathy, or perhaps intuition, but he possesses that rare ability to sense what dogs are thinking and feeling—perhaps even before they know themselves."

"He really made an impression," I said.

"You sound surprised."

I shrugged lightly. "I liked Nick a lot when I met him. And he seems like a nice guy. But I guess I expected you to be a harder sell. Or maybe I'm not convinced that the ability to talk to dogs is as rare a skill as you believe it to be."

"Perhaps I didn't make myself clear. It wasn't the way that Nick talked to the dogs that impressed me. Any pet owner can do that. But Nick possesses a much more important skill. He knows how to *listen*."

"I see." I stuffed a large bite of cake into my mouth. It tasted a little bit like crow. "So you'll introduce him to your friends?"

Aunt Peg nodded. "I thought I might throw a small party in a few weeks. Just a little something to put his name out there in the right kinds of places. Not that he appears to need my help."

"No?" I said. "I thought that was the whole point."

"Not as far as Nick's concerned. Apparently his Dog Whisperer business is rolling right along. It was your ex-husband who came up with the idea that Nick needed more clients. Bob's doing Nick's accounting now. Did he tell you that?"

"No," I said, surprised. "I had no idea. I just thought they were friends."

Aunt Peg sighed. "Melanie, *do* try to keep up."

"I'm working on it."

That's the story of my life unfortunately: I always seem to be two steps behind and running to catch up.

"Honey, I'm home!"

Sam stuck his head out of the living room, a bemused expression on his face. "*What?*"

"Just kidding," I said with a grin.

I love watching classic TV. There's nothing like old episodes of *Leave It to Beaver* or *The Andy Griffith Show* to make me feel like all is right with the world. But since Sam doesn't share my fondness for last century sitcoms, my Donna Reed moments often go right over his head.

"Davey, front and center," said Sam. "Your mom needs help."

He skirted deftly through the sea of Poodles that was milling around the hallway and took two bags of groceries out of my arms. Judging by the sounds emanating from the room behind him, Kev's and my arrival home had interrupted a hard-fought video game battle.

I heard a virtual explosion, followed by Davey's outraged yelp. "Damn it!"

"Excuse me?" I said.

"Sorry," my older son mumbled, appearing in the doorway.

Since Sam had the groceries, Davey was left with the choice of helping with either the dry cleaning or the library books. I was hoping he'd opt for the former, which needed to be carried upstairs and put away. Instead he bypassed the bundles I was carrying and grabbed his little brother's hand.

"Come on, Kev," he invited. "Let's go play!"

"Not exactly what I had in mind," I said. Sam and I both stared after the pair, who had disappeared back into the living room. "But it'll do."

I threw the dry cleaning in the hall closet, then followed Sam back to the kitchen. Together we put away the groceries. When that was done, Sam retrieved a couple of tennis balls from the toy pile in the corner and opened the back door. The Poodles knew what was coming next. Running as a group, they raced out to the middle of the two-acre yard.

Sam cocked his arm and let fly. He sent the first ball long

and wide toward a stand of trees. The second he hefted directly into the middle of what had once—briefly—been my vegetable garden.

"Good thing I didn't plant anything this year," I mentioned as the pack split in half and three Poodles went scrambling in that direction.

"Correct me if I'm wrong," Sam said mildly. "But I don't believe you planted anything last year either. Or the year before that."

"Gardening is a highly overrated skill."

"Says the woman with the black thumb."

"Hey, at least I know my limitations."

Casey was the first to return with a ball. She dropped it into Sam's hand. He waited for the other Poodles to get back into position, then threw it again. Tar was on his way back with the ball he'd fished out of the trees. Raven and Eve trotted along behind him.

"Beer?" I asked.

Sam nodded without turning around. He was busy lining up his next throw.

I was back in less than a minute and slipped the cold bottle into his hand. Sam was staring off into the distance. Noses lifted and sniffing the air, all six Poodles were now circling the thick trunk of the ancient oak tree that held Davey's tree house.

"Bad throw?" I inquired.

Sam shook his head. "Squirrels. Two of them. I think they're up in the tree laughing at all of us."

I plopped down on a chaise lounge and stretched my legs out in front of me. "I'm sure they're laughing at Tar," I said.

That silly Poodle was leaping up and down like a pogo stick at the base of the tree. Faith, the oldest and wisest of the crew, knew better than to waste her energy on a vain hope. She left the others and came back to join Sam and me on the deck. I patted the chaise beside me. Faith hopped up and lay down, pressing her warm body along the length of my legs.

"Bob called while you were out," Sam said. He picked up a deck chair and angled it in my direction, then took a seat as well. "He wanted me to tell you that he'd managed to locate some people named the Morrises . . . ?"

"That's great," I said. "It's about the ring." I had told Sam about Bob's unexpected find the day before. "Dan and Emily Morris are the people he and I bought the house from years ago. We're hoping they might know something about how the ring came to be there."

Sam nodded. "According to Bob, the family lives in Cos Cob. Right now, they're away on vacation with their kids. Home again in a couple of weeks, and happy to talk to you then. Bob said he didn't tell them what it was about, just that it had something to do with their old house."

"That works." I paused for a long, cold, drink. "The ring's been hidden for at least a decade and possibly a whole lot more. A few extra weeks isn't going to make any difference."

"You have to wonder why the ring was never found before," said Sam. "Surely whoever lost it must have looked for it."

"I'll let you know as soon as we find out the answers," I said lazily. "It'll be fun having a little project for the summer to keep me busy."

Sam smiled. "Because two kids, six dogs, and Aunt Peg isn't enough?"

"Not to mention you." I reached over, grasped his hand, and pulled him onto the chaise beside me.

Faith lifted her head and grumbled an objection under her breath as the chaise creaked and groaned beneath the three of us. Then she sighed and slipped off the other side. I scooted over to make room for Sam. He settled in beside me and I rested my head on his shoulder.

It was the perfect summer afternoon. The sun was high and warm in the sky. Davey and Kevin were keeping each other entertained. The Poodles had flopped down happily in the grass beneath the oak tree. At least for the moment, everything was just as it should be. Too bad, I thought, that I couldn't figure out a way to capture that peace and hold on to it.

And yet for the next few weeks it almost seemed as though I had. Sam cut back on his work schedule and we took the kids on outings to the beach and the Natural History Museum. Aunt Peg, occupied making new connections for Nick, barely had any time for me. Even Bob's renovations proceeded smoothly.

Life was good. This, I thought, must be how normal people live. It was definitely something I could get used to it. I was smiling in happy anticipation of another long, lazy, summer day when I answered the phone two weeks later.

And heard the news that Nick Walden was dead.

Chapter 7

"Dead?" I gasped. "How? When?"

"He was shot," Aunt Peg told me. "It happened last night. In his home."

My knees gave out. Thankfully there was a chair nearby. I sank down into it.

"Was there an intruder?" I asked.

"The police aren't sure what took place. But they're calling it a homicide."

A lump rose in my throat. I swallowed heavily. This was all too much to process.

"How did you find out?"

"It's on the morning news," said Aunt Peg. "A murder in Riverside is a big deal. Every local station had the story. How could you have missed it?"

"I was feeding the boys breakfast," I told her. "They're not allowed to watch TV while they eat."

"Well, someone ought to be keeping tabs," Peg said huffily.

"I just can't believe it." I realized I was shaking my head, as if denying the news would make it go away. "That's awful."

"What's awful?" asked Sam. He had Kevin with him.

I looked up and he saw the expression on my face. Unfortunately Sam and I have been here before. He knew what to do. "I'll bet *Sesame Street* is on now, isn't it?" he said to Kevin.

The toddler's face lit up. "Cookie Monster!" he said with a toothy grin.

Sam deposited him in front of the TV in the living room and quickly returned. By that time I'd found that Aunt Peg didn't have any more information than she'd already given me and ended the call. I was telling Sam the bad news when the phone rang again.

This time it was Bob.

"We've already heard," I said before he had a chance to speak. "Do you know what happened?"

"Just that Nick was shot late yesterday evening. I can't believe it. Who would do such a thing? Nick was a great guy. We . . . I . . . just had dinner with him a couple days ago."

"I'm sorry," I said. "I know the two of you were good friends."

Bob blew out a shaky sigh. "God, this is hard."

"I know," I said softly.

He didn't speak for a long time. I didn't push. I just waited until he was ready to continue.

"Listen, Mel," he said finally. "I need a favor. Can we talk? Is it all right if I come over?"

"Of course. Anything you want. But Davey's going to be spending the day at Joey Brickman's house. So I'll be dropping him off right down the road from you in just a few minutes. Do you want me to stop by?"

"No, I'm not home right now. I'm . . . somewhere else."

How very odd, I thought. The definition of *not home* would certainly seem to indicate that Bob was *somewhere else*. Was his current location a secret? Was there something he didn't want me to know?

Then I frowned and reined in my wandering thoughts. My ex had just been hit with news that had to have come as a huge shock. Under the circumstances, it was understandable that he might not be expressing himself clearly.

"Give me half an hour," I said. "Sam and I will both be here."

Alice Brickman, Joey's mom, has been a stalwart presence in my life since we'd met in a neighborhood play group when our boys were less than a year old. We'd quickly discovered how much we had in common and our sons' compatibility sealed the bond. Davey and Joey had become great friends, and Alice and I did too.

Over the years, she and I had supported each other through chicken pox, snow days, and endless numbers of school projects. We've also covered each other's backs. Alice knew I'd be there for her if she ever needed anything, and I knew she'd do the same for me. So now I didn't hesitate to strap Kevin into the car when I went to drop Davey off.

I made the drive to Flower Estates on autopilot, my thoughts consumed by the morning's terrible news. I hadn't yet had the chance to get to know Nick Walden well, but everything I did know about him made this tragedy seem all the more incomprehensible. Nick had been young, and talented, and eminently likeable. How could anyone have possibly wanted him dead?

Alice answered the door wearing a flowered sundress and flip-flops. Her strawberry blond hair was twisted into a careless knot on the top of her head, and her pale, freckled skin showed the beginnings of a summer tan. Before we even had a chance to say hello, the Brickmans' Golden Retriever, Berkley, shot through the open doorway. He flew past me down the steps and went careening into Davey. Spinning around, the dog jumped up to plop his big, hairy, paws on my son's shoulders.

"Berkley, get down!" Alice cried. "As if he ever listens," she muttered under her breath before treating me to a wide smile. "Great to see you. Do you have time to come in and visit?"

"Unfortunately no."

Behind me, Davey was giggling. Big dogs, even ones whose manners needed work, didn't bother him in the slightest. He pushed Berkley down, then ran into the house in search of Joey. The Golden galloped happily along behind, nearly knocking me off the step.

"Hello, Mrs. Brickman," I called after him. "How nice to see you. Thank you for having me."

The reminder to watch his own manners didn't even slow Davey down. He was already gone.

"Oh please." Alice laughed. "There's no need to stand on ceremony around here. Considering how much time he and Joey spend together, that child might as well be my second son."

True, that.

"So tell me what's wrong," said Alice. That's how well she knows me. "Is there anything I can do to help?"

"Actually yes," I admitted. "Do you think you could watch Kevin for an hour or two?"

"Sure." Alice nodded. "Carly has a friend coming over too, so I've already got four. I'll hardly even notice one more."

Carly was Alice's daughter. At nine, she was graceful as a willow and loved nothing more than dance. Except maybe kittens, and the color pink. I adored my rough-and-tumble sons, but sometimes I envied Alice her very girly daughter.

"Trust me, you'll notice this one," I told her. "He's two and into everything."

"Like I haven't been there," Alice scoffed. "At least he's still at an age where I can pick him up if I see trouble coming."

She accompanied me down the steps to the driveway. Kevin was still in his car seat. Before I could open the Volvo's door, Alice put out a hand to stop me.

"I'm happy to watch Kev, you know that. But it wasn't what I meant when I asked if I could help. Is everything all right?"

I shook my head. "A friend of Bob's was killed last night. He wants to come over and talk about it."

"Nick Walden." Alice's face fell. "I heard about it on the news. What an awful thing. He seemed like a great guy."

"You knew him?" I asked, surprised.

"I just met him once actually. I was walking Berkley—which is to say that Berkley was walking me. You know how that goes."

I did. Berkley was supposed to be the kids' dog but, not unexpectedly, Alice was the one who'd ended up taking care of him. And since no one in the family had the time to devote to consistent training, the young, rambunctious Golden Retriever tended to do things his own way. His walks with Alice often appeared to be less like a team effort than a wild ride that both participants hoped to survive.

"Berkley and I ran into Nick outside Bob's house one day," Alice said with a grimace. "As in, we literally ran into him. I guess I wasn't paying enough attention because when B saw something interesting and started to run, the leash flew right out of my hands. By the time I caught up, Nick was standing on the sidewalk with the lead wrapped around his legs. Even worse, Berkley—who obviously was stuck too—was barking like some demented hound from hell. Of course I immediately started to apologize."

"Of course," I agreed.

"And then I got a good look at Nick and all I could think was, Oh crap, why did I run out of the house looking like this? Would it have killed me to put on a little lipstick to walk the dog?"

That made me laugh. Yeah, Nick was that cute.

"But you know," Alice continued, "he couldn't have been nicer about the whole thing. Not only that, but in less than a minute the two of them were untangled and Berkley was sitting calmly beside him like a perfect angel. I have no idea how Nick did it. It was like watching someone perform magic."

"Nick was a dog whisperer," I said softly. My smile died as the enormity of the loss hit me again, making my chest feel hollow and empty.

"That's what he told me." Alice expression grew somber too. "He said that Goldens make great family dogs, but even great dogs need steady, dependable training. He offered to give me a few pointers."

"That sounds like Nick. He wanted the best for every dog he came in contact with."

"I took his card and tucked it away," said Alice. "I planned to take him up on his offer when the kids' camps start and I have more time. I'm sure he could have helped us."

Just one more way in which Nick's death had been a tragic waste. "I barely knew the guy," I said. "But I know I'm going to miss him."

"Don't make me cry." Alice reached up and scrubbed a hand across her cheek. Then she reached around me and opened the car door. "Kevin will be fine here until you're ready to come and get him. And you'll have to tell me what Bob says. Maybe he knows something that can help us make sense of what happened."

"Maybe," I replied. "But I wouldn't count on it. I don't think there's anything that could make me feel better about this."

* * *

I'd barely arrived back home when Bob's dark green Explorer turned in to the driveway. To my surprise, another car followed behind his. The second car was a small, red, Japanese hybrid. There appeared to be a woman driving it.

I stood in the front hall and stared shamelessly out the window, waiting for the pair to get out of their cars. I wanted to see who our second visitor was.

"What are you doing?" asked Sam, coming up behind me.

"Spying," I replied, my voice hushed. As if I was afraid that the people outside the house could hear me.

"On your ex-husband? I didn't know you were still that interested. Should I be worried?"

"I'm not looking at him." I pulled Sam over beside me and pointed out the window. "It's the woman I'm curious about."

By now she'd stepped out of the second car. She paused for a moment and gazed over at the house. Aviator-framed sunglasses covered her eyes; I couldn't read her expression. The woman was tall and slender, wearing a narrow linen sheath dress in a bright shade of pink that complimented her dark, glossy, hair. Her arms and legs were bare; she'd dressed appropriately for the warm summer day. Even so, she didn't look comfortable. Or maybe I was reading more into her stance than was actually there.

Bob had disembarked too. He stood next to the Explorer, waiting for her so that they could walk to the house together. When she reached his side, he slipped an arm around her waist and briefly pulled her close.

As I watched, Bob leaned down and said something to the woman. His lips brushed lightly across her silky hair. His hand continued to rest lightly on her hip. The contact between them appeared both supportive and intimate. Whoever the woman was, she and Bob knew one another well.

"Oh," said Sam.

I reared back and looked at him. "What does that mean?"

Sam didn't answer. Instead he slipped past me and opened the door. I stayed where I was and stared after him. Oh indeed.

Bob and the woman were already coming up the wide front steps. She lifted a hand gracefully and slid her shades up on top of her head. Her eyes were amber, flecked with bits of brown. She smiled briefly as Bob made the introductions.

"Melanie, Sam, this is Claire Walden," he said. "Claire is Nick's sister."

I did not see that coming. Choking on the greeting I'd meant to offer, I just stuck out my hand instead. Thankfully Sam's manners were smoother. He invited the couple inside. That gave me the minute I needed to regain control. But . . . Bob and *Nick's sister*?

"I'm so sorry for your loss," I said to Claire. "I only met your brother recently, but I was hoping to have the chance to get to know him better."

"Thank you," she said softly.

Her gaze slid past me and went to the pack of Poodles gathered at the back of the hall. The big black dogs had come running when the door opened. But instead of offering their usual exuberant welcome, today the Poodles seemed to sense the mood of our guests. A palpable feeling of sadness hung in the air and their response was equally subdued.

When Claire crouched down and held out a hand, the dogs didn't rush forward to overwhelm her. Instead they surrounded her quietly, pressing their bodies against hers and offering their own silent brand of support.

"What lovely Standard Poodles," said Claire. She looped an arm around Raven's neck and gazed at Augie, whose long hair was held in place by an array of protective bands and wraps. "Is that one a show dog?"

"They all were, at one time or another," I told her. It was easier for both of us to talk about the Poodles than about the true reason for their visit. "Augie is the only one who's being shown right now. He belongs to our son Davey."

"Davey," Claire murmured. "Of course."

My eyes widened. *Claire knew Davey?* I shot my ex-husband a questioning look over her head.

Bob, that coward, pretended not to notice.

Ignore me at your peril, I thought. Then my gaze shifted to Sam. How much did *he* know? Was I the only one who didn't have a clue what was going on?

Sam must have sensed the tension in the air. He moved quickly to change the subject. "Come on in and sit down," he said to Bob and Claire. "Does anyone want food? Or something to drink?"

Nobody took Sam up on his offer of refreshments. Instead we all followed him into the living room. Bob and Claire headed for the couch. I helped myself to a chair.

The Poodles came with us and Raven continued to remain close to Claire. When she took a seat on the couch, Raven sat down on her feet and leaned her warm body against Claire's legs. Bob, outmaneuvered by a Poodle, had to be content with a seat at the other end.

"Claire wanted to talk to you about Nick," Bob began.

I nodded, then waited for Claire to chart the course of the conversation. When she continued to remain silent, Sam said, "We only know what's been reported on TV. Do the police have a better idea of what happened than they're telling the media?"

"They have a few more facts, but not many," Claire said. She stopped and shook her head. "All they know for sure at this point is that Nick was shot last night in his home. There was no forced entry. They're speculating that he knew the person who shot him."

"Any sign of a struggle?" I asked.

"No. And Nick's dogs were there with him. He has two, a Rottweiler mix and little terrier. They're both pound puppies but they've been with Nick for years and are utterly devoted to him. If my brother had tried to defend himself, I'm sure they would have helped him if they could."

That was interesting.

"Who has the dogs now?" I asked.

"They're with me," Claire said. "I picked them up this morning. It was because of them that Nick was found."

"Apparently they started barking and howling." Bob picked up the story. "Nick's neighbor said the noise went on for more than an hour. She told the police that that was highly unusual. She said Nick never allowed his dogs to cause a disturbance. So she went next door around nine o'clock to check and see if everything was all right."

"She took one look in the front window and called the police," said Claire.

"So Nick had a nighttime visitor," I mused. "Someone both he and his dogs must have felt comfortable with. Did he have a girlfriend?"

Bob snickered, then quickly apologized. "Sorry. Yes, he did. Short answer, yes."

I turned to Claire. "What's the long answer?"

"There's one girl he's been involved with for several months. Her name is Diana Lee. But Nick is the kind of guy who attracts women. It's not unusual for him to be juggling several at once. I guess he and Diana are serious enough but my brother's not big on commitment."

"Was that a source of friction between them?" I asked.

Claire shrugged. "If it was, I never saw it. I never saw anything wrong at all. That's what's so awful about this. My brother was *fine*. He was building his business, he was happy with his life, he was in a good place. Until . . ."

Claire didn't finish the sentence. Out of the corner of

my eye, I saw Bob wince. Maybe that should have clued me in to what was coming. I hate it when I'm the last person in the room to catch on.

"Until?" I prompted her.

Claire lifted her head and jutted out her chin. "Until he got himself mixed up with your Aunt Peg."

Chapter 8

Oh, lordy, I thought. Had she just said what I thought I'd heard?

Judging by the expressions on Sam's and Bob's faces, she had indeed.

"You think that Aunt Peg had something to do with Nick's murder?" I asked incredulously.

Now let's get something straight. Aunt Peg is no angel. She can be tough, and manipulative, and sometimes downright scary. But murder? Even for her, that was pushing credibility. Besides, my aunt had adored Nick. She'd promised him her support. She'd even talked about throwing him a party.

I've been related to Aunt Peg for decades and she's never thrown a party for me. Just so we know where we all stand.

"That's crazy," I said flatly.

"Maybe," Claire replied. "And maybe not. All I know is that the police asked me if anything had changed recently in Nick's life and the only thing I could come up with was that he'd gotten involved with your aunt."

"You told the police you thought Peg Turnbull would make a good suspect?" Sam was biting his lip. He looked like he was trying not to laugh.

"Not in so many words. To tell the truth, I don't remember much of what I said. I had just found out that my brother was dead and I'm sure I wasn't thinking clearly."

Claire looked around the room, her gaze resting on each of us in turn. "But I thought about it afterward. The police seemed to think something like that—a new friend, a new business associate—was important. So maybe it is."

In spite of myself, I liked her for that. Claire was obviously upset and in pain. She was surrounded by the very people most likely to disagree with her opinion. And yet she still didn't back down. I had to admire her determination.

"You've come to the wrong place," I said to Bob. "You should have taken Claire to see Aunt Peg."

"No way." He shook his head vehemently. "I have too high a regard for my own good health for that. I figured you guys can break the news to Peg."

That was *so* not happening, I thought.

"And besides," said Bob. "There's the other thing."

The day wasn't even half over yet, I thought. How could there possibly be something else? Maybe a local outbreak of the plague? Or perhaps a tsunami bearing down on the Connecticut coast?

"What other thing?" I asked.

"You know," Bob said. "The mystery thing. You like to solve them. I told Claire that you could help."

I heard a low growl beside me. I was pretty sure that it had come from Sam. His patience with my ex-husband's antics tends to be even shorter than my own.

"That was nice of you, Bob," I said mildly. "But I doubt that Claire would want help . . . *from the chief suspect's family.*"

Bob blanched. I guessed he hadn't thought about that.

"Well, yeah," he stammered. "But Peg is probably innocent, right?"

There was no point in responding. I couldn't even believe that he'd felt the need to ask.

"Thank you, Bob," Sam answered for me. His tone was frosty but at least he didn't have his fingers wrapped around my ex-husband's neck. "Melanie and I will take your idea under advisement."

"I think I'd better be going," said Claire.

She stood up and we all walked her to the door. When Bob attempted to slip out with her, I laid a heavy hand on his shoulder and held him firmly in place.

"Not so fast," I muttered under my breath.

"I'll phone you later," Bob called after Claire.

She nodded and kept on walking. I waited until she'd gotten into her car and started down the driveway before closing the door. Then I used my grip on Bob's shoulder to steer him back into the living room. Left with little choice, he sat back down on the couch.

"Now," I said. "Suppose you tell us what that was all about?"

"What do you mean?" Bob managed a look of baffled innocence.

Like that was going to get him off the hook.

I stood next to the couch and glared down at him. "For starters, what's your relationship with Claire Walden? Why did you bring her here today? And most importantly, *how does she know Davey*?"

"Those are all good questions," Bob replied.

He cast a quick glance at Sam for support. I intercepted the look they shared and felt myself grow cold. For the second time, I found myself wondering what the two of them knew that I didn't.

Had my husband and my ex-husband been complicit in keeping secrets from me? I couldn't even fathom the possibility. And quite frankly, if I was about to discover that that appalling notion was true, I would rather have weathered the tsunami.

Since Bob seemed to have been struck dumb, I swung

my gaze in Sam's direction. "Maybe you'd like to start," I said.

He held up both hands and took a step back. A gesture denoting innocence or an attempt to ward off bad news? It was hard to tell.

"No, thank you," Sam said quickly. "This is all on Bob."

Now there were two of us staring at my ex-husband. Or eight, if you count the Poodles. They seemed anxious to hear what he had to say too.

"Oh for Pete's sake," Bob said. "This conversation has gone spinning off the rails for no reason. Claire is my girlfriend, okay? We've been together since spring. It's no big deal."

He was right, I thought. It *was* no big deal. So why all the subterfuge?

"And?" I asked.

Bob shrugged. "That's it, there's nothing more to tell. Claire and I are having a great time together. End of story."

"And where does Davey fit in?"

"Just where you'd expect, if you stopped and thought about it."

I would most certainly have done so. That is, if anyone had done me the courtesy of letting me know there was something that needed thinking about.

"Davey's my son," said Bob. "And Claire's my girlfriend. I spend as much time with both of them as I can. So it's kind of inevitable that those times would overlap. Davey and Claire met at my house a couple of months ago. They get along great."

A couple of *months* ago? Not only was Bob's explanation not helping, it was having the opposite effect instead. My head was starting to spin with the implications.

I sank into a chair opposite him. "Doesn't it seem odd to you that Davey would meet a woman at your house, apparently spend a significant amount of time in her company, and yet never think to mention her to me?"

Bob frowned uncomfortably. "Yeah, well . . . about that. I might have told him that talking to you about Claire was a bad idea."

And the other shoe dropped.

I sighed. It was either that or shriek. "Bob, why would you have done that?"

"I was trying to spare you."

"Spare me?"

"I didn't want you to be upset."

"Well, clearly that isn't working," I snapped. "How could I not find the fact that you told Davey to keep secrets from me, upsetting?"

"I guess I didn't look at it that way," Bob admitted. Then he brightened. "I told him he could tell Sam."

"Right." I turned and directed a frown at the second culprit. "You were in on this deception too. Just tell me one thing. *Why?*"

"Oh pish," said Aunt Peg, standing in the doorway. "Do we really have to explain this to you?"

I swiveled around in my seat. "Who let you in?"

"The door was unlocked. I let myself in. Eve and Augie were kind enough to come and greet me. Which is more than can be said for my relatives."

Vaguely I'd noticed that several Poodles had left the room. Too distracted by the conversation, I hadn't thought to stop and wonder why.

Sam hopped up and offered Aunt Peg his chair. Delighted to have my attention deflected away from him, he looked inordinately pleased by her arrival. Not that he was going to escape that easily.

"Your relatives were too busy arguing to answer the door," I told her.

"So I heard," Aunt Peg replied tartly. "Somehow—

despite the *truly* appalling news we've had today—Bob's relationship with Claire seems to be the issue under discussion?"

"You knew about her *too?*"

"Oh please." Peg sniffed. "You needn't sound so shocked. We all knew about Claire. You were the only one who was oblivious."

"Or kept in the dark," I muttered. "Depending on how you look at it."

"Bob had good reason for that. Even I understood."

"Then I wish you would explain it to me."

"It's really very simple," Aunt Peg said. "The other two times Bob was involved in a serious relationship, you became all out of sorts. None of us wanted to deal with that turmoil again."

My jaw fell open. Aunt Peg had to be joking. I looked around the room. Amazingly, I seemed to be the only one who found that blithe summation of past events absurdly simplistic. All out of sorts indeed.

"Bob's last girlfriend shot me," I pointed out.

"There was that," Sam agreed.

I was not impressed. His support was too little, too late.

"And the one before that was eighteen."

"Twenty," Bob corrected.

"Same difference!"

"Not really"

I silenced Bob with a glare. "It doesn't matter. What does matter is that I had valid objections to both those women. And the *only* reason I care about that is because any woman who is in your life, is also in Davey's. As you yourself just pointed out."

Bob nodded. "I feel much better having this is all out in the open," he said. "So what did you think of Claire?"

Seriously? He wanted to know that *now?* Hadn't he been listening to anything I'd said?

Apparently not. Because my ex-husband was sitting there, awaiting my reply.

"I've barely even had a chance to meet the poor woman," I told him shortly. "And that was under the worst possible circumstances. I'm still reserving judgment."

"I wish I could say the same," Aunt Peg muttered.

It turned out nobody had to break the news to her that she was a suspect in Nick Walden's murder. The police had already performed that duty for us.

Aunt Peg was not amused. "I hardly had time to assimilate the news myself before the police were knocking on my door and asking what I knew about it."

"What did you tell them?" I asked.

"The only thing I could. That Nick was a wonderful young man and I hadn't any idea who might have wanted to harm him. Then I advised them that they'd better hurry and get things sorted out, otherwise I might have to put my niece on the case."

"Oh, Aunt Peg, you did not say that!" I was horrified by the thought. "Please tell me you didn't."

The local authorities and I shared an uneasy and sometimes contentious relationship. Even when I managed to turn up information that they wouldn't otherwise have had, the professionals were never happy to hear that an amateur had been asking questions about one of their cases. And they really hated it when I beat them to the punch.

"Of course I did. There's nothing like the threat of a little competition to keep people on their toes."

"I'm sure the police are every bit as eager to solve this murder as you are to see it solved," said Sam. "There's no need to goad them along."

"That's precisely what Detective O'Malley told me."

"O'Malley?" I said faintly.

Aunt Peg nodded. "Do you know him?"

"We met several years ago," I said. "It's not a particularly happy memory."

"I can understand why. He had the nerve to ask me whether I possessed an alibi for the time in question. And unfortunately the good detective was not the slightest bit impressed by my answer. Apparently the law does not consider Standard Poodles to be reliable witnesses."

"You may not have an alibi," I pointed out. "But you don't have a motive either. Surely that has to count in your favor."

"I suppose it would have," Aunt Peg said slyly," if I'd gotten around to mentioning it."

Sam shook his head. "Peg, what are you up to now?"

"Since I was thrust into this situation without my consent, I've decided to take advantage of it," Aunt Peg replied. "Nick's death is more than a personal loss; it's also a blow to the local dog community. I want to see that his killer is brought to justice. And I can't think of a better way to keep tabs on the investigation than to allow myself to continue as one of the suspects."

For a minute there was only silence in the room. I think the three of us were too stunned to speak. Even the Poodles looked surprised by this turn of events.

Aunt Peg glanced in my direction. "Don't bother to thank me. It's the least I can do. You know I like to make myself useful."

"Thank you?" I echoed. "For what?"

"For keeping you in the loop, of course. Your own investigation will proceed much more smoothly if you know what the police are doing."

Really, I shouldn't have been surprised. Aunt Peg is the queen of ulterior motives. As soon as she appeared in the doorway, I should have known that she was up to something.

"What a great idea," Bob said enthusiastically. "Well done, Peg!"

Somewhere pigs were taking flight. Or perhaps there was a blue moon in the offing. Those were the only explanations I could come up with for this apparent detente between my ex-husband and my aunt.

"Everyone seems to have decided that I'm going to look into Nick's death," I said. "No one has bothered to ask my opinion. Doesn't anybody want to hear what I think?"

"Not particularly," Aunt Peg informed me.

To my surprise, it was Bob who took my question seriously. He reached his hands across the gap between us and placed them on top of mine. His eyes focused on mine with unnerving intensity.

"Here's what I need you to know," he said. "Claire is devastated by Nick's death. It's not just that her brother is gone, but also that she can't make sense of how or why it happened. She needs answers, and I'm betting you can find them."

I started to speak, but Bob didn't let me. He squeezed my hands and kept talking. "If you're willing to help me help Claire get through this, that's great. And if you're not . . . Then I guess I'll just have to do whatever it takes to change your mind."

This time when Bob paused, I found I had nothing to say. I couldn't remember the last time I'd seen my ex-husband so resolute about anything. This was a whole new side to him, one clearly prompted by his relationship with Claire. It looked like things might be more serious between them than I had initially thought.

"Let me think about it," I said. "Okay?"

"Sure. Just know that Claire will be very grateful for any help you can give us. And so will I." Bob released my hand and stood. He looked at the door, then looked back at me and arched a brow. "Am I clear to go now?"

"All clear," I agreed. "I'll walk you out."

On the way, I asked him if the Morris family had returned from vacation yet.

"Now that you mention it, they should be back in town by now. I'll give them another call and see if I can set up a meeting. The sooner we get that ring back with its rightful owner, the sooner James will stop driving me crazy."

Aunt Peg has ears like a bat. "James?" she said, following us out into the hallway. "Is that the man who was in jail?"

"He wasn't in jail," Sam corrected. "He just traveled a lot."

"Well, I wish he'd start traveling again," said Bob. "He comes over to my house every day now. Suddenly he's dying to help with the renovations."

"What's wrong with that?" asked Sam.

"For one thing, I don't need his help—especially since what that really means is that he stands around and supervises. And when he's not doing that, he wanders around the house poking into everything. I know he and Amber are short on funds. I'm guessing he thinks he's going to stumble upon another ring that he can stuff in his pocket and sell."

"That's ridiculous," I said. "Tell James he'd be better off buying lottery tickets."

"Or put a hammer in his hands and make him useful," Sam advised.

"Tell him to go home to his own house," Aunt Peg said firmly. "And then shut the door behind him."

As usual, she had the last word.

Chapter 9

"That was interesting," Sam said, a few minutes later as he closed the front door.

Bob and Aunt Peg had just left. Sam and I were alone—unless you count the Poodles, who'd followed us out to the front hall. They could sense the tension in the air, but hadn't figured out its source. Eve pressed up against my legs. Faith pushed her muzzle into my hand; her tongue rasped across my fingers. They didn't know what was wrong, but they were trying to offer comfort in any way they could.

I appreciated the thought, but I wasn't ready to give up my anger just yet.

"It was *very* interesting," I said to Sam.

"Oh?" He walked over to the sideboard and began to thumb through the day's mail. Unlike the Poodles, my husband was oblivious to my mood.

"What were you *thinking*?" I asked.

Sam looked up. "About what?"

Okay, I get that women are from Venus and men are from Mars. But surely after all this time, Sam couldn't be that dense about how his wife's mind worked, could he?

"Bob . . . and Claire?"

"Oh, right. I'm glad you know about that now. Keeping it under wraps was a real pain."

"*That's* the part that concerned you?" I asked incredulously. "Did you really think it was a good idea to keep Bob's relationship a secret from me?"

"Bob thought it was a good idea," Sam said slowly. "And it was his life. And his secret. So I honored his request."

"It's Davey's life too," I pointed out. "And now you and Bob have both taught him that it's all right not to tell me things he'd rather that I didn't know."

"Don't you think you're taking this a little too seriously?"

I stared at him across the width of the hallway. "No. I don't."

"Well, I do. Claire seems like a nice woman. Bob could do a lot worse. And has, actually."

Was he missing the point on purpose? I wondered.

"Bob could date a monkey for all I care," I snapped. "As long as I know about it so that I can keep an eye on what's going on with Davey."

"Davey likes Claire," Sam said.

Seriously, I wanted to smack him.

"I have no idea what you're so upset about," he continued. "For all I knew, Claire could have been a passing fling. So there was no point in your getting all wound up about a relationship that wasn't even going to last."

"That wasn't your choice to make," I told him.

"Sorry." Sam shrugged. "At the time it seemed like it was."

A lump rose in my throat. I fought it back down. I couldn't believe that Sam could be this flippant about an issue that was obviously so important to me. The problem went way beyond his depriving me of the ability to manage Davey's life as I saw fit. This was a matter of trust. And how we would deal with each other going forward.

"You are not forgiven," I blurted out.

The words sounded chilling, even to me. They also had the effect of finally alerting Sam to the seriousness of what we were discussing. He stopped and thought about that.

"I don't think I need your forgiveness," he said after a minute. "You may not have liked what I did, but I thought I was acting in your best interests. I didn't do anything wrong."

In the space of one heartbeat to the next, time seemed to stop. I felt as though a chasm was opening between us. One that I hadn't a clue how to cross. Worse still, I wasn't even sure that I wanted to.

Faith, still at my side, whined under her breath. Her body felt warm and solid. I wanted to clutch her like a lifeline. I knelt down and wrapped my arms around her neck. Then I drew in a deep breath and thought about what to do next.

If the morning's events had taught me anything it was that I'd allowed myself to become complacent. Clearly I'd been taking too much for granted. I needed to be asking more questions.

"You might as well tell me now," I said. "Are you and the rest of my family keeping any other secrets from me? You know, for my own good?"

Sam flicked a dismissive glance in my direction as he left the room. "Not that I'm aware of," he said.

"And then he just walked away," I said. "Like he thought the conversation was over. How do men do that?"

I was seated at a window table in The Bean Counter across from my sister-in-law, Bertie. She and my younger brother Frank have been married for four years and they're the parents of three-year-old Maggie. As is true with so many of my friends, Bertie and I met because of dogs. She's a professional handler with a thriving business based out of her home in Wilton. The only reason she'd missed the show where Davey had made his debut with Augie was because the family had been away on a trip to Disney World.

Bertie and I had touched base by phone since their return, but we hadn't had an opportunity to get together. So now we had a lot of catching up to do. When Sam had left to retrieve Kevin, I'd called Bertie. We'd agreed to meet at The Bean Counter for lunch. After the morning I'd just had, I was very much in need of Bertie's sensible, empathetic advice.

The Bean Counter had started out as simply a coffee bar but now, six years later, it also offers an innovative menu of sandwiches and gourmet pastries. The country bistro is a popular destination for everyone from soccer moms, to retirees, to local businessmen.

Bob takes care of the back office. He does the accounting, tracks inventory, orders supplies, and manages the payroll. Frank spends all his time in the front of the house. Most days, he's behind the counter himself. He greets patrons, offers suggestions, and concocts all kinds of custom-made sandwiches.

Bertie had grabbed a table for the two of us. I went to the counter to put in our order. When my turn came, Frank greeted me with a big grin.

He has hazel eyes that are much like my own, but other than that I've never been able to see much of a family resemblance. Frank is four years younger than me and half a foot taller. I tend to worry about things, Frank takes nothing seriously. I envy the ease with which my brother can simply take life as it comes, especially since it's an attitude that has served him well.

"What's today's special?" I asked.

I knew better than to try and order off the menu. No matter what I asked for, my brother was going to make me what he wanted me to have. Usually that meant I'd be trying a new novelty sandwich whose appeal he was undecided about. Some of Frank's innovations are wildly successful and go on to be added to the menu. Others are consigned to the garbage bin almost immediately.

Since I never know in advance which way the culinary wheel of fortune might roll, dining at The Bean Counter tends to be an adventure.

"Sriracha-infused breaded chicken in a wrap with spinach, tomato, and red onion."

I wrinkled my nose. "Isn't sriracha hot?"

"Some is. I'm using the Thai variety. It's sweeter, maybe a little tangier. Give it a whirl. If you don't like it . . ." Frank shrugged.

I knew what that meant. Try, try, again.

"Two then," I said. "One for Bertie and one for me."

Hopefully there'd be safety in numbers. Frank knew he could experiment on me with impunity, but I liked to believe that he wouldn't be so cavalier about his own wife's palate.

Even so, Bertie stared suspiciously at the two plates I delivered to the table. "What *is* that?"

"Something Thai," I said. "Start with a small bite."

"I have every intention of it," Bertie said with a laugh. "This isn't the first mystery meal I've had here."

As I slipped into my seat opposite her, I realized that three businessmen, lunching at the next table, were shifting in their seats and sending admiring glances her way. Ever since I've known her—probably ever since she was a little girl—Bertie's had that effect on men. She's tall and gorgeous with a mass of flaming auburn hair and the kind of body that wolf whistles were invented for.

The funny thing is, Bertie's lived with those attributes for so long that she's mostly oblivious to their effect on others. She's one of the sanest, most down-to-earth people I know, and I adore her. If—heaven forbid—she and Frank ever get divorced, the family is keeping Bertie and letting Frank go. We won't even have to take a vote. It's just the way things are going to be.

We each nibbled cautiously at the edges of our wraps. Then together we followed that with a bigger bite. The wraps weren't bad: perhaps not menu-worthy just yet, but certainly edible.

While we ate, I brought Bertie up to speed on everything that had transpired since we'd last spoken. She'd heard about Nick Walden, but the two of them had never met. So rather than dwelling on his death, she zeroed in immediately on what was bothering me. Bertie wanted to hear all about Nick's sister, Claire.

I told her everything I knew, which wasn't much. That topic led directly to my argument with Sam.

"Of course he walked away," Bertie replied. "In Sam's mind the conversation was over. And he won."

I looked at her with a frown. "That's a terrible thought."

"Sorry." Bertie looked unrepentant. "It's just life."

"I hope not. It was a disagreement, not a battle. Why does there have to be a winner and a loser?"

"That's just the way it works."

"But what about compromise? You know, trying to see each other's point of view? Meeting in the middle? Why isn't that an option?"

"I don't know," said Bertie. "You guys are both working on your second marriages. Maybe the rules are different for you."

"Geez, there are rules? Why didn't anybody tell me that?"

"This is basic man/woman stuff," said Bertie. "We just assumed you knew. So what happens when you guys usually fight? How does it end?"

"We don't fight. Ever."

"*Never*?" Bertie set down her wrap and stared at me across the table. "How is that even possible?"

"Okay, maybe we argue about little stuff like picking up

the towels in the bathroom and who forgot to pay the electric bill. But nothing big like this. And that was part of the problem: Sam didn't think this was a big deal. He didn't think it was important at all."

"*Men,*" Bertie muttered vehemently.

Frank, who'd been working the room, chose that moment to stop by the table. "So," he said brightly. "What do you guys think?"

"We've just concurred that men are idiots," I told him.

"Damn, if I'd known the wrap was that bad, I never would have served it." Frank picked up my plate. "Let me make you something else."

"It's not the food, honey." Bertie reached out and patted his arm. "More of a general observation."

"Oh." Frank put down the plate and backed away. "In that case I'll just make myself scarce."

"Good thinking." I waited until my brother was gone and then said, "I have to ask. Did you know too?"

"About Bob and Claire?"

I nodded. "That, and my family's plan to treat me like I was some kind of blithering idiot."

"No," Bertie said quickly. "I had no idea. Frank might have heard Bob talk about Claire, but you know your brother. Relationship stuff goes right over his head."

That wasn't all that went right over Frank's head, I thought. When something didn't affect him directly, Frank could be blissfully oblivious to just about anything.

"If I had known," Bertie continued, "I'd have told you. Absolutely."

"Thank you for that."

"In fact the more I think about it, the more angry I am on your behalf. If I found out that Mags was spending a lot of time with someone I didn't even know, I'd be livid."

After the grief I'd gotten from my other relatives, it was a relief to know that *someone* understood my feelings. As usual, Bertie had been able to make me feel better. Suddenly I was hungry again. I picked up the wrap and took another bite. The sriracha was beginning to grow on me. Either that or the heat had short-circuited my taste buds.

"So you met Claire for the first time this morning?" Bertie asked.

Still chewing, I settled for a nod.

"Did you like her?"

"I don't know yet," I replied honestly. "It's too soon to tell. But I hope I will. Bob's a good guy. He deserves to have someone great in his life."

"Maybe I'll wrangle an introduction and check her out for myself." Bertie's eyes glinted wickedly. "Do you think she and Bob are serious?"

"If they were, I'd apparently be the last person to know. But they've been together for several months. Plus he's introduced her to Davey. I'd like to think that counts for something."

Bertie polished off the last of her wrap and began to pick at the potato chips that had accompanied it. I watched her enviously. Frank had put baby carrots as a side item on my plate. Just another example of the many ways in which life isn't fair.

"Speaking of Davey . . . soccer camp again?"

"Yup. It starts next week. What's Maggie got lined up for the summer?"

"Preschool camp, if you can believe that. A little swimming and some arts and crafts. The session started on Monday; it's just a couple of hours a day. Since she's an only child, it's great for her to have a chance to hang out with kids her own age."

Been there, I thought. For the first nine years of Davey's life, he'd been an only child too.

"I have an announcement on that score myself," I said. "I'm going back to school too."

For the majority of my adult life I had been employed as a teacher, working first in the Stamford public school system and more recently as special needs tutor at Howard Academy, a private day school located in Greenwich. I had taken maternity leave after Kevin was born, and my scheduled break had now stretched through several extra semesters. I'd recently been contacted by the school's headmaster, however, and now it looked as though my sabbatical was coming to an end.

"That's great!" said Bertie. "I was beginning to wonder if you were ever going to go back."

"Me too," I admitted. "But it turns out that the wife of the man they hired to replace me is taking a job transfer to Belgium. So the position is open again and it's mine if I want it."

"Which you do," Bertie confirmed.

"You're right," I agreed. "I do want it. I miss being a teacher. And Howard Academy was a great place to work."

"What about Kev?"

"Sam and I have two months to get the details ironed out. He works at home and he says he'll manage. I'm going to ease back into the position gradually. I'll start in September with three half days a week."

Bertie picked up a handful of chips and dropped them on my plate next to the baby carrots. I considered them for about ten seconds, then dug in and helped myself.

"And in the meantime . . . ?" She let the question dangle.

"It's summer," I said. "And I'm taking it easy."

Bertie shook her head.

"Screw that," she said. "I've never seen you take the easy way yet. What about Nick Walden?"

"I don't know," I told her. "Bob was pretty vehement about wanting my help. So I guess I'll talk to Claire again. And then we'll see what happens after that."

Chapter 10

When I arrived home, Sam acted as if nothing had changed between us. Indeed he behaved as if nothing unusual had happened at all. He and Kevin were in the room off the kitchen that had become the locus for our Poodle grooming activities.

Kevin was on the floor in the corner, playing with a set of Legos. According to the picture on the Lego box, he was supposed to be building a castle. Instead his structure looked more like an igloo. Or maybe an ancient burial mound. He seemed to be having fun, however, so who was I to quibble with the results?

Sam had Augie lying on his side on the grooming table. The puppy was freshly bathed and Sam was busy blowing him dry. With a Poodle in show trim it isn't enough to simply get the moisture out of the hair. The coat must also be carefully straightened and detangled as it dries.

It's a painstaking job that requires patience. What it doesn't require is undivided attention. Once the large, freestanding dryer is correctly positioned, with the nozzle pointing where it needs to go, the fingers can usually fly through the exercise without much input from the brain. So I thought that we'd be able to talk while he worked.

Sam didn't agree however. Instead he mimed that the noise from the dryer would make conversation difficult.

And we both knew that if he turned the blower off midtask to talk to me, Augie's coat would curl and mat before he'd be able to finish it. So instead I left him to the chore, whistled up the other Poodles, and took them for a walk. The pack was delighted to take a spin around the neighborhood, and the exercise enabled me to work off some frustration.

I couldn't help but wonder why Sam had decided to give Augie a bath at the very time that would coincide with my return. Usually that was a job he and Davey did together. Not only that, but the puppy's coat had appeared to be in decent shape earlier. I hadn't noticed anything that would have required urgent care.

Or maybe I was just being paranoid, I thought. But now that I knew I'd spent the last several months in blissful ignorance, never dreaming for a moment that my own family was conspiring to keep secrets from me, I felt like I needed to question everything.

It was no way to run a marriage.

When Davey got home that afternoon he was delighted to discover that while he'd spent the day playing with Joey Brickman, his puppy had been given a bath and had his ears and topknot freshly rewrapped.

"Wow, he looks great." Davey wound his arms around Augie's neck and gave him a hug. "He even smells good. Thanks, Sam!"

Davey grabbed his little brother's hand. Together the two boys ran through the house and out to the backyard. The Poodles, who love a good chasing game, went flying after them.

"You missed a call from Bob earlier," Sam said as we heard the back door slam. "He wanted us to know that Nick is being buried at the end of the week. Claire's parents are flying up from North Carolina and they're having a private family funeral. Later on, after everything gets sorted out, there'll be a memorial service to celebrate Nick's life."

"Is Bob going to the funeral?" I asked.

Sam hesitated briefly, then nodded. "So he said."

That answer revealed more about the state of Bob and Claire's relationship than anything I'd heard previously. Good for Bob, I thought.

"I need to talk to Davey about Claire," I said.

"Why?"

Maybe I should have tried again to explain how I was feeling. Perhaps Sam's question was the opening I needed to start a discussion between us. But half of me was feeling mulish and the other half was more than a little afraid that Sam would simply blow off my concerns again.

So instead I gave him the answer he deserved. "Because Davey will tell me what's going on," I said.

I found the two boys in the middle of the yard at the foot of the old oak tree. A fork in the branches, ten feet above the ground, held the tree house that Sam and Davey had built together several years earlier. A rope ladder dangled down to provide access. Davey had wrapped Kevin's small hands around the sides of the ladder, and he was trying to hoist his brother up the length of the broad trunk.

The Poodles were circling the tree, observing the activity with varying degrees of interest and concern. Tar's tail was whipping back and forth eagerly. Faith, a mother herself, was pacing and whining under her breath.

It looked as though I'd arrived just in time.

"Davey, you know Kev's too young for the tree house."

A firm hand on my older son's shoulder separated the two boys. Then I reached around and pried Kevin's fingers loose from the ladder. As soon as he let go, I swung him down to the ground.

"He wanted to go up," Davey said in his own defense. "He asked me to take him, didn't you?"

The toddler nodded happily.

"Kevin's too young to know what's good for him and what isn't. That's why it's your job—as his big brother—to keep him safe."

"But Sam takes him up there!"

"Sam's a lot bigger than you are," I pointed out. "He climbs the ladder carrying Kevin in his arms. Can you do that?"

"No." Davey looked at the ground. "I guess not."

"In another few years, the two of you will be able to go up there together whenever you want."

"That's a long time," said Davey.

"Long time!" Kevin echoed. He pumped a fist in the air for good measure. Even when he has no idea what the conversation is about, he always agrees with his brother.

Looking at the two boys standing there side by side, united in their support for one another, a wave of tenderness washed over me. I suddenly felt like the luckiest woman in the world. Both my sons were happy and healthy. That was more than enough to make the other problems that had weighed down my day seem unimportant. I reached out and looped an arm around each of my sons and pulled them close in a hug.

"I love you guys," I said.

"Aww, Mom," Davey grumbled, his head pressed against my shoulder. "We already know that. You don't have to keep telling us."

"Yes, I do," I said.

Kevin disentangled himself and leaned back. "Love you, Mom. Want a Popsicle."

I laughed and let them both go. "You're a little manipulator," I told my younger son.

"I'm a 'lipulator," he repeated happily. "I want grape!"

"Go back inside," I said to Kev. I turned the toddler in the right direction and gave him a little push. "Dad will get you a Popsicle."

"I'll take him," Davey volunteered.

"No, I'd rather you stay out here with me a minute. I want to talk to you about something."

Kevin, accompanied by several Poodles, trotted dutifully toward the house. Davey sat down on the grass and crossed his legs. "What's up?" he asked.

Raven and Eve lay down beside him. I took a spot opposite the trio. "So your father has a new girlfriend," I said.

"Yeah, I guess." Davey ducked his head. I couldn't see his expression.

"And he told you not to tell me about her?"

"He said it would be easier if you didn't know," Davey admitted. "Are you mad?"

"Yes, I am," I told him. "I don't like secrets. But I'm not mad at you. It's the grown-ups who should have known better."

Davey lifted his head. He looked relieved.

"So now that I've met Claire, let's talk about her."

"You met her? When?"

"She was here earlier, with your dad." I didn't feel any need to explain the circumstances of their visit. "Do you like her?"

"Sure," Davey replied. "She's nice."

"Does she spend a lot of time with your dad?"

"I guess."

"Do you mind about that?"

"No." Davey frowned thoughtfully. "Why would I?"

"Maybe because it takes some of his attention away from you?"

"Nah, that's okay. Claire's pretty cool. Dad and I both like it when she comes over. She cooks sometimes. And she plays video games with me."

"Really?" I hadn't expected that.

"Sure." Davey grinned. "She's not very good. She screams and jumps around on the couch. Sometimes I let her win."

"That's big of you," I said with a laugh.

"Don't tell her. Okay?"

"I won't," I said. "On one condition. I don't want you keeping any more secrets from me. No matter who tells you to."

"Okay," Davey agreed readily. "It's a deal."

He pushed off with both hands and stood up. "Mom? About Claire . . ."

"Hmm?" I stood up as well.

"She makes Dad happy. He smiles a lot when she's around."

I reached out and ruffled his short hair. "That's a good thing."

"I think so too," Davey said. He sounded unexpectedly grown up. Then he grabbed Raven and Eve and took off running toward the house. Just that quickly, the illusion of maturity vanished.

"Where are you going in such a hurry?" I called after him.

Davey grinned back over his shoulder. "To get a Popsicle before Kevin eats them all!"

I waited until after the funeral to call Claire. She didn't seem surprised to hear from me and we agreed to get together that afternoon. By that time Davey's soccer camp had started, and Sam, who was between projects, agreed to watch Kevin.

Briefly I considered taking Faith with me. In a house with six dogs, it can be difficult to ensure that each one receives enough individual attention. And since Faith never takes advantage of her status as top dog, that makes me want to play favorites all the more.

But luckily before I loaded the big Poodle into the Volvo, I remembered that Claire had mentioned taking possession of Nick's two dogs after his death. A Rottie mix and a little terrier, she'd said. Considering that I barely knew Nick's sister, I wasn't at all sure how the visit might proceed. Things might be strained enough without adding the potential for canine tension to the mix.

Like her brother, Claire lived in Riverside, a subsection of Greenwich on the southeast side of town. GPS delivered me to a cute cottage at the end of a cul-de-sac near the turnpike. The house was set very near the road, and the yard behind it appeared almost non-existent. Based on Claire's description, Nick's dogs had sounded young and energetic. I wondered how all three of them—human and canine both—were dealing with the change in circumstance.

I hopped up two front stairs and rang the bell. Immediately I heard the rumble of heavy footsteps approaching the door. A cacophony of loud, deep-throated, barking sounded from within. If I'd been a burglar or a Jehovah's Witness, the noise alone would have been enough to make me reconsider visiting this address.

"Just a minute!" Claire called out.

Prudently I backed up. If the Rottie was about to come flying out when she opened the door, I didn't want to get knocked down the steps.

The same thought must have occurred to Claire because when she drew the door open a moment later, she had one hand on the knob and the other wrapped firmly around the big dog's leather collar. He was black with rust colored markings, and everything about him—from his deep chest, to his sturdy legs, to his broad, blunt, muzzle—gave the impression of barely restrained power.

Seeing me, the dog began to jump up and down in place. It was all Claire could do to hold him. It looked like any second he was going to drag her through the doorway and down the stairs.

"Thor, get down!" she commanded.

The dog dropped to all fours but continued to eye me warily. He didn't look like the kind of dog I'd want to meet in a dark alley.

"He's fine." Claire said quickly. "Really, he is." She only sounded half-convinced. "You're not afraid of dogs, are you? Oh no, of course not. You have big dogs of your own. Please come in. Thor will settle down as soon as he realizes you're not a threat."

That didn't sound very reassuring. Considering Thor's size and his territorial attitude, it seemed to me it would be better if he accepted me as non-threatening *before* I entered his domain.

"Will he run away if you let go of him?" I asked.

"No." Claire bit her lip. "But he might jump on you."

"Does he bite?"

"I don't think so."

Again, not the most reassuring answer I'd heard recently.

"Let's try it," I said. "Let go of his collar and let him approach me on his own."

Slowly Claire unwound her fingers. Once released, the big dog didn't charge at me. He did, however, rise up on his toes and lift his shoulders. The change in stance dropped his head into a more menacing position.

"Hey, Thor," I said quietly. "You and I are going to be friends."

I looked in the Rottie's direction, but not directly at him. When he advanced toward me, I held my ground and extended a hand. With luck, he'd inhale Faith's scent and realize I was an ally.

Or there was the other possibility: that he'd just go ahead and chomp my fingers before he took the time to sniff them.

Fortunately for all of us, Thor opted for the former. Claire exhaled the breath she'd been holding. I lifted my hand and ran it up over Thor's arched forehead. As I scratched between his ears, he managed a small wag of his stumpy tail.

"He really is a good dog," Claire said. "It's just that he has these protective instincts. Nick knew how to keep them in check. The two of them trusted each other implicitly. But Thor and I don't have the same kind of relationship yet. Who knows? Maybe we never will."

"It must be hard for him, having to adapt to a new living situation," I said.

"It is," Claire replied. "And on top of that he and Jojo really miss Nick. I know they have to be wondering where he is."

Claire and Thor both stepped back out of the doorway so I could enter the house. She closed the door behind us.

"Nick adopted both dogs from the pound," Claire continued as she led the way across a small hallway and into the living room. "So whatever happened to them before that is a mystery. But based on their behavior, they didn't come from good situations.

"When something startles Thor, his first response is aggression. Jojo, whom you haven't even met yet"—Claire waved a hand vaguely in the direction of the dining room—"hides under the table and won't come out. As you might imagine, Nick spent a great deal of time working with both of them."

Claire's lower lip began to quiver. She directed me to a seat on the couch and took a moment to gather herself. "He loved every minute of that. Being able to take damaged dogs and turn them back into good canine citizens was his life's work. And of course when he was with them, both dogs were totally reliable. But now they're just scared and confused. They don't know what to think or what they're supposed to do."

"It must be hard on all of you," I said quietly.

I chose a seat in the middle of the couch. In my house, a dog would have immediately jumped up on the furniture beside me. But either Thor had better manners than my Poodles, or else he hadn't totally accepted me yet. Instead of joining me on the couch, he lay down next to Claire's chair.

"It's harder than you can imagine," she said, trying, and failing, to hold back a sniffle. Claire fished a tissue out of her pocket and wiped her nose. "Nick and I were very close. I know siblings are supposed to fight and compete with each other, but even when we were little, Nick and I never did."

"You were lucky."

Claire looked up. "You have a brother, right?"

"Yes, Frank. He's Bob's partner at The Bean Counter."

"That's right. I'm pretty sure I knew that. Sorry, you'll have to forgive me. My brain is all over the place these days. I can't seem to concentrate on much of anything."

"You're forgiven," I said quickly. "No need to even ask. In fact, if you'd rather that I come back another day—"

"No. Please don't go." Claire's eyes were big and overly bright. She blinked several times, willing away tears. "I'm glad you're here. We need to talk."

"We do," I agreed. "But it doesn't have to happen today."

"The sooner, the better," said Claire. "Because I really need to apologize."

She was concerned about Aunt Peg, I thought. Claire must have had second thoughts about naming Peg as the chief suspect in Nick's murder.

"For siccing the police on Aunt Peg?" I asked. "You don't have to worry about that. Much as it pains me to admit it, she rather enjoyed the attention."

"Peg . . . what?" Claire looked confused. "Oh no, I wasn't worried about her. Your aunt strikes me as the kind of woman who can look out for herself."

She had that right.

"What then?"

"It's Davey. I'm sorry you didn't know that he and I are friends. Believe me, I had no idea about that until Bob told me that you were angry with him and why. You have every right to be upset about the way that was handled."

"Thank you," I said. "But you have nothing to apologize for. Just because Bob decided to act like an idiot doesn't mean I'm going to hold that against you."

"Even so, I never meant to cause any problems."

"Consider it behind us," I told her firmly. I thought for a moment, then added, "By the way, after I found out about your relationship with Bob, I asked Davey what he thought of you."

"What did he say?"

"That you make Bob happy. That he smiles more when you're around."

"Oh. Oh." Claire was once again blinking back tears. "Thank you for that."

"I'm glad that you two found one another," I said.

"Me too," Claire said softly. "I know Bob's your ex and that that isn't the easiest kind of relationship to navigate. But I hope, once we have a chance to get to know one another, that you and I will be able to get along too."

"I'm sure we will," I replied.

Claire straightened in her seat. She sucked in a deep breath and squared her shoulders. "Good," she said. "Because I need to ask you something."

"Go on."

"Bob is convinced that you have a knack for solving mysteries. Is that true?"

"Probably," I admitted.

"Then you're going to figure out who killed my brother. And I'm going to help you do it."

Chapter 11

"The police—" I said.

"I know," Claire broke in. She sounded exasperated. "They're working on it. I've spoken with them several times. They're exploring the usual avenues of investigation and they're doing their job to the best of their abilities."

Her voice had flattened to a monotone. It sounded as though she was reciting something she'd been told, probably more than once.

"I'm guessing you spoke with Detective O'Malley," I said.

In my previous acquaintance with the man—which thankfully had been brief—I'd found him to be someone who operated strictly by the book. He also had a certain Bulldog quality: stubbornness combined with an unflagging belief that he was always right.

"You know him?"

"I've been interrogated by him," I said dryly. "Does that count?"

Claire looked taken aback. For a moment I thought she might pursue that comment further. Then abruptly she thought better of it and switched tacks.

"Here's what I've learned in my job," she said. "The more people you get involved in an activity, the better things are likely to proceed. Frankly I can't see why this should be any different."

"What kind of job do you have?" I asked.

"I'm an event planner. I started out in the corporate world but after I did a few kids' parties on the side, I realized that was the career I really wanted. So I quit my job and went out on my own. I do mostly birthday parties, but also bar mitzvahs, graduations, or pretty much anything else that parents want."

"A party planner," I repeated faintly.

It was hard to see the correlation between that activity and solving murders. But maybe that was just me.

Claire stood up and left the room. I wondered if I should follow. She continued speaking as she crossed the hall and stood in the arched doorway that led to a small dining room opposite.

"Okay, maybe the parallels aren't exact," she said. "But look at the big picture." Claire squatted down and peered beneath the table. "Jojo, it's time to come out now. Melanie's a friend. She isn't going to hurt you."

"Big picture?" I asked. No wonder Claire enjoyed planning children's parties. This conversation was like a three-ring circus.

"You know," she said, glancing back over her shoulder at me. "it's like on a ship. When there's a crisis the captain says *'all hands on deck.'* He wants everybody with any sense to be working on solving the problem."

"Right," I agreed. I guessed I was still following her logic. More or less.

Frankly, dealing with the dog situation seemed easier than trying to keep up with the twists and turns of the conversation. Thanks to Aunt Peg's ongoing tutelage, I was pretty good at that stuff. So I got up and went and joined Nick's sister in the hallway.

When I knelt down beside her, I could just about see the little terrier through the forest of chair legs. Jojo had a wiry, wheat-colored, coat, V-shaped ears, and big dark eyes. His body was crouched just above the floor. His nails were digging into the rug beneath him. Poised to flee, the poor guy was also trembling.

"Is he always like that?" I asked.

Claire sighed. "Not when he was with Nick. But now, more often than not, I'm afraid so."

"Would he come out for a biscuit?"

"I doubt it."

"What does he like?" I asked. "I mean really like . . . more than anything?"

"That's easy. He loves to go for walks. I take him and Thor out twice a day. It's the one thing he gets excited about."

"Great," I said, rising to my feet. "Let's go."

"Now?" Claire looked up at me.

"Sure. Why not?"

She levered herself up beside me. "I thought we were going to talk about Nick. And what we're going to do next."

"I can walk and talk at the same time," I told her. "I've been doing it for years."

Claire tilted her head to one side and gave me a look. I imagined it was similar to the one she gave to misbehaving children at her parties. Being both a mother and a teacher, I've been known to use that same look to great effect myself.

So now I just waited her out. After a moment, Claire shrugged. She walked over to a closet near the front door. Two leather leashes were looped around the doorknob.

"Hey, guys!" she called out. "Who wants to go outside?"

Thor scrambled to his feet and came running into the hall. For a big dog, he was surprisingly agile. Jojo was slower to appear. He made sure that the path he took to Claire's side allowed for a very wide berth around me.

"What a good boy you are," I crooned in a friendly tone of voice as Claire snapped the lead to his collar. The terrier hid behind Claire's legs and ignored me.

"Don't take it personally." She handed me Thor's lead and kept Jojo for herself. Then she drew the door open and we both stepped outside. "He's like that with everyone. And you want to know the really stupid thing?"

"What's that?" I asked.

"Every time one of these dogs looks upset or does something that really worries me, the first thing I always think is, I'd better call Nick. He'll know just what to do."

A lump rose in my throat. Several seconds passed before I could even try to form an answer.

"Don't," said Claire, reading the expression on my face. "Let's just walk."

So we did.

"I didn't want to ask O'Malley," she said a few minutes later. "I find him a little intimidating, if you know what I mean."

I most certainly did.

"But what *are* the usual avenues of investigation?"

Claire had been right about what Jojo enjoyed. The terrier was hopping, skipping, and jumping along beside us. His tail was up over his back, wagging happily. His tongue slid in and out of the side of his mouth.

Thor meanwhile, kept his feet and his nose closer to the ground. He wanted to stop and sniff every bush and tree we walked past. The Rottie was strong and he enjoyed testing boundaries. He was also certain that his opinion counted for more than mine did. We'd had to discuss that a couple of times before we were able to settle into a harmonious walking rhythm.

"Principally the police are looking for someone with a good motive," I said. "Did Nick have any enemies?"

"No, of course not. My brother was the kind of guy who got along great with everybody."

"And yet it's likely that Nick was killed by someone he knew, possibly even someone he knew well." I nodded down the leash toward Thor. "Could you imagine this dog not trying to protect your brother, if he perceived that there was a threat?"

"No." Claire shook her head firmly. "Not for a second."

"Me either. So now we have to figure out who your brother knew that might have had a reason to want to harm him. Probably the first thing the police will do is look at Nick's finances. If you don't mind my asking, was he having any money problems?"

"Not that I'm aware of," Claire replied. "And I'm sure I'd have known if he was. Considering that we're both self-employed, we spent a lot of time comparing notes, you know?"

I nodded. "Aunt Peg said that he had plenty of clients."

Thor pulled me toward a particularly enticing tree and I stopped to let him lift his leg. Once he was finished, Jojo bounced over and followed suit.

"More than enough to keep him busy," Claire agreed. "Nick was happy with the way things were going. His business already brought in enough money for him to live on, and he expected to be expanding his client base in the near future."

"Because of Aunt Peg, you mean?"

"Precisely. She'd already begun introducing him to her friends. Nick loved all that. I know it sounds silly but there was nothing he enjoyed more than the prospect of getting to meet new dogs."

"That doesn't sound silly to me at all," I said. "I can totally understand why Nick felt that way."

"I bet you guys would have become great friends," Claire said softly. "If only there had been more time."

My breath caught on a sigh. "I was looking forward to it," I said.

Our positions were very different but we both felt the same keen sense of loss. I waited a beat then deliberately changed the subject.

"What about your brother's love life?"

"It was way busier than his professional life." Claire grimaced slightly. "If that's what you'd like to know."

"Maybe. You mentioned before that he had a girlfriend?"

"Yes, Diana."

"How long were they together?"

"I don't know. Three months, I guess. Or maybe six?"

"That's quite a time difference," I pointed out.

"I know. But as much as Nick and I talked about our respective businesses, he could be very reticent when it came to his private life."

"How come?" I asked curiously.

"When he was young, Nick was a shy, nerdy kind of kid. He didn't date much, even in high school. Our mother was always bugging him about that. You'd think she would have been happy with a son who got good grades and didn't get into trouble, but instead she kept asking him why he never brought girls home."

"That would have shut me up too," I said.

Claire nodded. "By the time Nick got to college, things turned around. He'd grown a couple of inches and gotten rid of his glasses. It wasn't so much that Nick discovered girls, as that they finally began to notice him."

"I can see why," I said. "Your brother was seriously cute."

"And he knew it." Claire laughed. "Thank God he was a nice guy and didn't take advantage of the situation. At least not too often."

Thor tugged me in the direction of a parked car. The

walk came to a halt while he examined every inch of the front tire.

"Thor likes rubber," said Claire. "Go figure. Nick had a thing for quirky dogs."

By now, Jojo had decided to add his scrutiny to that of the big dog. When Claire joined me beside the car, the terrier never even glanced in my direction as he pushed past my leg to get to the curb. We were definitely making progress. On the other hand, I didn't even want to think about what that tire might have run over recently to cause it to be such a source of fascination.

"Tell me about the times Nick did take advantage," I said as we waited for the dogs to finish their perusal.

"It was no big deal. Just that most of his clients were women. I was always teasing him about that."

"Do you think they hired him for more than his ability to help their dogs?"

"I'm sure some of them did. Nick once told me he sometimes felt like the Connecticut version of the hot, young pool boy. Not that he was complaining. It was all good for business."

"How did Diana feel about that?" I asked.

"I have no idea. I barely knew her. She and I met a couple of times, but that was the extent of our relationship. We don't have a lot in common. If it wasn't for Nick, we never would have spent time together at all."

"It sounds like you didn't like her much," I said, gathering up Thor's leash. It was time to move things along.

"It's not that exactly."

"Then what is it?"

Claire frowned as she and Jojo fell in beside us. "Don't take this the wrong way."

"I won't," I said.

"Diana's a snob."

I snorted out a laugh. "Is there a right way to take that?"

"I don't know." Claire looked flustered. "I'm not trying to be mean."

"Go ahead," I told her. "Have at it. Things will go much better if we're honest with one another."

"You're right," she agreed. "Okay, let me explain. Diana grew up in Greenwich, which couldn't have been more different from the little town in North Carolina where Nick and I are from. We both came north for college, then Nick ended up in Fairfield County with a girl. That relationship didn't last but he liked it here and stayed. I joined him last year. We both love Connecticut but we don't always feel like we fit in here."

"Did Diana make Nick feel that way?" I asked.

"I think so. Sometimes. Nick and I don't have a privileged background like she does. And that seemed to matter to her. I always felt like Diana wasn't sure that Nick was good enough for her."

"That doesn't sound like a great basis for a relationship."

"I could be totally wrong," Claire said quickly. "Like I said, it's not as though I ever spent a lot of time with her and Nick. It was just kind of a gut feeling I had."

"I'm a big believer in gut feelings," I told her. "More often than not, I think they're right."

Having circled several blocks of homes, we were now approaching Claire's house from the opposite direction. Thor and Jojo both knew where they lived. Despite having been so eager to leave the house only half an hour earlier, the two dogs now began to pull us toward it. It seemed to me that that spoke well of the relationship they were building with Claire.

She paused when we came to her driveway. "So we're going to do this, right? You'll help me find out what happened to Nick?"

My answer was inevitable. Claire must have felt the

same way because she didn't even wait for my reply. "So what's the first step?" she asked.

"I want to see Nick's client list," I said. "Do you have it?"

"No, but I can get it for you from Bob."

Right, I thought. Aunt Peg had told me that he was doing Nick's books. I'd forgotten about that.

"Don't worry," I told her. "I'll get it myself."

"And then what?" Claire asked eagerly. "Are we going to spy on them?"

That made me laugh. "No, I'm sure that won't be necessary."

"Or maybe you could tell Nick's clients that you've taken over his business. I saw how you handled Thor. He intimidates everybody, even me sometimes. But you knew just what to do with him. You could pull it off. It would be like undercover work."

"Claire, slow down. There's no point in making things more complicated than they have to be."

"What do you mean?"

"All I want to do is ask some questions. People love to talk about themselves, and Nick's murder will have been a shocking event in their lives. I don't think I'll have to trick anyone into talking about it."

"But the murderer—he'll clam up. Right?"

Maybe if we were in a B-movie, I thought.

"Let's wait and see what happens," I said aloud.

Claire tossed her head. "I don't want to wait. I want answers. Bob told me you were good at this stuff."

"I try hard," I told her. "Does that count?"

"I hope so." She didn't sound entirely convinced.

On the way home, I stopped at Davey's soccer camp and picked him up. He tossed his backpack, water bottle, and shin guards on the back seat of the car. A pair of muddy cleats landed on the floor. Not only did it take a village to raise my child, he needed one to outfit him as well.

"How was camp?" I asked, as he joined me up front and buckled on his seat belt.

"Okay."

"Just okay?" This was his fifth summer at camp. He'd always loved it before.

"All we did all day was run drills."

"I'm sure the coaches had a good reason for that." I drove back down the long driveway, paused to look both ways, then pulled out onto the road.

"They said it was good for us," Davey grumbled.

"Drills *are* good for you."

"Games are better."

I reached over and patted his knee. It was covered with grime. His T-shirt was grubby and there was a smear of mud on his neck. His short hair was spiky with sweat. That child was heading straight to the shower as soon as we got home.

"They said we were goofing off too much during scrimmage," Davey said with a frown. "So we had to run drills instead of playing."

I cocked a brow in his direction. "*Were* you goofing off?"

"Moo-om!" My son treated me to his version of every child's exasperated cry. "It's summer!"

"So?"

"It's not like we're in school or anything. Camp is supposed to be fun."

"You're right," I agreed. "But now that you're older, the coaches are expecting you to show some discipline too. Think of it this way: if you weren't a good player, they probably wouldn't care if you were goofing off."

"I guess."

I took my eyes off the road and glanced his way. "You guess? That's all I get?"

"Yup." Davey grinned at me across the seat. "We don't have to dissect my whole day or anything. I should have just said that camp was fine. I only told you what the coaches said so you wouldn't think I was keeping a secret."

"Oh." That thought hadn't occurred to me. "Thank you."

"You're welcome."

I pondered that for a minute, then said, "So . . . all those days when I picked you up at school and you told me everything was fine, is there anything else I should know about that?"

"Nope," he said cheerfully. "Definitely not."

Parenthood. It ought to come with a user's manual.

Chapter 12

When we got home, I sent Davey straight upstairs to take a shower. Then I went to look in the kitchen to see what kind of supplies we had on hand that could be turned into an appealing, healthy, low-cal, child-friendly, dinner. You know, the kind that sitcom mothers toss together with ease while also juggling three kids and holding down a full-time job.

Milk, peanut butter, and dog biscuits are the staples in my house. We always have those. But beyond that, Sam's and my food shopping habits are a bit haphazard. In our refrigerator, you never know what you might find. Sometimes you get lucky. And sometimes you kick yourself for not thinking ahead and stopping at the supermarket on the way home.

The first drawer I opened revealed packages of boneless chicken breasts and Portobello mushrooms. The crisper held a bag of romaine lettuce. There were fresh tomatoes from the farmer's market on the counter. It looked as though things were going to shape up nicely.

As I was closing the refrigerator, the back door pushed open. The Poodles came spilling through first. Tar, Augie, and Raven caused a bottleneck as they all tried to scramble through the doorway at the same time.

Faith and Casey had more sense. They both hung back

and waited their turns. Eve was walking more sedately behind the rest of the crew as Kevin had grabbed a fistful of her neck hair and was marching beside her across the deck. Sam brought up the rear.

Gently I disentangled my son's fingers from Eve's coat. The Poodle winced slightly as I performed the task. When she was finally free, she stepped away in relief and had a long shake.

"Good dog," I told her, giving the area a good rub with my hand. "You did such a good job."

Tar's ears pricked at the words. Our only intelligence-challenged Poodle, he sometimes struggled with basic commands. But Tar understood the words *good dog* readily enough. Not only that, but he had enough of an ego to assume that they always applied to him.

Now, certain that he'd heard himself praised, Tar was quite sure that I should give him a biscuit. He walked over to the pantry and waited. The other Poodles, catching on quickly, followed suit. So I got out the box of peanut butter biscuits and handed out treats all the way around. What can I say? My dogs have me beautifully trained.

"Where's Davey?" Kevin asked.

"Upstairs," I said. "He's taking a shower."

"Go see," my son announced. Small legs pumping, he trotted purposefully from the room.

Eve hesitated a moment, then followed. That Poodle is a glutton for punishment. Either that or she should be nominated for canine sainthood.

"So," said Sam, "did you and Claire have a good talk?"

"We did."

"And . . . ?"

I waited for him to elaborate, unsure which direction the conversation was going to go. Sam puttered around the kitchen for a minute before finally realizing I that hadn't yet answered.

"How did you two get along?" he asked.

"Just fine," I told him. "Claire seems very nice."

"That's great."

Sam nodded with satisfaction. As if he deserved some sort of credit for my belated opportunity to meet with my ex-husband's girlfriend. Which he most assuredly did not.

I was about to point that out when he said, "Then everything worked out. So what was all the fuss about?"

For a moment, I froze in place. I bit back the first retort that sprang to mind and reminded myself that it wasn't about winning or losing—no matter what Bertie had said. This was about us finding a way to work through a significant difference of opinion so that we could both come out whole on the other side.

"The fuss—as you call it—had nothing to do with Claire," I said slowly. "It was about everyone else trying to manage my life for me."

"I don't think so," Sam replied.

I tipped my head to one side. "Let me get this straight. Did I misunderstand what was going on? Were you and Bob *not* trying to keep me from finding out about Claire?"

"Really, Mel, you're getting all wound up over nothing again. This isn't a big deal; let's not try and make it one. I think you just need to take a deep breath and calm down."

Lord save me from a patronizing man. Especially one who flat-out refused to try and see my side of things. Nothing—short of threatening one of my children—could have lit my fuse faster.

"Thank you for your concern," I said shortly. "But I'm quite calm."

"If you stop and think about what really happened, I'm sure you'll realize that you read way too much into the whole situation. I know you're upset about Bob and Claire's relationship—"

I gasped in outrage. Sam couldn't really believe that, could he? If so, he and I not only weren't on the same page, we weren't even in the same library.

"I am not upset about Bob and Claire," I told him, speaking slowly and spacing my words for emphasis. "Whatever they want to do together is fine with me. I wish the two of them well."

"If you say so."

"I do," I said firmly.

"Good. Then whatever it is you *are* annoyed about, you need to put it behind you and get over it."

Sam left the room. I stood and watched him go. Even though we'd resolved nothing, I made no move to follow him. What's worse, I didn't want to. For the first time I could remember in all the years I'd known Sam, I had no desire to prolong the time we spent together.

And I wasn't happy about that one bit.

That evening I asked Bob for Nick's client roster. He ascertained that he had Claire's permission to release the list, then called me back.

"When I took over the accounting for Nick's business in the spring, he gave me all his records," Bob said. "They go back three years, to when he was first getting started. How far back do you want me to go?"

"I'd like to see all the current clients, certainly. And then how about everyone else from the last year? Can you give them to me in reverse chronological order from when they started using Nick's services?"

"Sure, no problem."

"Rough idea, how many names are we talking about?"

"Probably around twenty, give or take. And most of those are still listed as current. Even when Nick had finished working with a particular dog, he'd still check back with the client periodically to make sure that things were continuing to go well. That kept their accounts open in the books. Nick always said that in order to understand what was going wrong with the dogs, he first needed to understand their owners. It seems like a number of his clients ended up also becoming his friends."

As he was speaking, Bob e-mailed the list to me. I opened the file and ran my gaze down the list of names and addresses. Also included were the names and breeds of each client's dogs. They ran the gamut from large to small, and mixed breed to purebred.

"I hope Nick's clients will be as happy to see me as they apparently were to see him," I said.

"They will," Bob said with confidence. "And, Mel?"

"Hmm?" I was still busy reading.

"Thank you. Claire and I both appreciate what you're doing."

"You're welcome," I replied. I felt unexpectedly touched by his gratitude. "Let's just hope it works."

The next morning I picked up the phone and started at the top of the list. The first two numbers I called resulted in nothing more than the opportunity to leave a message on an answering machine. It looked as though summer vacation might play a role in determining how many of Nick's former clients I could talk to. I left a brief message on each machine and moved on.

With my third try, I was luckier. Fran Dolan picked up on the first ring. I explained who I was and what I wanted and Fran assured me that her schedule was clear and that she'd be delighted to meet with me that morning.

"And Barney too," she said.

Thanks to Bob's detailed notes, I knew that Barney was Mrs. Dolan's Basset Hound. "Woof!" I replied.

Sam and I managed to split up our parental duties with a minimum of conversation. I agreed to drop Davey off at soccer camp and Sam volunteered to take Kevin to swim class at the Y. Sam had a meeting in White Plains after that, and I assured him I'd be home to see to the dogs. If our schedules continued to dovetail so neatly, it seemed conceivable we might reach the point where we barely had to speak to one another at all.

Mrs. Dolan lived in Greenwich, just a short trip away down the Merritt Parkway. Her house, like so many in the area, was a traditional Colonial in style. Painted white with black shutters, it was situated on a wooded, multi-acre lot north of the parkway.

Mindful that there was a dog in residence, I drove slowly up the gravel driveway. Barney didn't put in an appearance, however. Nor did he accompany his owner to the front door when she let me in.

Mrs. Dolan was a plump, pleasant-looking woman in her mid-fifties. Her blond hair was gathered into a low bun but the day's humidity had caused a profusion of curls to escape and frizz around her face. Dressed in a caftan that swirled with bright colors, she had a ready smile and a firm handshake.

"Please call me Fran," she said as she ushered me inside. "Everybody does."

"And I'm Melanie," I replied. "Thank you for agreeing to see me."

"Don't thank me. I was glad you called." Fran's hand fluttered in the air. "What happened to that poor young man was awful. I'm happy to have the chance to talk to someone who knew him like I did."

Caftan swishing around her legs, Fran turned and went striding down the hall toward the back of the house. I fell into step behind her.

"Do you live here alone?" I asked.

"My son lives on the property. He's in his twenties and doesn't want to admit that he lives with his mother, so he's made himself an apartment over the garage. Mr. Dolan and I are divorced."

"I'm sorry," I said.

Fran smiled at me back over her shoulder. "I'm not. It's been ten years. Best thing I ever did was get rid of Jerry. He lives in Fort Lee with his ex-secretary. Let me pour us some coffee and we'll go sit in the sunroom and chat."

Our first stop was the kitchen and it was there that I got my first look at Barney the Basset. The low-slung hound was lying on the floor, asleep in a wide shaft of sunlight. The dog's broad body was settled heavily on its side, which left his lower legs resting on the tile surface beneath him and his upper ones simply extending outward into space.

Awakened by our arrival, Barney rolled into a semi-upright position. He lifted his head, opened his eyes, and regarded us both balefully. Long silky-looking ears puddled on the floor beneath his head. Then he sighed heavily and flopped back down. Within seconds he was snoring.

"That's Barney," said Fran. "I'd introduce you but he'd probably sleep through it. He's not much of a watchdog."

"So I see," I said with a laugh. "I'm pretty sure that Bassets aren't known for their vigilant qualities."

"I know that now," Fran admitted. "But back when I got Barney, I just assumed that any dog would run to the door and bark when somebody arrived. His disinterest in guarding the house came as a big surprise."

"Is that why you hired Nick?" I asked.

"Oh no. Far from it."

Fran poured us each a cup of coffee from the pot on the counter. I added a measure of milk to mine from the pitcher beside it. Fran helped herself to a generous teaspoon of sugar. Then we carried our cups to the sunroom: a bright, step-down alcove located behind the kitchen. White wicker chairs with plump, chintz-covered, cushions were grouped in front of oversized windows that overlooked a spacious backyard.

The area wasn't fenced, I noted idly. Having been trained by Aunt Peg, I shared her belief that dogs should always be safely contained. Toward the back of the yard was an old, wooden shed with warped walls and a sagging roof. A pile of new lumber was stacked beside it. Maybe a fence was coming, I thought, as we both found seats in the sun.

"Nick was a fine young man," Fran said. "You have no idea how sorry I was to hear the news that he'd been killed. He was nothing short of genius when it came to understanding dogs and knowing what made them tick. Is that how you met him too?"

"No, he was a friend of my ex-husband," I told her.

"Well, if you never saw him in action, let me tell you that Nick Walden had a real gift. Barney can be a little hardheaded. He listens when he wants to and ignores me when there's something else more interesting on his agenda."

Hounds, I thought. You had to love them.

"Watching that dog interact with Nick was like seeing two friends who spoke the same language. It was uncanny the way they communicated with one another. I told Nick he must be psychic, but he said no, that he was just an empathetic dog trainer."

"Hardly *just,*" I said. Truly empathetic dog people, those who possessed an instinctive understanding of canine thoughts and behavior, were few and far between. "That's a rare skill."

"That's what I told him." Fran nodded. "But Nick was modest about what he was able to do. I swear he even knew what Barney was thinking."

"If you don't mind my asking, why did you hire Nick's services?"

"I was at the library one day and I saw an ad Nick had left pinned to the bulletin board there. I figured it was like a sign from God that I ran across it because Barney had been driving me crazy."

As one, we turned to look at the sleeping Basset. If that was his usual level of activity, it was hard for me to see how the dog might arouse strong emotions at all, much less go so far as to drive someone crazy.

Fran laughed. She must have been reading my thoughts. Her cup and saucer clinked as she set them down on the wicker table between us.

"Maybe he doesn't look like it now," she said. "But when Barney's outside, he's a live wire."

"Really." I smiled politely.

"Not fast necessarily. But determined to go where he wants to go when he wants to go there."

Now *that* I could readily see.

"Barney's also kind of food motivated," said Fran. "That dog will eat anything. And with that nose of his, it seems like Barney can sniff out something interesting half a mile away. So he has a tendency to wander off. Sometimes I would put him in the yard, come back five minutes later, and he'd just be gone. I was always having to go out looking for him."

"I can see how that would be a nuisance," I agreed.

"I called the number on the card and told Nick that I needed someone who could train Barney to stay home. He asked me a lot of questions and then came for a home visit."

"And was he able to help you?" I asked.

"Yes, and no." Fran smiled ruefully. "Like I said earlier, he and Barney got along like a house on fire. That part was great. Nick was the one who told me about Barney being a scent hound. And that scent hounds follow their noses. He said that's what Barney was bred to do."

"Did he have a solution for you?" I asked.

"He most certainly did. He told me I needed a fence."

Fran started to giggle. After a few seconds, I was laughing with her. Barney didn't open his eyes, but his tail thumped up and down on the floor. I guess even he was in on the joke.

"When he said that I felt pretty dumb," Fran admitted. "But Nick delivered the news in the nicest possible way.

That was how he did things. He was very clear about that fact that our problems weren't Barney's fault, that he was only doing what generations of selective breeding had taught him to do."

I nodded.

"And then Nick told me said that the problems we'd been having weren't my fault either. How could I have understood something I didn't even know? So then I didn't feel like such an idiot anymore."

Nick not only had a way with dogs, I thought. He knew just how to handle their owners too.

"I had an invisible fence installed the following week," Fran said. "And now when Barney goes outside, he wears the collar. And he stays where he's supposed to be."

"I'm glad everything worked out. So I guess you only needed Nick's services for one visit?"

"Oh no," Fran said quickly. "That's not how it worked at all. After I had the fence put in, Nick came back to teach Barney how the system worked. First Barney had to learn where the boundaries were and how to stay inside them."

"And after that?"

"Nick was just such pleasant company. And he never made it seem like it was an imposition to stop by and see how we were doing. We even started teaching Barney some basic tricks. Just fooling around and having fun. Nick would come over and spend an afternoon, and Barney and I always looked forward to his visits . . ."

Fran's voice trailed away unhappily. She glanced at the dog in the kitchen. Barney was still snoring. Every so often his feet would paddle in the air or his tail would wag, but for the most part he was oblivious to his surroundings.

"I'm not the only one who will miss Nick," she said with a sigh. "He and Barney got to be great friends. Now Barney won't have anyone to talk to."

"It sounds as though both you both got to know Nick pretty well," I said. "Were you aware of any problems Nick might have been having?"

Fran thought for a minute before answering. "No, nothing," she said finally. "Nick was always the same happy, sunny guy. He never seemed to worry about stuff at all. If I had to guess, I'd say that whatever happened to Nick . . . he never saw it coming at all."

Chapter 13

Back in my car, I pulled out Nick's client roster and had another look.

The majority of his clients had lived in Greenwich, including a woman named Missy Alexander whose address placed her no more than a mile or so from my current location. I could call ahead and see if she was home, but that would give Mrs. Alexander a chance to turn me away. I decided I'd probably have better luck simply showing up at her house and seeing what happened.

The Alexander residence was large and impressive. Built of stone, it was set back from the road and surrounded by several acres of well-manicured lawn. Considering the grandeur of the approach, I wasn't expecting to find the lady of the house on her knees in a flower bed, up to her elbows in dirt.

Unlike the house I'd just visited, here I was greeted by the dog first. As I stepped out of my car, a tiny, amber-colored, ball of fluff came hurtling across the lawn, barking wildly. As it drew near, I saw that the little golden missile was a Pomeranian, six to eight months of age, with a big grin and a very high opinion of herself.

Reaching my legs, the puppy began to spin in mad circles around them. Brief, high-pitched yips accompanied each bouncing stride. I didn't dare take another step for fear of putting a foot on her.

Over by the front walk, the slim, blue-jean-clad woman rocked back on her heels but didn't rise. Instead she lifted a hand, shaded her eyes from the sun, and stared at me and her small whirling dervish. A look of annoyance crossed her face.

"Primp!" she called, without much conviction. "Come back here."

The puppy paused her playful assault long enough to glance back and forth between me and her owner. Seizing the opportunity, I used the brief moment of inaction to reach down and scoop the little dog up in my hands. The plush appearance of the Pom's red-gold coat made her appear bigger than she really was. I've worked out with dumbbells that were heavier.

Now the woman rose to her feet. She was tall and slender to the point of skinniness. Handsome rather than pretty, she wore little make-up, though I imagined she was probably well lathered in sunscreen. Her hair was covered by an old kerchief.

Still frowning, the woman yanked off a pair of gardening gloves and let them fall to the ground at her feet. She wiped her hands on her jeans and the sun glinted off a diamond the size of a grape on her left ring finger. Lips pursed, she strode in my direction across the lawn.

"Be careful. She'll nip you if she gets the chance."

Having already discovered that for myself, I now had my fingers angled discreetly out of range as the puppy wriggled within my grasp. I carried her across the driveway to the edge of the lawn and set her down. Happily Primp scampered back to her approaching owner.

"Are you Missy Alexander?" I asked.

Her nod was curt. "Whatever you're selling, I don't want any. I like the religion I already have. And if it's a donation you're looking for, you'll need to send the request to my husband's office."

"I just want to talk," I said. "My name is Melanie Travis."

"I don't have time to talk to strangers." Missy spun on her heel. "Please see yourself out."

"We haven't met, Mrs. Alexander, but we have a friend in common."

Her retreating steps slowed fractionally. She still had her back to me but she was listening.

"Nick Walden," I said.

The woman stopped and turned. "What about him?"

"I was a friend of his, and I'm also a friend of his sister. We're trying to make sense of what happened to him."

"What does that mean exactly?"

Her words were clipped, her tone abrupt. I don't intimidate easily but Missy Alexander made me want to take a step back. If she was looking for a job, she would have made a wonderful headmistress. Or maybe chief warden of a women's prison.

"We want to know how and why Nick died," I said.

"He was shot," Missy informed me. "I read that in the newspaper. As for why, what does that have to do with me?"

"Probably nothing," I said. "But if you could give me just a few minutes—"

"One." She folded her arms over her chest. "No more."

The clock was ticking. I'd talk fast. In my experience, everybody likes to talk about their dogs. Maybe starting there would loosen things up a little.

"I'm guessing you engaged Nick's services because of your puppy?"

"That would be correct."

"Normal new baby adjustment issues, or one problem in particular . . . ?"

"How is that germane?" Missy snapped impatiently.

So much for loosening things up. It was time to cut to the chase.

"Were you aware of any problems Nick might have been having in his business—"

"No. None."

"—or his personal life?"

Missy's eyes narrowed. "How would you expect me to know that?"

I shrugged in what I hoped was a disarming fashion. "Nick became friends with many of his clients." So Bob had told me. And my conversation with Fran Dolan had certainly supported that claim. "It wasn't unusual for him to discuss other things besides dogs when he was with them."

"I'm afraid I don't know what you're talking about," Missy replied shortly. "Our relationship was nothing like that."

My gaze drifted downward. While we'd been speaking, Primp had sat down beside her owner's sneaker-clad foot. One tiny paw reached over and quickly worked the shoelace free of its bow. The puppy drew the narrow cord into her mouth and began to chew happily.

Primp might be light on training, but damn, she was cute.

"So yours was strictly a business relationship?" I said.

For the first time, Missy didn't snap an answer right back. Something I wasn't quite able to read came and went in her eyes.

"Of course," she said after a brief pause. "I have no idea what would make you think otherwise."

Pointedly she lifted her arm and had a look at her watch.

"Were you satisfied with Nick's services?" I asked quickly. Any moment now, my time was going to be up.

"Very much so. Of course he still had further work to do. But both I and my husband thought that Nick had made a very good start to Primp's training."

I found it interesting that Missy thought to mention her husband just after I'd inquired about her relationship with Nick. It was almost as if she was trying to remind me of his existence. Or maybe she was trying to remind herself.

"I assume we're done?"

Missy made an attempt to turn away once again. But Primp, still holding tight to her shoelace, forestalled the movement and bought me another few seconds.

As she leaned down and prized the fastener from between the Pom's sharp teeth, I said, "Can you think of any reason at all that someone might have wanted to harm Nick Walden?"

Abruptly Missy straightened. She now had the errant puppy clasped in her arms. Her shoelace was still untied.

"I heard that Nick had a new sponsor of some sort," she said. "Someone who was supposed to be helping his business to grow. Maybe you want to check with that guy."

Or that woman, I thought as Missy spun around and strode back to her flower bed. Regardless, I was pretty sure that Aunt Peg was in the clear.

It had been an interesting morning and I had plenty to think about as I drove home. I'd spoken to two of Nick's clients and each had portrayed her working relationship with Nick very differently. From what I'd seen of the dog whisperer, I had to assume that Fran's description was the closer to the norm. But maybe I was wrong about that.

On the other hand, Missy had told me several other things that hadn't rung true either. According to the list Bob had given me, Missy and Primp had been clients of Nick's for the last three months. So how come the puppy still didn't seem to have any training? And if, during the time Nick spent at her house, the two of them had discussed nothing but dogs, how did she know about his new sponsor?

I might have spent more time debating those questions, but when I got home, it turned out that the Poodles had other plans for me.

This is what usually happens when I arrive home: I pull the car into the garage and enter the house through a connecting door. The adult Poodles, having heard the garage door rumble open, come running to cluster in the hallway and clamor for my immediate attention. Augie, the puppy, doesn't join the fray because he has to wait for me to release him from his crate. Our only Poodle currently "in hair," he's confined when Sam and I are both away because his show coat is a precious and fragile commodity.

A Poodle's hair starts growing when he's born and is protected every day of his life until his show career ends. A hole in the wrong place can spoil a dog's look and keep him out of the ring for months. For that reason, Poodle puppies learn at an early age that certain kinds of behavior are off-limits. No rubbing, no scratching, and definitely no play involving hair pulling, are allowed.

I trust my Poodles to obey the house rules even when I'm not looking. But I also enforce that trust with a nice, big, comfy, crate. Augie might be almost twelve months old, but he was still a puppy. Not only that, but at his age he was entering the canine teenage rebellion stage—that several-month-long period when dogs act out, ignore their training, and generally make you wonder what you ever liked about them in the first place, before reaching the other side and blossoming back into the wonderful pets you always knew they were.

You know, kind of like kids.

So when I opened the door leading into the house from the garage, the first surprise was that no flying scramble of Poodles came running to greet me. The second was that from my vantage point just inside the door, I could see that the big crate in the corner of the kitchen where Sam and I stow Augie when we're both going to be out, was clearly standing open. And empty.

That wasn't good on so many levels that I didn't even want to stop and think about it. Instead I tossed my purse and keys on a nearby side table, remained where I was, and called out, "Hey, guys! Where is everybody?"

Purposely I kept my tone light and welcoming. *Nobody's in trouble yet,* it said. *Let's see what we have to deal with first.* The fact that the Poodles hadn't appeared when I first walked in the door meant that something was wrong somewhere. Now I wanted them to come to me.

And then they did. One by one, black heads began to pop around the corner of the entrance that led to the living room. Faith, Raven, Eve; I counted noses and identified faces. So far, so good. Casey took an additional few seconds to appear, but then she joined the bunch as well.

That left only Tar and Augie who continued to be AWOL. Only an idiot wouldn't have seen *that* coming.

Faith sidled out into the hallway. Eve was beside her. Then Raven and Casey followed suit. The bitches had their heads lowered and their ears flat. Their tails hung down and swung slowly from side to side, a silent plea for clemency.

This was clearly a group of dogs who felt very guilty about something. I wondered whether the four had actively participated in whatever mayhem I was about to discover or whether they'd merely been powerless to prevent it from happening. At least there weren't any big, black, hunks of hair littering the hallway, I thought as I strode toward them. It wasn't much, but it was better than the alternative.

"What did you guys do?" I asked them. "Who's in trouble?"

Acting as one, the four Poodles turned to look back into the living room. They couldn't have answered my question more clearly if they had drawn me a diagram. Faith gazed at me imploringly. *Don't be too mad,* her dark, expressive eyes said.

Reaching the group of bitches, I dropped a hand onto Faith's head and ruffled it through her topknot reassuringly. Her tail lifted slightly. She leaned in close against my legs.

"I'm not angry at you," I told her. "You know that. You never do anything wrong."

Hearing that, the other three bitches came and crowded around us. If forgiveness was available, they wanted to get in on it too. Either that or they were hoping to distance themselves from whatever I was about to see in the living room. Neither possibility seemed very reassuring.

Not yet ready to offer general absolution, I turned the corner and had a look. For the first, startled, moment, everything simply looked white. It was as if the room had been blanketed by an explosion of confetti that seemed to have been strewn randomly over floor and furniture alike. And of course, lying there right in the middle of the debris, were my two missing Standard Poodles.

It took me a moment to process what was going on. Tar and Augie were on the floor facing one another. Something—it appeared to be a giant, fabric toy—bridged the distance between them. Each Poodle had grasped an end of the object between their teeth and they were engaged in a fierce game of tug-of-war.

Then all at once my heart sank as I realized what I was

seeing. The prize the two dogs were wrestling over wasn't a toy at all. It was the middle cushion from the living room couch. Or what remained of it anyway.

Even worse, what had appeared at first glance to be confetti was instead the former insides of that ripped-open cushion, now gleefully deposited around the room. Aside from that lovely mess, an end table and lamp had been overturned, and a stack of books was scattered across the floor.

It looked as though I'd missed quite a party.

"Drop it!" I said in the meanest voice I could muster.

Behind me, the bitches immediately exercised prudent discretion. All four backed out of the room and away from the scene of the crime, making their escape on quiet feet so as not to draw attention to themselves.

Tar and Augie should have watched and learned. Instead the two boys were so busy arguing with one another, they didn't even seem to realize that they were being yelled at.

"I said drop it!"

I advanced on the pair like an avenging angel and snatched away the ragged cushion cover. Game *over*. At least that got their attention.

Augie looked up inquiringly, then bounced to his feet ready to continue playing. He jumped in the air and tried to grab the shredded fabric out of my hands. Rather than retreating, I leaned into his advance. As the puppy rose, he bonked his nose on the fist I'd closed around his prize.

Ow! Augie might as well have said the word. His expression made it that clear. Confused, the puppy dropped back to all fours and waited to see what would happen next.

For the moment, I ignored him and turned to Tar. That big fool of a dog was now sitting up, wagging his tail. "What were you thinking?" I asked him sternly. "You're the adult, you're supposed to know better."

Tar's expression never wavered. His tail continued to slap back and forth happily. *Mom's home! Mom's home! Mom's home!*

I know. Why did I even bother to ask? Tar never knew better. He had a big goofy grin on his face and not a clue in the world that he'd done something wrong.

I showed him the ruined cushion cover. I put it right in front of his nose. "No!" I said firmly. Tar didn't care. He was just pleased that I was paying attention to him. It didn't seem to matter in the slightest why.

At least when I gave Augie the same stern reprimand, I got results. The puppy had the grace to look chastened when faced with the evidence of what he had done. "This isn't a toy," I told him. Augie hung his head and looked away. It was nice to see that someone had learned something.

I gazed around the room and sighed. It was going to take me a while to clean up the mess. And then I'd need to figure out how to go about replacing the cushion that had been destroyed.

A better woman would have gotten started on all that right away. Not me. I sank to the floor where I stood.

"Come here," I said to Augie.

I patted the rug beside me. The puppy, inferring correctly that he'd been forgiven and delighted to find himself back in favor, couldn't get there fast enough.

"How come you aren't in your crate?" I asked him. If Sam had put the puppy away before he and Kevin left that morning, this whole problem could have been avoided.

Augie gave a short, sharp bark in reply. He wiggled happily in place. *Not my fault,* he told me.

I already knew that.

I reached over and ran a practiced hand through his copious topknot and neck hair. The puppy's bands and wraps were still in place. There were no jagged holes where hair was missing, no sticky saliva causing new mats.

That discovery improved my mood enormously. The couch might have taken a hit for the team, but hairwise we had come through the melee unscathed. I've had worse days.

Chapter 14

Later I vacuumed up the evidence of the dogs' misdeeds and shoved an old bolster into the space where the missing couch cushion should have gone. Then I hid the whole mismatched problem under a fringed afghan. None of my efforts helped much.

If Sam had an opinion about my odd decorating choices, he didn't mention it. So I didn't bring up the fact that he had neglected to put Augie in his crate when he went out. Apparently it was just one more thing that we weren't going to discuss.

The following morning he and I switched parental duties. Sam dropped Davey at soccer camp and I strapped Kevin into the Volvo and drove to Greenwich to visit Nick's girlfriend, Diana Lee. I didn't have to worry about calling ahead. Claire had made all the arrangements for me. Not only had she set up the meeting, she'd even e-mailed me directions.

That woman was a gem. How Bob and Sam could ever have thought that she and I wouldn't get along, I have no idea.

Diana Lee lived in a multi-storey brick building only a few blocks from Greenwich Avenue. Her condominium was on the fourth floor. As Kevin and I exited the elevator, I could see through the window at the end of the hallway that the view—looking out over Long Island Sound—was spectacular.

Diana answered the door wearing a silk sundress and sandals. Long blond hair, fastened with tortoiseshell clips above her ears, fell in rippling waves to the middle of her back. Her manicure and pedicure were both flawless; the nails on her fingers and toes were painted a matching shade of hot pink.

I had on cropped pants and sneakers, in case you were wondering. My linen shirt had been tucked in when I left home and my hair was mostly clean. By my standards, I was having a good day.

Standing beside me, small hand clasped firmly in mine, Kevin looked perfectly presentable too. He was wearing his favorite blue T-shirt and matching shorts. All the Velcro clips on his sneaks were neatly fastened. I had let Kev ring the doorbell and he had a big smile on his face when Diana opened the door.

It didn't matter. We did not make a good first impression.

"Oh," she said, looking at the two of us like we were refugees from a traveling circus. "I was only expecting an adult."

"I'm Melanie," I said. I released Kev's fingers and held out my hand. "And this is my son Kevin."

Diana glanced at my outstretched hand like she thought I might be carrying something contagious. "Sorry," she said, holding up her own hands and backing away. "I don't do sticky."

"We don't either," I said brightly.

Kev was freshly scrubbed. Even his hair was combed. Maybe I'm a little biased, but it was hard to see how anyone could find fault with his appearance.

Even so, Diana's expression remained dubious.

"May we come in?" I asked.

"Um . . . look."

Since she was clearly stalling for time, I did look. Her condo was all bare floors and stark planes. The walls were white; so was the upholstered furniture. Her tables were fashioned of chrome and glass. Everywhere I gazed, I saw breakable objects and sharp edges. If there was a comfortable place to sit down in that apartment, I couldn't find it.

"I'm not child proofed," Diana said.

"I'll hold Kevin's hand," I told her.

She wrinkled her nose delicately. "I don't like kids."

"I can tell." I nodded down at Kevin. "So can he, for that matter."

That got her interest. "He can?"

"Of course. Why wouldn't he?"

Just to make me look bad, Kevin favored Diana with another toothy grin. Obviously he's too young to take rejection seriously.

"I don't know. I thought . . . maybe he didn't understand yet."

"He talks too," I mentioned.

Diana looked at Kev and arranged her features into a fake-looking smile. "Can you make him say hello?"

Frickin' A, I wanted to say. He's a child, not a parrot. But before I had a chance to answer, Kevin took matters into his own hands.

"Hello," he said happily, waving his free hand up at Diana. "Pretty lady!"

"Oh my." Diana looked briefly startled. Then she laughed. "I didn't expect that."

"I didn't either," I told her truthfully.

When it comes to appearances, Kev isn't much of a connoisseur. The adults he's drawn to are usually those holding toys or cookies. Maybe he'd been attracted by the mango-colored silk dress or the ornate fake flowers decorating Diana's sandals. Either way, I figured I ought to strengthen my grip on his small hand.

Diana leaned down. There was still a good four to five

feet between them, but at least now she was on Kevin's level. "Thank you," she said.

" 'Welcome," Kevin chirped, beaming another smile. He was full of surprises this morning.

"Your son has very nice manners."

"Sometimes," I said.

Rarely, I thought to myself. But who was I to argue with success? At the rate he was going, Kev would be the one who charmed our way in the door.

"Look," I said, holding up the ever-present diaper bag, "I've brought some of his favorite toys with me. Kev can sit on the floor and play while we talk. He won't be any trouble at all."

Diana still didn't look entirely convinced. "What if he gets . . . cranky?"

I shrugged. "Then we'll leave."

"Okay. I guess." She stepped back out of the doorway and we finally entered the condo. "But you'll keep an eye on him, right?"

"Absolutely."

"And you won't give him any juice boxes, or string cheese, or fruity things to eat."

"None at all," I agreed solemnly. Whatever worked.

Diana and I took seats on either side of a glass-topped table. My chair must have been artistically designed, because it certainly wasn't built for practicality. Narrow and slippery, it should have come with arms for me to hold on to. And maybe a seat belt.

Luckily Kevin had no such concerns. As soon as I unpacked his Matchbox cars, the toddler was happy to find a spot on the shiny tile floor. He giggled with delight as the cars zoomed over the highly polished surface. I'd never seen them move so fast before, and I was pretty sure Kev hadn't either.

"Claire said you wanted to talk to me about Nick,"

Diana said. She kept a wary eye on the child beneath the table as if she was half-afraid that he might leave fingerprints on the chrome table legs, or attempt to blow his nose on her silk dress. "What do you want to know?"

"What went wrong," I said flatly. "I want to know why Nick is dead."

"Then you've come to the wrong place because I have no idea." Diana shook her head. "I mean, really *no* idea. It's not like Nick ever had anything worth stealing."

"The police don't think there was a break-in," I told her. "And neither does Claire."

"Claire." Diana sniffed dismissively, as if she wouldn't expect Nick's sister to be on top of anything. Her fingers drummed on the tabletop, nails clicking on the glass, hand refusing to stay still. I wondered if she was wishing for a cigarette.

"Tell me about your relationship with Nick," I said. "How long were you together?"

"We met over the winter. In Whole Foods of all places."

"Better than a bar," I said.

"Oh, I agree. Nick was buying some sort of disgusting, all-natural, dog food." She shuddered lightly. "I was there for the fresh produce. We met in the checkout line."

"I guess you don't like dogs," I said.

"Some dogs are okay. If they belong to other people. And they're small. And quiet. You know."

Actually I didn't. But what I did know, suddenly, was that this woman would never have been Nick Walden's soul mate.

"How did you get along with Thor and Jojo?" I asked curiously.

"Nick was a dog *trainer*."

"Yes, I know."

"So he trained those two to stay away from me. And then we were all happy."

Oh, I thought, then reconsidered. Make that oh my.

"That's great," I said. "That you and Nick were happy together."

Diana's eyes narrowed. "You sound like you're doubting me."

"Not at all. Just asking."

"Of course we were happy. We wouldn't have stayed together otherwise. Nick's business was growing. He was someone who was going places."

Interesting juxtaposition, I thought. "And that was important to you?"

"Of course it was important. I want to marry a successful man, not just one who can make a living."

"Were you and Nick . . . talking about getting married?" I asked.

"Not in so many words. But I'm twenty-eight years old. I've had enough *boy*friends. If I don't see the possibility of a future with a man, what's the point of even starting something?"

"I see. Then I guess what I heard was wrong."

Diana looked up. Her fingers stilled. She looked like a beautiful doe, sniffing the wind and sensing danger.

"What did you hear?"

"That your relationship with Nick wasn't entirely exclusive."

"Who told you that?" Diana wanted to know.

I just shrugged.

"Nick was a cute guy. In his line of work, he got offers. And I guess maybe he thought he still had a few wild oats to sow before settling down."

"Did that bother you?"

"It might have if I thought about it," Diana said firmly. "I chose not to."

She was lying, I realized as her gaze slipped away from

mine. Not only that, but the nails were tapping on the table again.

"You wouldn't happen to have any idea who was with Nick the night he was killed, would you?" I asked.

"No," Diana snapped. "None."

"What about you? What were you doing that night?"

"I was here."

"Alone?"

Diana's gaze hardened. "Yes, I was by myself. Just because Nick only believed in monogamy when it suited him to do so, doesn't mean that I felt the same way."

"You could have been out with girlfriends," I pointed out.

"I wasn't."

Diana looked smug. I wondered whether it had occurred to her that in her rush to castigate Nick for his behavior while defending her own, she'd also managed to establish the fact that she had no alibi for the night of his death.

"Do you know anyone who might have wanted to hurt Nick?" I asked.

She didn't answer right away. I wouldn't have expected the question to require that much thought. Surely the police would have asked her the same thing.

Kevin, meanwhile, was now pushing a Matchbox car over my shoe and up my shin. He was growing bored. I needed to get this conversation wrapped up.

"Taran Black," she said finally. "If I had to pick someone, he'd be the one."

"Who is he?"

"An old friend of Nick's who borrowed some money from him last year. He promised to repay Nick but he never did."

"Was it a large sum of money?"

"Big enough, I suppose. I know that Nick wanted it back. He and Taran fought about it a couple of times."

"Anyone else?"

"No." Diana shook her head. "Nick was the kind of guy who got along with everyone. Which was why I always thought it was so odd what he chose to do for a living."

"Odd in what way?"

"Nick had charisma. People were drawn to him. I used to see it all the time. He could have had his choice of good careers. Sales, or maybe something in marketing. But instead of putting his talents to good use, he chose to waste them on dogs. I mean really, *dogs*." She smirked. "Can you imagine it?"

"Actually I can," I said. "I happen to like dogs too."

Diana blew out a breath and looked exasperated. Like she'd expected us to be reading from the same script and I'd had the temerity to disappoint her.

"Okay sure, you *like* dogs," she said. "But could you imagine devoting your whole life to them?"

I thought of Aunt Peg, and the dozens of other dedicated breeders and exhibitors I'd met at the shows. Nick might have taken a different approach, but he was far from the only person I knew who held his dogs in the same high esteem as he did people.

"I live with six Standard Poodles," I told her. "They outnumber both the kids and the adults at my house."

Kev was now standing beside my chair, hugging my knee. I suspected he needed a diaper change. The mere thought would probably give my hostess a fit of the vapors.

"Kids?" she repeated. "You have others?"

"Just one," I replied. "Two, total." As I stood up, Kevin lifted his arms. I reached down and swung him up onto my hip. I couldn't resist adding, "So far."

"Good Lord, you might have more?"

"You never know," I said cheerfully.

"Dogs *and* children." She shuddered delicately. "You must live in a barn."

"Some days it feels that way," I admitted.

"Pretty lady," Kevin said a few minutes later as we rode the elevator down to the ground floor. "Nice."

"You're too easy," I told him with a laugh. "You like everybody."

That thought reminded me of Nick. The more time I'd spent in Diana's company, the harder it had become to imagine the two of them together. If she had ultimately forced Nick to choose between her and his canine companions, I was betting that he'd have opted for Thor and Jojo.

Had Diana realized that? I wondered. And if so, when did she figure it out? For a woman on the hunt for a husband and tired of wasting her time, that realization could have come as quite a blow.

Despite what Diana claimed, she could have been at Nick's house that night. The neighbors wouldn't have thought twice about her presence. Her fingerprints were already all over Nick's place and Thor and Jojo would have accepted her company with equanimity.

I wondered if Diana had a temper. And if she owned a gun.

Nick's girlfriend hadn't seemed as distraught about his death as I might have expected. Maybe she was good at masking her emotions. Or maybe she was already lining up someone else to take Nick's place. Someone who didn't like dogs. Or whose lifestyle dovetailed more neatly with her own.

One thing I did know. My visit with Diana had raised more questions than it had answered.

We could have gone straight home from Greenwich, but honestly, I couldn't come up with a single reason why that would be a good idea.

Sam was undoubtedly there. It couldn't have taken him more than half an hour to drop Davey off at camp. A month earlier, it would have seemed like the most natural thing in the world for me to drive home and make lunch for the three of us.

But now when I pictured Sam and me sitting across from each other at the kitchen table, I couldn't imagine what we might find to talk about beyond some mundane topic like the weather or the price of gas. Everything else—in fact any subject of substance—seemed like it might be fraught with risk.

I still couldn't get past the festering resentment I felt about the cavalier way in which I'd been treated by my own family. Even worse had been Sam's complete dismissal of my feelings when I'd tried to discuss the matter. Sadly the end result was that I'd been left with no desire to talk to my husband at all.

So instead of going home, Kevin and I detoured to Alice's house in my old neighborhood. Over the course of the last decade, Alice and I have spent numerous hours sharing our problems and secrets, and our joys and frustrations. She and her husband, Joe, had been married for nearly fifteen years. Their relationship hasn't always charted the smoothest course, but somehow Alice always finds a way to make things work. Her methods rely on diplomacy, consideration, and perseverance, leavened with the occasional touch of brute force. If anyone could give me sane and sensible advice about how to reset my relationship with Sam, I was sure it was going to be Alice.

"Good," I said when she answered the door. "You're here."

Alice grinned and shoved open the screen door with a swing of her hip. She grabbed Kevin—whose diaper I'd changed when we got back to the car—and pulled us both inside the compact, cape-style home that had obviously been built from the same blueprint as Bob's house just down the block.

Alice planted a loud, smacking, kiss on Kevin's mouth, rubbed his nose with her own, then deigned to look at me.

"You might have called first before driving over here," she pointed out as Kevin squirmed in her arms and shrieked with delight.

"What, and ruin the suspense?" I said with a laugh. "Besides, Kev and I were already out gallivanting."

"Oh, I loved that." Alice sighed. "I used to gallivant. You know, when I was still young and carefree. Like you."

She lowered Kevin to the floor. Immediately the toddler took off toward the back of the house. I had no idea what he was looking for, but he seemed to have an agenda. Alice and I watched him go. Neither of us was in a hurry to follow.

"Young and carefree," I said. "What's that?"

"Says the baby of the group." Alice huffed.

"Alice, we're the same age."

"We are not. You're in your mid-thirties. I'm staring forty in the face."

I shrugged. "So look the other way."

"Easy for you to say." Alice refused to be mollified. "When it's your turn, you'll understand how I feel."

"When it's my turn," I said with a grin. "I'll come to you for advice."

"Perfect. I'm good at that."

"I know," I agreed. "That's why we're here."

"Really?" Alice looked interested.

"That's one reason. The other is because Kev and I were just visiting a woman who lives in an all white condo and hates dogs and kids. After that, I needed someone to reacquaint me with the real world."

"That's right up my alley," Alice said happily. She started down the hallway and I fell in beside her. "Though I should probably confess that there are some days when I don't like dogs and kids either."

"Is today one of those days?"

"Nope. You're good. Carly and Joey are both at camp. Berkley's entertaining himself in the backyard. So you arrived during the midday lull. Well, if you don't count the fact that I'm doing laundry and trying to get a pot of beef stew on the stove for dinner."

"Can I help?" I asked.

"No, you can sit and talk to me. In fact, I'll sit too. We'll drink lemonade."

"How very civilized."

Alice grimaced. "At least you didn't say sedate. We older women are sensitive about things like that."

"Yeah, right."

We found Kevin rooting through Alice's kitchen cabinets, pulling out pots and pans and lining them up on the floor. Based on past experience, I guessed he was either planning to construct a teetering tower or grab a wooden spoon and make music. Alice took in the scene and offered a suggestion.

"How about if I set him up in the living room with a peanut butter and jelly sandwich and a DVD? Then we can talk in here."

"Sounds perfect," I said.

Five minutes later, Kevin was chortling over cartoons in the other room and Alice and I were parked at the kitchen table.

"Start at the beginning," she said. "And don't leave out a single detail. I want to hear everything that's wrong."

Chapter 15

"This could take a while," I told her.

"That's okay, I have time." Alice looked at me across the table. "Are we going to talk about Nick?"

"No. Claire."

"Who's that?"

"Claire Walden. She's Nick's sister."

"Oh my God." Alice sounded shocked. "Is she dead too?"

"Thankfully, no," I said quickly. "Claire is alive and well."

"But she's a problem?"

"Not of her own making. Actually she's more like an innocent bystander in this whole mess."

"Okay, so there's a mess." Alice was pleased to be moving the story along. "I'm good at messes. What does this one involve?"

"Mostly me and Sam," I replied. "But also Bob, and Aunt Peg. And of course Claire."

Alice nodded. "So we're talking about a *big* mess. Start with you and Sam."

"I wish I could, but it makes more sense if I start with Bob and Claire."

"Just so long as you don't start with your Aunt Peg. She scares me."

"You're in good company," I said. "Aunt Peg scares most people. I'm pretty sure she does it on purpose."

"So tell me about Bob and Claire," Alice prompted.

"They're in a relationship. Probably a semi-serious one. They've been together for several months."

"Bob's allowed," Alice said carefully. "Right?"

"Of course," I agreed. "Bob can do whatever he wants with whomever he wants."

"So what's the problem? Is it Davey?"

I heaved a sigh of relief. Trust Alice to cut straight to the heart of the matter. She got it. I had known she would.

As Alice had requested, I went back to the beginning and explained everything. She leaned back in her chair, sipped her lemonade, and listened with her heart open and her mouth shut. By the time I reached the end, she looked disappointed. And maybe a little sad.

"So there you have it," I said. "What do you think?"

"For starters, I'd have expected better of Sam."

"Me too," I admitted.

"And Bob needs a swift kick."

"Not for the first time," I muttered.

"As for Peg . . . I'm not even going there."

"Okay, but here's the sixty-four-thousand-dollar question. Now what? Where do Sam and I go from here?"

"First thing," Alice said practically, "is that you two need to talk."

"I've tried that. Sam doesn't think we have anything to 'talk' about."

"*Men.*" She snorted.

"That's what Bertie said."

Alice nodded. Men and communication were not a good match. We all agreed on that part.

"Keep thinking," I said. "What's your second idea?"

"Forgive and forget?"

I shook my head. "I'm not that nice a person."

"Yes, you are."

"Good try." I laughed. "No. I'm not. And besides, if I let Sam slide this time, what's to prevent him from doing something stupid like this again in the future?"

"He thought he was acting in your own best interests," Alice pointed out.

"So what?" I replied mulishly. "He was wrong."

"He meant well. Surely that counts for something."

"But he was still wrong," I repeated.

"But maybe that's not the most important thing. Stop and think for a minute, Mel. If you really want to hold on to your anger, then keep telling yourself that Sam was wrong. And every time you do that, you'll get mad all over again. But what are you really accomplishing?"

"Damn," I said.

"Now what?"

"I'm doing just what I told Bertie I wouldn't do."

"Which was?" Alice asked curiously.

"Making this about winning and losing."

"Bingo," said Alice. "Give the girl a gold star."

"Forgive and forget," I mused. "So that's what you would do if this was you and Joe?"

"Sometimes marriage is about rolling with the punches—metaphorically speaking, that is. You can't always fix things to your own satisfaction so there's no point in insisting that you can. Sometimes you just have to put stuff behind you and move on."

I sighed once again. I wasn't in love with the idea, but it made sense. And it might be the only viable alternative I had.

"And then if it were me," said Alice, "for the next month I'd burn Joe's dinner and overstarch his shirts. You know, just because."

I looked at her and laughed. "You have an evil streak."

"I should hope so."

Alice raised her glass. I raised mine. We clinked in the middle.

"To moving on," she said. Then she cocked a brow in

my direction. "And all that other stuff. Peace on earth, good will toward men."

"I'll work on it," I told her.

My cell phone rang as I was finishing my lemonade. It was Bob. "Are you busy?" he asked.

"Always," I replied. "But I think I can spare some time. Are you at home?"

"Yeah. Why?"

"I'm right down the block. Kev and I will see you in ten minutes."

We walked the distance between the two houses in less time than that, even with Kevin stopping every few feet to examine a crack in the sidewalk or a wayward leaf. At his age, the world is endlessly fascinating. If I could recapture even half the wonder he finds in everyday objects and events, I'd be a happy person.

Bob's front door wasn't locked; no surprise there. It would have been more polite to knock and wait to be admitted, but having spent nearly a decade calling that house my home, it felt entirely natural for me to simply let us in.

Bob's Siamese cat, Bosco, was lying draped along the top of the couch in the living room. Awakened by our intrusion, he opened his eyes and stared at us standing in his hallway. What is it about cats that they always seem to be judging me and finding me wanting?

"Pretty kitty," said Kev, immediately spinning in that direction.

Bosco slowly sat up. His long tail lashed up and down. I could swear he was sneering at us as I caught Kevin's hand and pulled him back.

"Pretty kitty has claws," I said.

Undaunted, Kevin continued to tug. Luckily Bob saved us from the argument that was about to ensue.

"I'm up here," he called from the second floor. "Come on up."

Kevin is great at going up steps and it didn't take much

to redirect his energy toward the staircase. I let him lead the way. If he got distracted and missed a step, I'd be right behind to catch him. Climbing with both hands and feet, Kev set a speedy pace.

"Hey, kid, good to see you." Bob was standing in the bathroom doorway. He squatted down and opened his arms and Kevin ran right into them. "Look how much you've grown."

"Big now!" Kevin announced happily.

"Yes, you are. Want to come in the bathroom and see my tools?"

"Tools?" I hurried up the last few steps to follow close behind. "*Real* tools?"

"Sure." Bob smirked. "For breaking down real walls and putting up real tile."

"Cut it out. That's not what I meant. Nobody's casting aspersions on the quality of your renovations . . ." I paused and sucked in a startled breath. "Wow, this place looks great."

The small, dark, bathroom that Davey and I had lived with was now only a memory. In its place was a room that had nearly doubled in size and had a new, larger window bringing in more light. There was cream-colored paint on the walls, an elegant new vanity with brass hardware, and an updated shower and tub.

"I should hope so," Bob said. "I've done a ton of work in here."

"It looks it." I ran my finger along the smooth marble countertop. "I'm impressed."

"I still have the new floor to install and a bit more tiling to do, but it's beginning to come together."

"Hammer," Kevin said suddenly.

While Bob and I had been admiring his handiwork, my son had been digging through the tool chest on the floor. Now he stood up and swung around. Both of his small hands were gripping the handle of a full-sized hammer and as he spun, the heavy tool lifted. Its face just missed smacking Bob in the knee.

"Yikes!" Bob jumped back. "That kid has an arm on him."

"That's what I meant about real tools," I said. I crossed the room and gently unwrapped Kevin's fingers from around the hammer's grip. "His next trick might have been to bash in your pretty new vanity."

Bob considered that. He moved toward the still-open toolbox. "Then I guess we don't want him playing with a screwdriver either."

"Nope."

Kevin puckered up his face and thought about crying as I removed the hammer from his grasp. Then he got a better idea. He turned around and looked at Bob hopefully.

"Pliers?" Bob asked, dangling a pair just above Kevin's reach. "No sharp edges."

"But they pinch," I pointed out.

"Oh. Right."

Bob withdrew the pliers and tucked them away. Deprived of a second toy, Kevin's lower lip began to quiver. Any second now, we were going to be treated to a full-blown meltdown.

I nudged Bob aside and had a look for myself. There had to be at least *one* child-friendly item in that damn tool chest. If not, we were in trouble.

"Oh look!" I cried, treating Kevin to my sunniest, happy voice. "Bob's work gloves! I wonder if they might fit on your hands? Let's see, shall we?"

Kev didn't even stop to think. He held up his hands and I slipped a thick suede glove onto each one. His small fingers were swallowed up inside; the gloves reached all the way to his elbows. Kevin flapped his hands from side to side and giggled happily.

"Crisis averted," Bob said with relief as Kev sat down on the floor to play with the gloves.

"For the minute," I told him. "What did you want to talk to me about?"

Bob reached over and slid open a drawer in the new vanity. A velvet jeweler's pouch was nestled within.

"You're keeping that ring in your bathroom?" I said.

"Sure, why not? Where else would I put it?"

"A safety deposit box maybe?"

Bob shrugged. "It's safe enough here. Nobody's going to go pawing around in a half-renovated bathroom looking for expensive jewelry."

I gave him a scornful look. "Except maybe your acquisitive next door neighbor."

"That's another reason why I'm keeping it close," Bob told me. "I needed to have the ring on hand because I talked to Dan and Emily Morris. It isn't theirs. Emily even stopped by this morning and had a look to make sure. She said she'd never seen the ring before."

"So much for the easy answer. I guess we'll just have to keep digging. Did you think to ask her if she remembered the name of the people that she and Dan bought the house from?"

"I did," Bob confirmed. "But she didn't. Apparently that was twenty years ago."

"I'm pretty sure we can get that information at the Town Hall," I said thoughtfully. "Probably from the Town Clerk or the Register of Deeds."

Bob nodded. "I was thinking the same thing. I'll try and stop down there sometime this week."

Kev was beginning to fidget again. There was only so long that he was going to be entertained by a pair of floppy gloves. Now he tossed them on the floor and pushed himself to his feet. When he headed for the stairs, I turned and went after him. At his age, going down steps is much harder than going up. Hand in hand, we descended to the first floor.

Bob followed us and opened the front door.

"Let me know what you find out," I said as he walked us out.

"I will."

Bob glanced at his driveway, then out at the curb. Finally he sent a puzzled look my way. I could understand his confusion. The Volvo was still parked down the street in front of Alice's house.

I was explaining that when a battered pick-up truck came rolling down the road and turned into the Fines' driveway next door. The truck's engine sputtered and wheezed as if we were hearing its last gasp. James was sitting in the passenger seat. His buddy Phil was driving.

Phil turned off the engine and the truck coughed, jerked twice, then quit. The side door creaked as James pushed it open. He came bounding out and sketched us a wave.

"Hey, neighbor!" he called. "Find any more hidden treasure?"

"Not today," Bob answered with a tight smile. You didn't have to be a relative to hear the annoyance in his tone.

Momentarily distracted, I realized too late that I should have been holding Kevin's hand. Before I could grab him, the toddler took off toward the neighboring driveway. For someone so small, he could move with surprising speed when he wanted to. Now his little legs pumped up and down like pistons as he raced headlong toward his favorite thing in the world.

"Big truck!" Kevin cried happily.

Phil had climbed out of the driver's seat and come around the back of the pickup. "Hey, little guy," he said as the toddler came barreling toward him. "What's your name?"

"Kevin," my son announced. He barely spared Phil a glance. "Big truck!"

"Big enough," Phil agreed. "Do you want a ride?"

"No, thank you." I moved quickly to intercept my son. "Kev doesn't need a ride."

James had lowered the tailgate and I saw that the bed of the pick-up was filled with pre-cut lumber, large tools, and gardening supplies. James leaned in, grabbed a heavy bag of potting soil, and hauled it back toward the opening.

"Ride," Kev said firmly. "Ride in big truck!"

"Not today," I told him, equally firm.

When his small hand eluded my grasp, I swooped down and picked him up. I intended to settle him on my hip but Kevin had other ideas. He continued to wiggle in protest. Fully occupied by my squirming toddler, I didn't even notice Phil's approach. So I was startled to look up and find him standing right next to me.

Phil reached out, circled his hands around Kevin's shoulders, and tried to lift him out of my arms. "Let me just put him in the bed for a minute," he said.

That was *so* not happening. Kev did not need to climb in the back of a rusty old truck filled with sharp objects. And Phil needed someone to acquaint him with the concepts of boundaries and personal space. If he didn't get out of my face in the next three seconds, that person was going to be me.

Holding Kevin to me securely, I backed away. "I said no," I repeated.

Finally Phil got the message. He held up his hands in a gesture of injured innocence. "Sure, Mom. Whatever you say. Sorry, buddy."

Kevin began to wail. In the space of an instant he morphed from over-stimulated to over-tired. He probably had a headache too. I know I did.

Phil turned his back on us and went to help James unload. Good riddance, I thought, as I carried Kevin back to where Bob was waiting.

My ex fell into step beside me as I carried the crying child down the sidewalk in the other direction. "Sorry about that," he said.

I just shook my head. It wasn't Bob's fault. "What's

with those guys anyway? Don't they seem kind of weird to you?"

"I don't know. And frankly I don't care. The two of them are hatching some kind of bogus get-rich-quick scheme. Whatever it is, I don't want any part of it."

Lulled by the motion of my walking, Kevin's wails had subsided. I switched him to my other hip. His head fell back to rest on my shoulder. In another minute, he'd be asleep.

"Bogus?" I said. "In what way?"

"I have no idea. But if their plan was legit, I'm guessing that they would have told me what it was instead of dangling the opportunity in front of me like bait and waiting for me to jump on it."

"They wanted you to give them money?"

"They wanted me to *invest*. I was promised a big return."

"Wow," I said with a laugh. "Lucky you."

"Tell me about it." Bob grinned. His mama didn't raise no fool. At least not when it came to finances.

We reached the car and Bob opened the back door. Kevin was finally asleep. I slid his boneless weight into the seat and fastened the straps.

"What are they doing with the building supplies?" I asked.

The Fines' backyard was no bigger than Bob's. I knew from firsthand experience that there was barely room for a swing set and a sandbox. Construction of any kind was pretty much out of the question.

"You got me. James mentioned something about a project he's working on in his basement. To tell the truth, I wasn't paying that much attention. The guy likes to talk a lot. I don't always listen."

In his place, I'd have probably done the same. "Are you seeing Claire soon?" I asked.

Bob nodded. "Tonight."

"Tell her I said hi."

"Really?" Bob looked surprised.

"Yeah. Give her my best."

I left him thinking about that, climbed in my car, and drove home.

Chapter 16

I meant to follow Alice's advice. I honestly did. I figured I would start doing so just as soon as the smoldering kernel of resentment that flared to life every time Sam opened his mouth died a withering death.

Unfortunately I didn't have a clue how to make that happen.

So instead I worked on keeping myself busy. If forgiving and forgetting was too hard to manage, maybe absence would make the heart grow fonder. My life was turning into a succession of clichés. The teacher in me found that utterly demoralizing.

I spent the next several days talking to five more of Nick's clients. They all had the same thing to say. Nick had been terrific with their dogs, an enthusiastic and intuitive trainer, and they'd been very sorry to hear of his demise. Several asked if I had any recommendations for a replacement trainer. I told them I'd think about it and get back to them.

Nearly a week had passed since I'd spoken with Claire about finding her brother's killer and I was beginning to feel like I was spinning my wheels. Everyone had loved Nick Walden—except for the one person who hadn't. But I was no closer to discovering that person's identity than I'd been in the beginning.

There's something about talking to Aunt Peg that always clears my head. Alice would probably say that's because Peg scares the rest of the extraneous clutter right out of my brain. I prefer to think it's the fact that I feel the need to stay on my toes while in her presence. That alone seems to sharpen my focus.

The three things Aunt Peg enjoys most in life are her Poodles, solving puzzles, and showing up her often-deficient niece. That would be me, in case you had any doubts. So when I called the next morning to see if I might drop by—and even volunteered to bring a Poodle with me, thereby serving up the trifecta of wish fulfillment—I wasn't expecting any resistance on Aunt Peg's part.

Nor was I expecting the level of enthusiasm that my suggestion produced.

"Perfect," she said. "Come right now."

"Now?" I squeaked.

"Yes, now. As in right this minute. Is there something wrong with that idea?"

Where to begin, I thought. For starters, it was barely eight A.M. and my family had yet to sort itself out for the day.

Kevin was sitting at the kitchen table with a half-eaten bowl of Cheerios and a spoon he'd decided he'd rather use as a drum. Davey was out on the deck brushing the previous day's mud off his shin guards. His backpack was sitting on a chair, half-full. I had yet to grab him a clean jersey from the laundry or make his lunch.

The pack of Poodles was split between the two boys. Half the dogs were outside, the other half were under the table waiting for spillage. Sam was leaning against the counter sipping a cup of coffee. He tipped his head and raised a brow at my startled response.

"I'm a little busy," I said.

"Then why did you call?" Aunt Peg sounded miffed.

"I thought maybe later—"

"Later will be too late."

"Aunt Peg, what are you up to?"

"I've invited Detective O'Malley to come and give me an update on his investigation. Unlike you, he thought this sounded like a fine time. I expect him within the half hour."

"No way," I said incredulously. "O'Malley agreed to drive all the way out to your house just to give *you* an update?"

"He did indeed," Aunt Peg replied. She paused briefly, then added, "I may have sweetened the pot a little."

Of course she had. My aunt was a master at manipulation. Ask me how I know—but only if you have several hours to listen to the answer.

I leaned over, plucked the spoon out of Kevin's hand, and put it back in his cereal bowl. For several seconds he wavered between protesting and eating. Luckily hunger won out. He scooped up a spoonful of Cheerios and shoved them in his mouth.

"What did you tell him?" I asked.

"I alluded to a tidbit of information about Nick that I'd previously forgotten to mention."

"What is it?" I asked.

"If you want to know that, you'll have to come. At the same time, you can hear what O'Malley has to say *and* take the opportunity to dazzle him with a few deductions of your own."

"I don't have any deductions," I told her. "Dazzling or otherwise."

"You have half an hour," Aunt Peg said impatiently. "Perhaps you should come up with some."

Davey chose that moment to come clumping in from outside. I had no idea why he was already wearing his cleats, but the knocking sound they made when they hit the hardwood floor caught Tar's attention. The big Poodle jumped up and went to investigate. Head lowered for a closer look, he pounced on Davey's feet like he thought my son's shoes were small animals that needed killing.

Davey laughed and did an impromptu tap dance. That clatter caused the rest of the Poodles to jump up and run over to see what was making all the noise. Oblivious to the mayhem he'd provoked, my older son deftly eluded the oncoming canine mob and strolled over to the table. He tucked his shin guards into his backpack, then looked up at me.

"What's for breakfast?" Davey asked brightly.

Around us, the commotion in the kitchen had increased sixfold. In the time it took to blink I found myself standing in the midst of a swarm of Poodles. All the dogs were now running wildly around the room, sticking their noses into corners, and trying to figure out what the source of the excitement had been and where it had disappeared to.

"Aunt Peg, I'll have to get back to you," I said.

Sam straightened, walked over, and took the phone out of my hands. "Peg," he said, "she's on her way." He listened for a minute, then hung up the phone and handed it back to me.

"But—" I began.

Sam didn't wait for me to finish. "Go."

"Davey's lunch—"

"I'll make it."

"His jersey—"

"In the laundry," Davey piped up helpfully.

"I'll find it."

"Kev—"

"He's with me," Sam said firmly. "Go."

"Go!" cried Kevin.

The toddler punctuated the command by bouncing his spoon off the table. A stray Cheerio went catapulting through the air. Raven caught it on the fly.

"I have things under control here," said Sam, appearances to the contrary notwithstanding. "Go keep Peg from getting herself arrested."

So I went.

I had intended to take Augie with me to visit Aunt Peg. But under the current circumstances, the puppy's company would be superfluous. With Detective O'Malley due to arrive at any minute, she and I were going to have plenty of other things to keep us busy. I'd start by passing along a stern warning about the police detective.

The first time O'Malley and I met, we hadn't exactly hit it off. Three years had passed since then, but I still had a very clear memory of him asking me if my dogs were licensed and reading Davey his rights. The latter was supposed to have been all in fun. At least that was what I'd thought until O'Malley had begun grilling me as though he was sure my life was filled with deep, dark, secrets that needed to be uncovered.

The detective hadn't liked my Poodles, he hadn't liked my answers, and he'd treated me like a simpleton. His interrogation technique was both dogged and pedantic. By the end, I'd almost wished I had something to confess just to liven up the proceedings. I could only hope that today's meeting turned out to be an improvement on our previous encounter.

When I got to Aunt Peg's house, I saw that O'Malley had beaten me there. Apparently the detective drove faster than he talked. A plain, dark blue sedan was already parked beneath the Japanese maple tree in the front yard.

I parked the Volvo and got out, then stood and stared at the house. Something was different. It took me a few seconds to figure out what it was. Then abruptly I realized this was the first time I'd ever shown up at Aunt Peg's and not immediately been greeted by her rambunctious canine horde.

Nor did I hear a joyous cacophony of barking from

within. That was also decidedly odd. The Poodles should have been announcing my arrival. I hoped the surly detective hadn't shot them.

"*Well?*"

Aunt Peg's sharp tone roused me from my morbid thoughts. The front door was open and Peg was waiting. Her arms were folded over her chest. She glared down at me impatiently.

"Are you just going to stand there," she asked, "or are you coming inside?"

"Coming," I replied quickly. I hopped up the three steps and crossed the porch. "Where are the Poodles?"

Aunt Peg pulled me inside and shut the door. "Apparently Ed is *not* a dog person."

"I know."

"You might have warned me."

"I might have," I said mildly. "If I'd had any notice at all of what you were up to." Then abruptly I stopped and stared. "Wait a minute . . . *Ed?*"

Aunt Peg nodded. "Detective O'Malley."

"You called him Ed."

"That's his name. Ed O'Malley. He and I are eating scones and comparing notes. We're getting along famously. Really, Melanie, must you make *everything* so difficult?"

Apparently so. I'd left home thinking I was on my way to an inquisition, only to arrive and to find myself at a tea party. This must have been how Alice felt when she dropped down into the rabbit hole.

Aunt Peg was entertaining Detective O'Malley in the kitchen, either because she wanted to set a tone of friendly informality or-more likely—because that placed them closer to the food. The detective clearly didn't mind. He was seated at the butcher block table, munching on a blueberry scone that was liberally slathered with butter. A large mug filled with freshly brewed coffee sat beside his plate. I could smell its heady aroma as soon as I entered the room.

Aunt Peg's preferred drink is Earl Grey tea. When I visit, she's apt to pull out a stale jar of instant coffee and slap it on the counter. Obviously Detective O'Malley rated better treatment.

Seeing me, he swallowed, wiped his mouth on a linen napkin, and rose to his feet. O'Malley was just shy of six feet and built like a linebacker. He had bushy dark eyebrows and hair to match. Both were now threaded with strands of gray. That was new since the last time I'd seen him. He looked like he might have put on a couple of pounds too.

When Aunt Peg performed the introductions, O'Malley gazed at me with a perplexed frown as if he wasn't quite sure whether he recognized me or not. That being the case, I felt no compunction to jog his memory. He was the detective; he could do his own detecting.

I poured myself a cup of coffee and took a seat at the table.

"You look familiar," he said finally.

"We met a couple of years ago," I told him.

"In what connection?"

"You were investigating a murder at the Winston Pumpernill Nursing Home."

"That's right." O'Malley nodded slowly. "Mary Lennox. She was a lovely lady. I believe her nephew belonged to some kind of dog group?"

"The South Avenue Obedience Club. We made therapy dog visits to Winston Pumpernill."

I could see the recognition dawn. O'Malley's gaze sharpened.

"You had a big black Poodle," he said. The words came out sounding like an accusation. "Just like these here."

He waved a hand as if to indicate that he was talking about Aunt Peg's Poodles. Except of course that none of them were in evidence.

"Exactly like that," I agreed. "I got my Poodles from Aunt Peg."

"And maybe your curiosity level too?"

"Quite possibly." No need to point out that Peg and I weren't blood relatives. It would only confuse matters.

"Ed and I were just talking about Nick's laptop." Aunt Peg finally interjected herself into the conversation. I wondered what had taken her so long. "The police retrieved it from Nick's house."

"Was there anything interesting on it?" I asked.

"Nothing out of the ordinary, unfortunately. Nick Walden appears to have been just what everyone thought he was: a young guy with a clean record and no prior connection to trouble."

"Except that everyone was obviously wrong," Aunt Peg said acerbically. "What about his cell phone?"

The detective had broken off a piece of scone and popped it into his mouth. It didn't stop him from answering. "I believe I'm the one supposed to be asking the questions. You mentioned on the phone that you had a piece of information that might be useful to our investigation . . . ?"

"I have something to share," Aunt Peg replied. "I can't promise it will be useful."

She rose from her chair, collected O'Malley's mug, and refreshed his coffee from the pot on the counter. I couldn't decide whether the delaying tactic was meant to ratchet up the suspense, or whether Aunt Peg's promise of new evidence had merely been the lure she'd dangled in front of O'Malley and me to get us to dance to her tune. For her sake, I sincerely hoped it was the former.

"Why don't you let me be the judge of that?" the detective told her. He sat and waited expectantly.

"Nick has a sister," Aunt Peg said as she replaced his mug on the table.

"Yes. Claire Walden, two years younger. We've spoken with her several times." O'Malley paused, then added, "If you're going to tell me that I should look into her further, let me assure you that the young lady has a firm alibi. One, I might add, that was provided by a member of your own family."

"Ex," I muttered under my breath.

"Excuse me?" O'Malley turned his gaze my way.

"Ex," I repeated, louder this time. Why did I have to keep reminding people of this? "Bob is my *ex*-husband."

"Amicable, though. Right?"

I nodded.

"You still use his name."

I sighed. "It's a long story."

"Anything I need to know?"

"No," I replied firmly. "Definitely not."

"Good," said the detective. "Now this Bob Travis is the one who introduced Walden to you."

"That's right."

He swung back to Aunt Peg. "Which is how he got to you."

"Right again," Peg agreed.

"Is there a problem with any of this that I should know about?"

"No," Aunt Peg and I said simultaneously, a rare moment of mutual accord.

O'Malley braced his elbows on the table and stared at Aunt Peg. "So why'd you bring it up?"

"I did no such thing. Talking about Bob Travis was your idea. It suits me to have as little to say about the man as possible."

That piqued O'Malley's interest. "So you're telling me that the two of you don't get along?"

"I have no need to get along with Bob. As Melanie pointed out, he's merely an ex. A *former* relation. Nothing more than that."

"And yet you agreed to do him a favor."

"No," Peg corrected. "I agreed to do Melanie a favor. She was the one who approached me about meeting with Nick. Bob had the very good sense to stay clear."

"Even so, it was Travis's idea for you to help his friend."

"Perhaps, but that wasn't what I agreed to. I said only that I would talk to Nick and see what I thought of him. Frankly, given the source of the recommendation, I expected to kick him to the curb shortly thereafter."

"And yet that didn't happen."

Grateful to be ignored, I sat in silence and watched the two of them spar.

Clearly Aunt Peg had thought she'd lulled O'Malley into a state of amicability with her buttered scones and her easy banter. But he was proving to be a wilier adversary than she'd anticipated. Now that the detective was the one asking the questions, he appeared to be enjoying himself. With one deft turn of the conversation, Peg had unexpectedly found her agenda superseded by O'Malley's own.

Or so I thought. I should have known that no one gets the better of Aunt Peg. At least not that easily.

"Ed," she said, holding up a hand to stop the flow of questions. "You're heading in entirely the wrong direction."

O'Malley leaned back in his chair and folded his arms over his chest. "Is that so?"

"My relationship with Nick Walden is not what we need to be discussing. Nor my lack of one with Bob Travis."

"Then maybe you'd like to tell me what is?"

"Just as I said earlier. Nick's sister."

"Not Claire," I said quickly.

I *liked* Claire. Not only that, but I was certain her grief was genuine. I refused to believe that she'd had anything to do with her brother's murder.

"Quite right," Aunt Peg agreed. "Not Claire. I'm talking about Nick's other sister. Anabelle."

Chapter 17

Anabelle?

I set my coffee cup down on the table with a sharp thump. Who on earth was Anabelle? And why was this the first time I was hearing about her?

Aunt Peg looked very pleased with herself. Evidently O'Malley's and my befuddled expressions were everything she'd hoped for. In her game of Stump the Relatives and Authorities, Peg had just produced the winning hand.

O'Malley recovered first. "Anabelle Walden?" he asked. He drew a notebook and pen out of his pocket.

"I believe she goes by the name of Anabelle Gifford now."

"And you say that she's the deceased's sister?"

"His older sister," Aunt Peg confirmed. "Estranged from the family."

Okay, I thought. That answered one question. Maybe. But not a host of others. Luckily for me, the detective felt the same way.

"Nobody's mentioned anything about her to me before," said O'Malley. "Why is that?"

"Apparently Claire and Nick don't have any contact with her. They haven't been in touch for at least a decade."

O'Malley started to say something, but he was moving too slowly for me. I leapt ahead with a question of my own.

"How do you know about her?" I demanded.

"Nick and I were talking one day and he seemed very distracted," Aunt Peg said. "I asked him what was the matter and he told me that he'd just received a phone call from his sister Anabelle. He said that he hadn't spoken to her since he was a teenager—"

"Did he tell you why?" I asked.

"No, he did not. And you know me—I certainly would have wormed the information out of him, but we were interrupted and the opportunity was lost. I thought perhaps I'd ask him about her the next time we saw one another."

"But you didn't," said O'Malley.

"I never had the chance," Peg replied. "I never saw Nick again."

"You might have told me this sooner," he said sternly.

"In the commotion of everything that came after, that brief conversation simply slipped my mind," Aunt Peg said with a sigh. "Unfortunately I am not as young as I used to be."

She paused, as if waiting for one of us to correct her. O'Malley and I both remained silent. I didn't know about him, but my thoughts were spinning willy-nilly in other directions. I had more pressing things to ponder than Aunt Peg's vanity.

"When Nick mentioned his estranged sister," she continued, "Anabelle was merely an object of curiosity. The fact of her existence didn't seem that unusual. After all, estrangements happen. Even in the best of families."

Aunt Peg glanced my way. Until we'd bonded seven years earlier over a dead body, a stolen stud dog, and a mutual love of Poodles, Peg had been a virtual stranger to me. Money and the disposition of a will had created a rift in our family that no one had crossed for nearly a decade.

"And now that you've *remembered*"—O'Malley lingered on the word with palpable irritation—"you think this Anabelle Gifford might be somebody important."

"She might be." Aunt Peg refused to be cowed by his tone. "In any case, it seems to me that she's someone you ought to talk to. All I know is that she contacted her brother out of the blue. And then just a few days later, he was dead."

"I'll have to check again to be sure, but I don't think there were any calls on Walden's phone from someone by that name." The detective made another note on his pad. "Nevertheless, if she's out there, we'll track her down."

"I wonder why she got in touch with Nick after all these years," I mused aloud.

O'Malley sent me a stern look. "That's a question for the police to answer."

"Of course it is," I agreed demurely.

Aunt Peg pursed her lips and said nothing. I took that to mean that it would be a race to see which one of us would succeed in getting to Claire Walden first. If anyone could fill in some of the blanks, she'd be the person to do it.

"This Anabelle Gifford," O'Malley said to Peg. "Any idea where she lives?"

"None whatsoever. Nick only spoke of her the one time. And then just briefly."

"Nick's family is from North Carolina," I told him.

"And how would you know that?" he asked.

"Claire told me."

O'Malley frowned. He sat and thought for a minute. "I seem to recall that the last time we met, you were acquainted with both the deceased and the woman who was found to have killed her," he said finally.

"That's right."

"In fact, you summoned the Darien Police to the murderer's home where a brawl was in progress and where they were subsequently able to extract a confession."

Right again, I thought. But somehow, agreeing with Detective O'Malley too readily was beginning to seem like a bad idea.

"And now you've turned up again," he said.

"Not exactly," I corrected him. "I've been here all the time."

The detective was not amused. "It sounds like you have very bad luck. Either that or you make a habit of injecting yourself into situations where you don't belong."

"Nick Walden was my friend," I said steadily. "His sister is almost family." That was stretching things a bit, but I wanted to make my point. "I don't think it's up to you to tell me where I do or do not belong."

O'Malley shoved back his chair and rose to his feet. "Don't try to do my job for me, Ms. Travis. Killers are dangerous people and they do desperate things. I would hate for you to find yourself in the wrong place at the wrong time."

"I would too," I replied.

"You happen to come across any information you think I should know, you'll bring it to me, right?"

"Of course." I nodded.

"*Before* acting on it yourself."

"I'll try."

O'Malley's brow drew downward. His features set in a scowl. "Try *hard,*" he snapped.

Aunt Peg walked the detective to the door. She even convinced him to take along another scone for the road. They parted with a handshake and a smile. Apparently O'Malley's frowns were reserved for me.

"That was fun," Aunt Peg said when she returned. Along the way, she'd detoured to open the library door and a flurry of Poodles came bounding into the kitchen with her.

"Fun, my foot," I said huffily. "You certainly took your own sweet time remembering to tell us about Anabelle Gifford."

"I can assure you it wasn't done on purpose. Considering the brevity of the conversation, you're lucky I remembered her at all. It seems to me that if Claire Walden thought the police needed to know about her sister, she was perfectly capable of informing them herself. Naturally I assumed that she already had."

And yet, judging by O'Malley's reaction, the information had been as much of a surprise to him as it had been to me.

"Were you telling the truth when you said that you didn't know how to get in touch with Anabelle?" I asked.

Peg drew herself up to her full height. Since she approaches six feet, that had her towering over me. An effect she clearly intended.

"I always tell the truth," she informed me.

I struggled not to laugh.

"At least when I need to."

"Or when it's expedient," I said.

"Ed and his minions will use their resources to find Anabelle." Aunt Peg stared down at me and added, "And while the police are making themselves useful, I suggest you do the same."

"I've already spoken to half a dozen of Nick's clients," I told her. "And I'm trying to line up the rest."

"And?"

"They all thought he was a great guy."

"That's hardly news."

"It's all I've got," I admitted.

"Then it's a good thing I didn't leave it to you to pull something out of *your* hat for the detective."

We'd talked ourselves around in a circle.

"Anabelle Gifford," I said, standing up and heading for the door. "I need to see Claire."

"I imagine Ed felt much the same way. Rather than stepping on his toes, you might want to wait your turn."

Aunt Peg—the most impatient woman I'd ever met—counseling prudence? Somewhere in the world pigs were flying.

"How very unlike you," I said.

"Pish." Peg snorted. "With your proclivity for finding trouble, you never know when you might need to call for back-up. Best to at least attempt to stay on the good side of the authorities, don't you think?"

That sounded like the Aunt Peg I knew and loved.

"I'll try to remember that," I told her.

"I should hope so," she said.

I spent the rest of the morning running errands and catching up on all the minutiae of my daily life which—when allowed to grow unchecked—threatens to rise up and overwhelm everything in the vicinity. Sam and Kev were out when I got home. So I took the dogs for a quick run then went out again too.

At the pet food warehouse, I stocked up on dog food and got guilted into purchasing a jumbo bag of rawhide bones. Downtown at the library, I returned a stack of books, some of which weren't even overdue. Back home by noon, I scheduled Davey's yearly appointment with the pediatrician and debated whether it was too soon to think about taking Kevin to the dentist.

It was nice to feel on top of things for a change.

About that time, it occurred to me that I'd missed breakfast. Usually my meal choices are heavily influenced by Sam and the kids. Most days I simply end up with whatever they're having. So the luxury of choosing my own menu required some serious thought. I was still considering my options when the doorbell rang.

The Poodles are usually quicker on the uptake than I am when guests arrive. But since I'd just passed out new rawhide bones, now they were conflicted. Should they stay and chew or run and bark?

Tar, who tried to do both, predictably lost his bone in the middle of the hall. That occasioned the inevitable scrambling among the rest of the pack—a canine version of musical chairs, played with rawhide toys. Eve dropped her bone and scooped up Tar's. Raven grabbed Eve's discarded bone and made a dash for the safety of the stairs. Faith ended up with Raven's bone. Tar just stood there and barked.

I opened the door and found Claire standing on the step, glowering.

"What did your aunt tell Detective O'Malley?" she asked before I even had a chance to speak.

"Umm . . ."

"As soon as Nick got involved with her, I knew that woman was going to be trouble!"

Claire stalked past me into the house. Then stopped dead. Her eyes widened as she took in the ongoing melee in the hallway.

"Goodness," she said. "Did you have this many dogs the last time I was here?"

"I'm afraid so. Don't worry, they'll settle down in a minute."

"I'm not worried." Claire's neat sidestep removed her from the path of a pair of careening canine missiles both holding a knotted end of the same bone. "They're Poodles. Them, I can understand. Peg is an entirely different matter."

Welcome to the club, I thought.

"I was just going to make myself some lunch," I said. Maybe a nice meal would defuse the situation. "Want to join me?"

"No. I'm too mad to eat."

Claire strode down the hallway. Given little choice in the matter, I tagged along behind. Reaching the kitchen, she yanked out a chair at the table and sat down. I hesitated in the doorway, waiting to see what would happen next.

"Well?" said Claire. "Aren't you going to cook, or eat, or something?"

"I got the idea you wanted to talk."

"I'll talk. You eat. What are you having?"

"Tuna salad on rye," I said, making the decision on the spot. Ease of preparation had begun to seem like a priority.

"With celery and onions?"

"Lots of celery, no onions." I opened the refrigerator and began pulling out ingredients. "Parsley and a little bit of tarragon."

Claire considered my answer. "That might work. Rye with seeds or without?"

"With." I straightened and turned to face her. "For someone who isn't eating, you're very picky about what's being served."

"I like food," she said with a shrug. "Homemade mayo?"

"Not in this universe." I laughed. "Two kids, one husband, six dogs. Does that sound like the kind of place where you'd find homemade mayonnaise?"

"You would if I lived here."

Said the woman without young children.

I propped my hands on my hips and tipped my head to one side. "So are you eating or not?"

"I guess I could manage a small sandwich."

I grabbed two cans of tuna and a loaf of bread out of the pantry. "I have pickles," I mentioned.

"Sweet or dill?"

"Seriously?" I said. "How do you ever eat out? You must be a waiter's worst nightmare."

Claire brushed away my comment with a wave of her hand. "I tip very well. Waiters find a way to deal. I care about the food I put into my body. You should too."

"Some days I'm lucky if I get three meals and my shoes match. Around here, it usually doesn't pay to be any pickier than that."

Claire muttered something under her breath that I didn't quite catch. Figuring it was probably just as well, I went to work making us a couple of sandwiches. While I did that, Claire set the table.

How she knew where everything was, I have no idea. People who feel at home in other's people's kitchens baffle the heck out of me. Most days, I barely feel comfortable in my own.

"Back to Aunt Peg," I said ten minutes later as I slipped a plate of food down in front of Claire and joined her at the table. "I gather you have a complaint to make. But why come here? You should have gone directly to Peg."

"That's not happening," Claire said firmly. "I've been told that your aunt is a holy terror."

Bob's work, no doubt. Then again, he had a point.

"She can be," I admitted. "But Aunt Peg liked Nick. She'll like you too."

For someone who'd claimed to be too angry to eat, Claire was making very short work of her sandwich. On the other hand, her sweet pickles still sat on the side of the plate, untouched. Since I'd already scarfed mine down, I was tempted to steal hers. Only the realization that someone as picky about her food as Claire probably wouldn't appreciate my fingers dancing around her plate, kept my hands in my lap.

"Peg will associate me with Bob," she said. "She'll probably hate me on sight."

"She's not *that* bad."

"Nevertheless, you're easier."

"Thank you," I said. "I think."

Claire polished off the last of her sandwich and daintily wiped her lips with her napkin. It was time to get down to business, and the first words out of her mouth dispelled the notion that the meal might have improved her mood.

"Detective O'Malley showed up at my house an hour ago," she pronounced. "I hoped he'd come because he had something to report about his investigation. Imagine my shock when instead he brought up a name that I haven't heard since I was in high school."

"Anabelle Gifford," I said.

"Anabelle Walden," Claire corrected me. "That's was my sister's name the last time I saw her."

"When was that?"

"Nearly ten years ago when she walked out of my parents' house. My mother was crying, my father was raging. Nick was trying to placate everyone, all to no avail. I think I was in shock. Mostly what I remember about that day is my father saying, *'If you leave us for him, you're not a member of this family anymore. If you walk out that door, it will be closed to you forever.'* "

I swallowed heavily. The food I'd just eaten turned over in my stomach. No matter how angry I was, I couldn't imagine ever saying something like that to a child of mine.

"What had she done to make your parents so angry?" I asked.

"You'll probably think it's silly."

"You've met my family," I said. "I don't have any room to judge."

Claire nodded. Hard not to agree with the truth.

"My parents are southerners," she told me. "Conservative, religious, still not entirely sure that the Confederacy didn't win the war. They can be a little closed-minded about people who don't agree with them." She paused, then added, "They're big on family values."

It sounded just the opposite to me. But I kept quiet and let Claire continue speaking.

"Anabelle was in her senior year of high school. She'd just turned eighteen. She was about to graduate with honors."

"She met a boy," I guessed.

"Worse than that, she met a *man*. My father probably could have handled a boy. Or at least exerted some influence over what he and Anabelle did together. But Zane was in his twenties and out of school. He had a job tending bar, he played in a band on the weekends. He swept Anabelle right off her feet."

"Was that so terrible?" I asked. "Eighteen isn't that young."

"It was in my father's eyes. He still thought of Anabelle as his little princess. She was the oldest, the cheerleader, the baton twirler, the girly girl he'd always wanted. He always thought she could do no wrong."

"That's a tough pedestal to balance on forever," I pointed out.

Claire sighed. "The stupid thing was, Anabelle wasn't even trying to rebel. She just met a guy and fell in love. I don't think it ever crossed her mind that doing so would change her whole life. And that after that none of us would ever be the same."

Chapter 18

"At eighteen it's hard to think so far ahead," I said.

"I'm sure it never occurred to Anabelle that she would have to," Claire replied. "Zane's band got an opportunity to go to New York that summer. Supposedly they had a promise of a meeting with a record label. Now it sounds crazy—the idea that some big music producer would be interested in a local, southern, bar band—but when you're that age anything seems possible. Zane told Anabelle to pack her bags and she did."

I could see where that was going, and it didn't look good.

"Anabelle had everything all planned out before she even told my folks. She gave up her waitressing job and figured she'd pick up another one in New York. Probably even make better money. She said she'd be back in plenty of time to start her freshman year at Wake Forest, just like Daddy expected her to."

"I take it he didn't like that idea?"

Claire sighed. "He hated it. He didn't even stop to think before he forbade her to go. Daddy said that no daughter of his was going to turn herself into a low-class, trailer trash, groupie and follow some long-haired musician around from gig to gig. He and Anabelle fought about it for a week."

"It sounds as though neither of them won in the end."

"They were both too stubborn for their own good. And neither one would give an inch. Finally Zane just said that he'd go to New York without her. Well, that idea made Anabelle crazy. She was stuck in the middle between Zane and Daddy, trying desperately to keep both men in her life happy. But no matter how hard she tried, she couldn't make it happen."

"So when she had to choose, she chose her boyfriend over your family," I said.

"No." Claire shook her head. "Not on purpose. Anabelle left with Zane, but I know she believed that Daddy would get over being mad once she was gone. She thought he'd miss her and be ready to forgive her when she came back. You have to understand, Anabelle had always been his favorite. She could get away with just about anything. She had no reason to think this would end up any differently."

"But it must have," I said with a frown. "Because it sounds as though she never did come back?"

"No, she didn't. But that wasn't Anabelle's doing; it was Daddy's. He was dead serious about locking the door behind her. Mama tried to change his mind. Nick and I did too. He wouldn't listen to any of us. It was as if Anabelle's running off to New York was a personal rejection of him. Daddy was so bitter about what she'd done that he wouldn't even let us mention her name.

"When fall came, I thought even if Anabelle wasn't coming home, surely she'd go to Wake Forest. But that didn't happen either. I know because I called the school and checked. Daddy wouldn't pay her bills and it was too late to apply for financial aid. She just disappeared. After Anabelle left the house that day, it was as if she fell off the face of the earth."

I exhaled slowly. "How awful."

"It *was* awful," Claire agreed. "It tore our family apart,

bit by bit. We were like a group of strangers living under the same roof. Nick couldn't wait to get away. That's why he decided to come north for college. When my turn came, I did the same. We both wanted a fresh start."

"And in all the time since, you've still never had any contact with your sister?" I asked.

"Not even once. Back when I first came up here for school I thought about trying to track her down. But so much time had already passed. Plus Anabelle had never tried to get in touch with me either. So I thought maybe she didn't want to be found. Maybe Daddy was right and Anabelle had forgotten all about us and gone on with her life."

"You never even wondered—"

"Of course I wondered!" Claire snapped. Tears shimmered in her amber eyes. "But what was I supposed to do? I didn't know where Anabelle was. As it turns out, I didn't even know her name. I certainly had no idea that Nick had been in touch with her.

"What happened with Anabelle was like some hideous family secret that I've spent the last ten years trying to put behind me. Then this morning, out of the blue, Detective O'Malley brought it all up again. Apparently your Aunt Peg knows things about my family that I didn't even know myself! I was totally blindsided by his questions. I couldn't begin to answer them. It's bad enough that I don't have any information about Anabelle. Even worse, this whole thing makes me feel like maybe I didn't even know my own brother."

"I'm so sorry," I said.

I picked up our plates and carried them over to the sink. Returning to the table, I brought a box of Kleenex with me.

Claire shook her head. "I'm not crying," she said. The statement sounded more determined than factual. "I hate to cry. And now I seem to be doing it all the time."

"You're allowed," I said gently. "Crying might make you feel better."

"It won't, trust me. My eyes swell up and my nose gets red. I look like a clown when I cry." Now Claire sounded annoyed. She snatched a tissue from the box and blew her nose noisily. "Nick was my best friend. I thought I knew everything about him. Now I don't know what to think."

"The police will need to talk to Anabelle," I said.

Claire nodded. "They're looking for her now. O'Malley said he'd let me know when they find her."

"Will you want to see her?"

"Of course. How could I not want that? Especially now, knowing that she'd gotten in touch with Nick before he died. After all this time, I don't even know who Anabelle is anymore. But she's still family."

"It might be nice to have a big sister again," I said.

"Maybe." Claire didn't sound convinced. "Or maybe it's been so long that we won't have a single thing in common anymore. I guess I'll just have to play that part by ear."

She pushed back her chair and stood. Claire picked up her purse and slung it over her shoulder. Together we headed for the door.

"I hope Aunt Peg is forgiven," I said. "I'm willing to let her take the blame for a lot of things but this really wasn't her fault."

"That's not what Bob would say." Claire managed a small smile. "He uses her as a scapegoat for just about everything."

"She feels the same way about him," I said with a laugh. I paused beside the door. "One quick question before you go?"

"Shoot," said Claire.

"When I spoke with Diana, she mentioned someone named Taran Black. She said he owed Nick money. Do you know who he is?"

"Sure. I've known Taran since grade school. Nick has

too. He's a little on the flakey side but basically harmless. I can't imagine him and Nick having a disagreement serious enough to yell about, much less . . ."

She didn't finish the sentence, but we both knew what had been left unsaid. Much less murder.

"Even so," I said. "I'd like to talk to him."

"I'll track down his phone number."

"Thank you."

"No. Thank *you*." Claire surprised me by wrapping her arms around me and pulling me close in a hug. "This morning I was ready to kick the dog and scare the chickens. Talking to you helped a lot. I feel much better now."

"I'm glad," I said. I stepped back and looked at her. "You and Bob. If you don't mind my asking, how's that working out?"

"Good." Claire nodded thoughtfully. "Really very good."

"I'm happy to hear that," I told her. "If . . . if that should change at some point, I hope that you and I will be able to stay friends."

Claire blinked several times. I got the impression she might be blinking back more tears. Then unexpectedly I got another hug.

"I'd like that," she said softly. "I really would."

I stood in the doorway and watched her drive away. I don't make friends easily. Despite the uncomfortable circumstances under which we'd met, I was pretty sure Claire was going to be a keeper.

Since Sam and Kevin still hadn't reappeared and Davey didn't need to be picked up until four-thirty, I decided to make myself useful by talking to a couple more of Nick's clients. Bethany Grace lived in Shippan, a wealthy neighborhood in southern Stamford, located on a peninsula that juts out into Long Island Sound. Sara Owens's address was in Belle Haven, an equivalent coastal community of beautiful waterfront homes in Greenwich. The two destinations were only a short distance apart via the Connecticut Turnpike.

Luck was on my side. Bethany and Sara were both at home and each of the women agreed to see me that afternoon. Starting in North Stamford, I drove to Shippan first.

The Grace family lived in a large, cream-colored, Colonial on a corner lot near the yacht club. The house was set back from the road and surrounded by a profusion of low trees and flowering shrubs. A quick estimate revealed that the Graces probably spent more money on landscaping than I do on my mortgage. The overall effect was lovely however, so maybe that was just jealousy on my part.

When I got out of my car, I could smell the sharp tang of saltwater on the breeze that blew inland off the Sound. I wondered if a house like that came with its own private beach. As it turned out, I didn't have to speculate for long.

Bethany Grace opened the door to her home with her hand holding tight to the collar of a medium-sized, fluffy, white puppy. I recognized the prick ears and foxy face. American Eskimo Dogs, like Standard Poodles, compete in the Non-Sporting Group. I'd seen plenty of them at the shows.

This one, however, was leaping up and down in the doorway with the kind of frantic energy not usually seen in the show ring. It was also barking loudly enough to make my ears sting. White nails scrambled on the marble floor each time the puppy hit the ground briefly before launching itself back up into the air.

"Come in so I can shut the door," Bethany said quickly. She was younger than the other clients I'd spoken with, probably in her late thirties with stick-straight blond hair and the face of a pixie. At the moment, a very disgruntled pixie.

"Snowy, stop that!" she ordered. "Behave yourself!"

I slipped past the squabbling pair and into the house. As soon as Bethany closed the door and released the puppy's collar, the little Eskie darted away, still barking shrilly. Halfway down the hallway, he spun to one side and dove under a cherrywood table positioned along the wall.

"Sorry about that," Bethany said. "Snowy thinks he's in charge of the front door. And unfortunately he's not great at listening."

As we introduced ourselves, Snowy came racing back. Now a big blue ball was clutched in his mouth. Tail flipped up and over his back, the puppy skidded to a stop in front of us. He dropped the ball at Bethany's feet and looked up expectantly. She pretended not to notice him, so I did too.

"Thank you for agreeing to see me," I said.

"No problem. To tell the truth, I never turn down the opportunity for adult conversation. Especially during summer vacation."

I recognized that feeling readily enough. "You must be a mother too." I laughed.

Waiting below us, Snowy was growing tired of being ignored. He picked up the ball and dropped it again, then nudged it closer with his nose. After a few more seconds, the Eskie's paws began to dance impatiently on the polished floor. When we still didn't respond to his antics, he began to bark once more.

"Snowy, cut that out!"

The command had no discernible effect on the puppy's behavior, so Bethany repeated it. Once, and then again.

Good thing Aunt Peg wasn't there, I thought. She would have felt obliged to point out that a dog that wasn't corrected the first time it ignored a command was even less likely to respond appropriately the second time the command was given. Either that, or she simply would have smacked the woman. Fortunately, I was able to exercise more restraint.

Bethany looked at me and rolled her eyes, a mute plea for commiseration. I shrugged and waited to see what would happen next. Bethany leaned down and scooped up the ball. Before she'd even thrown it, Snowy was already scrambling away down the hallway in pursuit. No wonder the Eskie thought he was in charge.

"Come on," she said. "Let's go sit on the terrace. "It'll be quieter out there."

I wondered if that meant that we'd be leaving the puppy inside the house.

"He knows how to push your buttons," I commented.

Bethany sighed. "Nick told me the same thing. We were working on turning that around."

Then she opened the French doors at the other end of the hall and I forgot about talking and simply stopped and stared. The vista that opened out before us was incredible. Beyond the terrace, a manicured lawn sloped down to a narrow private beach. Sunlight glinted off the gently rolling waves of the azure blue Long Island Sound. Two sailboats were racing side by side and tacking into the light breeze.

"Wow," I said.

"I know. It's gorgeous, isn't it? I see the view every day, so I've gotten used to it. But it's always nice when someone sees it for the first time and reminds me how lucky I am."

We found seats in a pair of matching bamboo chairs. Snowy, who'd followed us outside, carried his ball into the middle of the yard. He lay down and began to chew.

"Here's the crazy thing," said Bethany. "I have two teenagers who could be out here swimming or sailing, or over at the club playing tennis. Instead, Kyle's up in his room on the Internet doing God knows what. And Tyler's at the mall with her friends."

"That seems like a shame on a beautiful day like this," I agreed.

"How old are yours?"

"Eleven and two. Both boys."

"That's quite a spread in age." She stopped abruptly, her face growing pink. "I'm sorry, that was rude of me."

"Not at all," I said easily. "Probably a lot of people wonder how that happened."

"I'm guessing that most have better manners than to ask."

"I don't mind. The boys are from two different marriages, and somehow without meaning to, I took ten years off in the middle."

Bethany nodded. "I get that. Sometimes it seems like half of parenting is dealing with things you didn't mean to have happen." She gazed out into the yard. "Like Snowy there."

"Was he supposed to be Kyle and Tyler's puppy?"

"He *is* their puppy," Bethany said firmly. "Not that you'd ever know it from the amount of attention they pay to him. Richard—that's my husband—brought Snowy home with him from a business trip. He'd been away for two weeks and I guess he was feeling guilty. He had a box of chocolates for me and a puppy for the kids."

Bethany's expression wavered somewhere between exasperated and resigned. "Richard told them that Snowy was some rare, exotic, Eskimo dog who'd been born in an igloo. That's how the puppy got his name."

With that sixth sense all dogs have that lets them know when someone's talking about them, Snowy lifted his head and gazed in our direction. Briefly it looked as though he might get up and come over to join us. Then the puppy thought better of the idea. He lowered his muzzle and went back to chewing on his ball.

"Kyle and Tyler were all excited about their new puppy—for about a week. Then they went back to their friends, and their sports, and their video games. Frankly, my chocolates lasted longer than their interest in the new dog did."

"That's really too bad," I said.

"Tell me about it."

"It's a shame for Snowy, as well as for you," I pointed out. "Much as you don't want to have an untrained puppy, Snowy's probably not too happy about the lack of structure in his life either."

"Are you kidding me? That dog has a great life. He gets to do whatever he wants."

"Snowy's what, five, maybe six months old?"

Bethany nodded.

"He's a baby," I said. "Not only does he need adult guidance, he's *looking* for it. The reason he does whatever he wants is because you haven't set enough boundaries."

"I set boundaries," Bethany said. "Snowy ignores them."

"Because you let him."

"No, I don't." She stopped. Then frowned. "Well, maybe I do. But why do I have to be the enforcer?"

"Because no one else wants the job?"

"It's like having a third child," Bethany muttered.

"It's worse," I said. "Because of the language barrier. But only for a little while. And then it gets much better."

"That's what Nick was doing here. He was trying to teach me how to communicate effectively with Snowy. He said the problem wasn't that Snowy didn't want to behave but that he didn't understand what I wanted him to do."

"That sounds about right," I agreed.

"Nick was like Dr. Dolittle," Bethany said. "He knew everything that puppy was thinking. It was amazing to watch the two of them together. They were totally simpatico. How did he do that?"

"He had a rare gift," I said softly. "Nick was a lucky guy."

Bethany looked up. "Right up until the day he wasn't."

"Do you have any thoughts about that?"

"I think Nick needed a new girlfriend."

Interesting. "Why do you say that?" I asked.

"The one he had wasn't good enough for him."

"You met Diana?"

"Diana?" Bethany looked confused. "Who was she?"

"Nick's girlfriend."

"Not the one I met. Her name was Carol."

Oh, I thought. Here we go again.

Chapter 19

"Wait a minute," I said. "Was her name Carol Luna?"
"I don't know." Bethany shrugged. "It's not like we were formally introduced. I just heard Carol."

There was a woman named Carol on the client list Bob had given me. *Carol Luna, four months duration as client, Doberman Pinscher puppy.* I had left a message on her phone asking if she'd be willing to talk to me. Carol Luna had never called me back. Could she be the woman Bethany had met?

"What didn't you like about her?" I asked.

"For one thing, she was a lot older than Nick. Although she'd probably be pissed that I noticed, considering how much work she'd had done. Not that I'm a prude about stuff like that—the age difference or the plastic surgery—but Nick was a great guy. I just thought he could do better."

Bethany looked at me and grimaced. "Plus her manners left a lot to be desired."

Fair enough, on all points.

"What made you think that she was Nick's girlfriend?"

"Who else but an angry girlfriend would follow a man to his place of business and stand there yelling at him where anyone could overhear? And if she wasn't someone close to him, how did she even know where to find him?"

I could see why Bethany had come to that conclusion. And for all I knew, maybe she was right.

"So this woman Carol showed up uninvited at your house," I prompted.

"That's right. She parked in the driveway and let herself in through the side gate. Nick and I were in the yard working with Snowy, when she came marching around the house like she thought she had every right to be here. Trust me, that's not the way people do things around here."

In a neighborhood of multi-million-dollar beachfront mansions, I should think not.

"When I saw her," said Bethany, "my first thought was to call the police."

"And did you?"

"I got out my phone, but almost immediately it became clear that Nick knew who she was. He seemed pretty shocked to see her though. He left Snowy and me, and walked over and grabbed her arm. He tried to turn her around and make her leave."

"I take it that didn't work?"

"Not even close. She just started yelling at him. That's when I heard her name. Nick said something like, 'Carol, please, you need to calm down. You shouldn't even be here.' It didn't help one bit. She just kept screaming. That was one angry lady."

"What was she yelling about?"

"Considering everything that's happened since, I really wish I knew. But at the time . . ." Bethany stopped and shook her head. "I thought it was a lovers' spat. It never even occurred to me that it might be something more. I liked Nick, you know?"

I nodded. Everybody had.

"I didn't want to embarrass him. It wasn't his fault his girlfriend was a shrew. So even though they were standing in my yard, I made myself scarce. I figured that whatever was going on wasn't any of my business."

"Too bad," I said.

"I'll tell you what's really too bad. When I went in the house, Snowy stayed outside. That puppy always did prefer Nick's company to anyone else's." Bethany gazed at me with her head tipped to one side, considering. "Nick could talk to Snowy like they were members of the same family. It was amazing the way they understood each other. I don't suppose you can do that too?"

I snorted softly. "I wish."

"Me too. Because then you could ask him. Whatever was going on out here that day, Snowy overheard the whole thing."

After that, my conversation with Sara Owens was anticlimactic. Like Bethany, Sara lived in a wealthy seaside neighborhood. Her Normandy style mansion was a block away from the Sound but fortunately for its owner, still managed to offer a coveted, unobstructed, water view.

Sara was a divorcee in her mid-fifties. Her children were grown and gone. Her husband had had a midlife crisis and left her for a younger woman; the two of them were now living in the south of France. After his defection, Sara had felt lonely rattling around her huge home with only the housekeeper for company, but she'd won the house in the divorce and improbably continued to cling to the hope that her husband might someday return to it—minus the company of his new wife, of course.

I learned all that in the first five minutes of our acquaintance. Sara was friendly, pert, and very talkative. Her dark blond hair was threaded with gray that she didn't bother to hide. Her figure was curvaceous and slightly plump, and she was dressed in a designer ensemble that seemed overly elaborate for an at-home visit on a hot summer day.

But then my usual hot weather ensemble starts with a pair of shorts. Or maybe khakis. So what do I know?

Sara and I sat in a morning room whose temperature

had been lowered to just above glacial. We sipped sweet tea, served by the housekeeper, who also set a plate of crunchy homemade oatmeal cookies on the table between us. Sara ate three for every one of mine.

"Go ahead," she said, poking me in the arm and gesturing toward the plate. "Indulge yourself. Life is short, and things you think will last forever never do. You've got to grab everything you can get your hands on when the opportunities arise. Trust me, I know."

So I had another cookie. It wasn't a hardship. They were chewy and buttery and studded with plump raisins. Maybe I'd have another after that and skip dinner. And breakfast tomorrow morning.

"If you don't mind my asking," I said, "where is your dog?"

"Oh, Elan is out back somewhere." Sara waved a hand dismissively. "That silly hound has a mind of his own. He isn't much of a house dog."

"Your choice, or his?" I asked.

Sara's lovely home bore the unmistakable imprint of a high-priced interior designer. On the short walk from the front door to the room where we were sitting, I'd seen antique furniture, Oriental rugs, and pristine upholstery. It was hard to imagine how a silly hound might complement the décor.

"Both, actually." Sara lowered her voice as if confiding a secret. "Elan and I? We don't really get along. Starting when he was a puppy, we just never got on the same page. After Harold left, I thought a dog would be good company. But the only company Elan seems to enjoy is his own."

"What kind of hound is he?" I asked.

"An Afghan Hound, the most beautiful breed of dog you could possibly imagine. His hair is silver blue and feels like silk. I wanted a classy looking dog, and that's Elan all right. He looks like he ought to be owned by royalty."

An Afghan, I thought. What a shame. Sara could hardly

have made a worse choice. The breed was famous not only for its stunning beauty and aristocratic dignity, but also for its aloof and independent temperament. Not the best idea for a woman alone and seeking companionship.

On the other hand, it turned out that I'd been wrong earlier. The dog *would* complement the décor. He probably looked gorgeous draped over Sara's designer furniture.

"I'm sorry," I said.

"Don't be. It wasn't your mistake. I take full responsibility. And believe me, Nick Walden read me the riot act about that. He told me that I should have put as much thought into getting a puppy as I would have into adding a member to my family. And I guess he was right."

Indeed. Aunt Peg would have told her much the same thing.

"But at least you found Nick," I said. "He was great with dogs and their owners. Was he able to help you and Elan get along better?"

"That was the original idea. But after a couple of weeks, Nick and I both came to the conclusion that Elan and I just weren't suited to one another. He needs room to run and an owner who will give him plenty of exercise. I need a dog that's little and fluffy and wants to snuggle with me on the couch. Once we figured that out, Nick started looking around for me. He was going to find a good home for Elan and then help me shop for a replacement."

"Not another hound," I said with a small smile.

"No way. I learned that lesson the first time around. But I'll tell you what. Nick Walden was really nice about it. He could have made me feel stupid for getting the wrong dog but he never did." Sara shook her head. "I mean, what kind of idiot doesn't even like her own dog?"

"It happens," I said. "And depending on what you're looking for in a pet, hounds can be tough."

"That's what Nick told me. He said he was working with another client whose hound dog got along fine with its owner but caused all sorts of problems for her son. It made me feel a lot better, just knowing that I wasn't the only one who got the whole dog-ownership thing wrong."

"Believe me," I told her. "You're *far* from the only one. That's why Nick's services were in such demand."

"What happened to him is a real shame," Sara said with a sigh. "I talked to the police, but I don't know if they even have any suspects. It seems like every time there's a break-in somewhere, we're told that it's kids looking for drug money. Nick seemed like the kind of guy who spent every penny he had on his dogs. There couldn't have been much left over for someone to steal."

"When Nick was here working with you and Elan," I said, "did he ever seem worried about anything? Did he talk about any problems he might have had?"

"No, never. Although as you may have noticed, I like to talk. Could be that I didn't give him much of a chance."

We smiled together. Sara did have a lot to say. She would definitely dominate just about any conversation.

"My impression of Nick was that he was a doer, not a talker," she added. "He was the rare man who knew how to listen. Maybe because he spent so much time listening to his dogs."

I nodded in agreement. "So what will you do with Elan now?"

"I haven't figured that part out yet. I guess I'll follow Nick's advice and start looking for a home for him on my own."

"My aunt's involved with a lot of dog people. She might be able to help. She breeds Standard Poodles, but I'm sure she can put you in touch with an Afghan rescue group."

"Poodles?" Sara's face brightened. "I was thinking I might try one of those next."

"One thing at a time," I told her. "Let's get Elan well situated first."

"Sure, there's no hurry. I'll be working on making some other changes in the meantime."

"Dog related?" I asked. "Or something different?"

"I've been thinking about what Nick said the last time I saw him. He told me that when something isn't working, you have to learn to let go. It might seem hard at the time, but you have to keep looking forward and not back. Nick Walden was pretty wise for someone so young. Finding a better home for Elan may be just the beginning."

"Good for you," I said. "And good luck."

"Thanks," Sara replied. She sounded less sure than her brave words might have indicated. "I'm going to need it."

On my way home from Greenwich I swung by Davey's camp. I'd arrived a few minutes before the four-thirty dismissal so while I waited for Davey to appear, I pulled out my phone and gave Carol Luna's number another try. She still didn't pick up. I left a second message, explaining more fully why I wanted to speak with her. Hopefully she'd get around to returning my call this time.

As I disconnected the call, Davey came trotting over to the car. He threw his gear in the back, climbed in up front next to me, and asked, "What's for dinner?"

I leveled him a look. "A more polite child might have started the conversation with, *Hi Mom, how was your day? Thank you for picking me up and not complaining about the mud I tracked into your car.*"

"Maybe." Davey considered for a moment, then shook his head. "But I don't think so. That part doesn't need to be said. It's assumed."

No doubt about it, the kid was a smarty-pants. I hated to think where he might have gotten that from.

"Good manners should never be taken for granted," I said primly as we pulled back out onto Newfield Avenue.

All at once, hearing *those* words coming out of *my*

mouth made me frown. Good Lord, I sounded just like my mother.

That thought brought a sharp pang. Even after twelve years, I still felt the loss. Davey had never had the chance to know either of his grandparents. They had been killed in a car crash in the first year of my marriage to Bob. I was newly pregnant when I heard the news.

Looking back now, I remembered that year as a jumble of emotional peaks and valleys. I'd had to mourn the passing of two lives while celebrating the beginning of another.

My mother would have loved Davey with all her heart. She had liked Bob enough and I was sure she'd hoped that their relationship would deepen with time. Neither she nor my father protested when we announced our engagement, even though they both thought that we were marrying much too young. Of course, as it turned out, they were right.

My father's love for Davey would have been more restrained, perhaps a bit gruff in its expression, but no less heartfelt. He would have taken his grandson fishing, teaching him how to thread a line and construct a lure, just as he'd done with Frank and me when we were young.

By the time Davey was old enough to learn those things, Bob was already gone from our lives. My parents would have made the effort to fill that gap. They would have made sure that even with only one parent, Davey never felt any less surrounded by love.

If only they'd had the chance.

I sighed loudly.

"*Now* what did I do?" Davey asked.

"Nothing." I gave my head a quick shake. "It wasn't you."

"That's good." He plucked at his jersey. It was stiff with sweat. "Who is it then?"

"Nobody," I told him. "I was just thinking about something."

"It's Sam."

"Hey!" I said, surprised. I took my eyes off the road long enough for a quick glance in my son's direction. "I didn't say that."

"You were thinking it."

"No, I wasn't."

"Mom, I'm not dumb."

"What does that mean?" I asked.

"I'd have to be stupid not to know that you're mad at Sam. Even the Poodles know." Davey paused for a grin. "All except Tar."

"Sam and I had a disagreement," I said carefully.

"About what?"

I reached over and gave him a poke. "None of your business."

"So fix it," Davey told me. The wisdom of youth.

"I'm going to," I replied. The decision had been made only a minute earlier. "I thought the whole problem was Sam's fault, but now I realize it doesn't matter who was right or wrong."

"Why not?" Davey wanted to know.

"Because life's too short to spend worrying about stuff like that."

"Not at my age." He shook his head slowly. "When you're eleven, life takes forever to happen."

"Consider yourself lucky," I told him.

We were both lucky, I thought. Lately I'd allowed myself to forget that. It was time to put things right.

Later that night after the kids were in bed, I sat down in the living room with Sam. The Poodles were spread out around us, some lying on the furniture, others draped across the floor. The couch was free. Sam and I both found seats there.

Usually Sam picks up the remote, turns on the TV, and looks for a crime drama. Tonight he turned and looked at me instead. "Long day," he said.

"Ditto," I agreed. "But you had Kevin. He uses up a lot of energy."

"Tell me about it." Sam groaned softly and leaned back into the soft cushion. He passed his hand over his eyes, then cradled it under his head. "The only time Kev stopped moving was when we were in the car."

"That's why he went straight to bed," I said. "Now you get to reap your reward."

Sam opened one eye. "What's that?"

"An apology from your wife."

"What do you need to apologize for?"

This is the answer to why men lead happier lives. Emotionally speaking, they haven't a clue. I'd spent the last week obsessing over our relationship, consulting my friends on how to remedy what had seemed to me to be a dire situation, and generally moping around the house like the apocalypse was imminent.

And Sam hadn't even noticed anything was wrong.

For Pete's sake, according to Davey, even the Poodles knew.

"I guess I shouldn't have gotten so upset about your keeping Claire a secret from me."

"Oh that."

Yes, *that,* I thought.

Sam levered himself up. "Then I probably ought to apologize to you too. I realize now that I didn't give the whole thing enough thought. Bob said all he wanted to do was keep the peace, and that seemed like a good idea at the time. I never stopped to think about the fact that you might feel betrayed. Believe me, that was never my intention."

"I know," I said softly. "But you made me feel like maybe I couldn't trust you."

Sam reached out and took my hand in his. "You can *always* trust me."

"I don't like secrets," I said. "Especially ones that concern Davey."

"I know that." His thumb stroked back and forth gently across my palm. "I made a bad decision. I wish I could promise you that it will never happen again but I'm new to this parenting stuff and, as I'm learning, I'm far from perfect at it."

"Me too," I said.

Sam chuckled. The sound bubbled up from deep in his throat as he used his free hand to reach for me. "Come over here, you. Let's join forces and be imperfect together."

I scooched toward him along the couch. God, I had missed this, the easy rapport we'd always shared, the laughing and touching that went along with it. Our connection had frayed but it wasn't torn. Now I could feel it knitting back together.

I leaned toward Sam and placed my lips right next to his ear. "You're on," I said.

Chapter 20

I woke up the next morning feeling refreshed, revitalized, and ready to do something useful. When I checked my e-mail I saw that Claire had sent me contact info for Taran Black—the guy who owed his old buddy Nick a sizeable sum of money that he didn't want to repay. It turned out that Taran lived in Port Chester, a medium-sized, mostly blue-collar city just on the other side of the New York/Connecticut border.

I waited until after nine A.M. to call. Even so, I got the impression I might have woken Taran up. He coughed and grumbled under his breath while I explained who I was and why I was getting in touch. When I mentioned that it was Nick's girlfriend, Diana Lee, who'd been the one to point me in his direction, I was pretty sure I heard a disgusted snort.

Nevertheless, Taran agreed readily enough to meet with me. Maybe he just wanted to get me off the phone so he could go back to sleep. I let him choose the time and the place, and our meeting was set for five o'clock that afternoon at a bar in downtown Port Chester.

That left my entire day unexpectedly free. Since it was Saturday, Davey didn't have camp, so Sam and I decided to take the kids to the beach at Tod's Point. Technically the beach pass belongs to Aunt Peg because she's the Greenwich resident, but Peg hasn't been on a beach in decades. At the beginning of each summer, the sticker seems to find its way into our hands and we always find an opportunity to put it to good use.

I packed a picnic lunch and plenty of sunscreen and we spent most of the day playing in the sun and the surf. By midafternoon, Kevin was half-asleep and even Davey's energy was beginning to flag. We got home in plenty of time for me to shower the sand out my hair and make my appointment in Port Chester.

When I left the house, Sam, Davey, and Kevin were zonked out in front of a baseball game on TV. The Poodles had brought a selection of toys into the living room, hoping for a game of catch or tug-of-war. It didn't look like that would be happening anytime soon. Five hours in the sun and waves had left my human family totally beat.

"See you guys later," I said.

Sam sketched a half-hearted wave. Nobody else even looked up. As I let myself out, I made a mental note to pick up something easy for dinner on the way home.

It took me half an hour to get to Port Chester and an additional ten minutes to locate the small, slightly dilapidated, neighborhood tavern where Taran had wanted to meet. I entered the establishment and pushed the warped door shut behind me. The bar's interior was cool and dimly lit, and I paused for several seconds to let my eyes make the adjustment from the bright sunlight outside.

Before I'd even had a chance to take a look around, a man seated by himself at a quiet corner table, pushed back his chair and stood. He was an inch or two under six feet tall with a pudgy body and soft, fleshy features. His jaw was lined with several days' worth of stubble. His T-hirt, straining to fit around his torso, pictured a palm tree and a sliver of moon. Its motto extolled the virtues of the South Carolina coast.

He walked toward me, holding out his hand, and when

he spoke I could hear the remnants of a southern drawl. "Hi, I'm Taran Black," he said. "You must be Melanie."

"I am," I agreed, and we shook on it.

Taran led the way back to his table. Even this early in the evening, the bar was half full. I wondered how he'd picked me out so easily. When I asked, Taran just laughed.

"This place is like Cheers," he told me. "Half the neighborhood hangs out here and everybody already knows everyone else. That's why I chose to meet here. I figured we wouldn't have any trouble finding each other."

A blue-jean-clad waitress skirted her way to us through the closely grouped tables and took our order. Taran asked for a draft. I opted for club soda with a twist of lime.

We made small talk until she returned with our drinks and a bowl of unshelled peanuts. Taran's draft arrived in a tall, frosty, mug with a rim of foam on the top. He lifted the heavy glass and took a long drink.

Then he set the mug down on the scarred, dark wood table, and gazed at me with an expression that conveyed both annoyance and resignation. "So Diana sent you," he said. "What does she want now?"

"Nothing," I replied. The word just popped out. Too late, it occurred to me that Taran might have been more forthcoming if he'd thought I was there at Diana's behest.

"Nothing? That's a pleasant change." He paused to take another hefty gulp from his glass.

So far I'd only sipped at my club soda. Taran's beer was already half gone. He lifted his hand and signaled the waitress to bring him another.

"Then why are you here?" Taran asked.

"I wanted to talk to you about Nick," I said.

Taran's thick fingers scrambled around in the bowl of peanuts. He drew out a handful and closed his fist to crush the shells, then let the pieces dribble down onto the tabletop. One by one, he tossed the peanuts into his mouth.

"Nick was a great guy," he told me as he chewed.

"That's what everybody says," I told him. "So how come he's dead?"

Taran shrugged. "When your time's up, it's up."

"So you think fate is responsible?"

"Sure. What else?"

"Nick was shot," I said. "Fate didn't pull the trigger."

Taran polished off his first beer and slid the empty mug to the edge of the table. As if on cue, the waitress set the refill down in front of him.

"Why do I get the impression you think I might know something about that?" he asked.

"Do you?"

"Look. Nick and I were old friends, we'd known each other for years. Sure we'd had our differences of opinion. I gave Nick a black eye in fifth grade. He retaliated by knocking out one of my teeth. But that's the way these things go."

Not among my friends, I thought.

"It sounds like you had a pretty contentious relationship," I said.

"Nah, that was just kid stuff."

"And now?"

"People grow up, things change. It turns out that we don't have that much in common anymore. Maybe we got together for a beer every so often, but that was about it. Our lives went in different directions. It happens."

"So you wouldn't have any idea why someone might have wanted to harm Nick?"

"None," Taran said firmly. "Like I said, Nick was mostly someone from my past. I didn't really know him that well anymore."

I wasn't buying that for a minute. Taran was stonewalling. I wondered why.

"And yet," I said, "Nick felt that he still knew you well enough to lend you a sum of money."

Taran scowled. "Did Diana tell you that?"

I nodded.

"You don't want to believe everything that bitch says."

Despite the hostility of the words, Taran's tone remained matter-of-fact. And that wasn't the only thing that seemed contradictory about the man sitting across from me. I got the impression that he wasn't telling me the whole truth—parts of it possibly, but certainly not all of it. Claire had called him harmless. I wasn't sure that I'd agree with her assessment.

I wondered what kinds of secrets Taran was keeping from me and how much it meant to him to keep them hidden.

"Then it isn't true?" I asked. "You didn't borrow money from Nick and refuse to repay it?"

"Refuse to repay it?" Taran snorted. "That's rich."

"Why?" I asked curiously.

"I didn't have Nick's money. By the time he came looking for it, it was long gone. He knew that in the end."

I leaned toward him across the table. "What do you mean *in the end?*"

"Nothing ominous, so don't go trying to make it sound that way. Geez." Taran shook his head. "All I'm saying is that everything got cleared up a couple days before he died. It was just a little family matter."

"Family matter?" Now I was confused. "Your family or his?"

Taran didn't answer my question. Instead he said, "Tell me something. Why is this any of your business?"

"Nick was a friend of mine too. I want to know what happened to him."

"Then you should be talking to the police."

"They don't know either," I said. "If they did, I wouldn't be here. And Nick's sister, Claire, wouldn't be wondering how something so awful could have happened to the only sibling she had left—"

"Hold on!" Taran's hand snaked across the table and grabbed my wrist. "You know Claire?"

"She's the one who gave me your phone number."

My arm was secured tightly within his grasp. When I tugged at it, offering a small amount of resistance, Taran looked down in surprise as if he hadn't even realized he was holding me.

His fingers snapped open. His hand jerked back.

"You and Claire," he said deliberately. "You're like . . . friends?"

I thought of our last conversation and nodded. "That's right."

"Wow. Okay. Good!" Taran appeared to be digesting that information. "Let me think."

I certainly wasn't stopping him.

Something very odd was going on here. Taran had maintained his cool throughout our discussion of Nick's murder and his suspicious, unpaid debt. But now with one mention of Nick's sister he suddenly seemed flustered, almost agitated.

"Look," he said after a minute. "You have to do something for me."

I lifted a brow. "That depends on what it is."

"You have to give Claire a message."

"I can probably do that," I said carefully. "But I would need to know what the message is about. Or you could call her yourself."

"I can't." Taran's head jerked back and forth in a sharp shake. "I promised."

"Promised whom?"

Out of the corner of my eye, I saw the waitress heading back toward our table. Taran lifted a hand and waved her impatiently away. Then he hunkered down and stared at me across the pitted tabletop.

"How much do you know about Nick and Claire's family?" he asked.

"Mostly just the basics." Taran was keeping a close hold on what he knew. I had every intention of doing the same.

He frowned at my reply and seemed to be considering whether or not to press on. "Maybe I shouldn't be doing this," he said.

"I wouldn't worry about that if I were you," I told him. "Because I have no idea what you *are* doing."

"Breaking a confidence. At least considering it."

And then it hit me. All at once I knew what the topic we were dancing around, had to be. Taran had been Nick's childhood friend. If he'd known the Walden family that long, he must have known Anabelle too. Nick's big sister, last seen a decade earlier heading north to New York City—a city only thirty miles away from where we now sat.

"Anabelle," I said softly.

Taran shot up straight in his seat. "What about her?"

"Do you know where she is?"

"I might. Who wants to know?"

"The police, for one," I told him. "They're working on finding her. And Claire wants to know too. She hasn't seen or heard from her sister in ten years."

"That wasn't Anabelle's fault."

"Nor Claire's either," I pointed out. "They both got caught up in something beyond their control. I know that Claire would like to have the chance to get reacquainted with her sister. If that's possible."

"It's possible," Taran said slowly. "We just have to figure out how to make it happen."

"We?"

He nodded. "There are a few stumbling blocks in the way."

"Are you aware that Anabelle spoke with Nick only a few days before he died?"

"Yeah. That was my fault."

"*Your* fault?"

Taran looked glum. "It wasn't supposed to happen that way."

"What way?"

"It was about the money. You know, that I borrowed from Nick?"

This conversation had more unexpected detours than a Kentucky highway. Taran's thoughts were skittering all over the place. Rather than trying to make sense of everything now, it seemed smarter to just keep agreeing with him in the hope that that would keep him talking.

"Sure," I said. "What about it?"

"It was for Alexander."

"Who's he?" My voice croaked. Hastily I reached for a sip of my soda.

"Anabelle's son." Taran frowned. "I guess you probably know about Zane?"

"I know that he took off for New York to look for a record deal and that Anabelle went with him."

"That was the idea in the beginning, but it didn't work out. His band may have been a big fish in the small pond at home, but up here they were nobody. They couldn't even get gigs in bars."

"And the record producer?"

"Never even met with them."

No surprise there.

"The band stayed together for a couple of years. You know, looking for their big break? But it was pretty clear to everyone but them that they were never going to make it."

"What about Anabelle?" I asked.

"She hung in there. What choice did she have? Zane was the only family she had left. Along the way, they went to City Hall and got married. She clung to the idea that they were living this romantic fantasy. You know, like the Romeo and Juliet of the Bronx?"

Taran shook his head, looking disgusted. "Pretty soon she was working two jobs a day. She ended up supporting Zane and whatever other musicians happened to be crashing on their couch at the time. Even after she got pregnant.

By that time, Zane had found work as some other band's roadie. He was always looking for ways to follow his dream. That was the only thing that ever mattered to him."

"Are they still together?" I asked.

"No way. Zane is long gone. He met some guy who said he could introduce him around in L.A. and Zane bought a plane ticket and took off. He never even looked back. I guess he didn't want a wife and kid tying him down anymore."

"Bastard," I muttered under my breath.

"You got it."

"What's your part in all this?" I asked him.

Taran looked at me and shrugged. "Old friend who reminded Anabelle of better days? Occasional baby-sitter and shoulder to cry on? Anabelle and I reconnected when I came up here for a job after college. Mostly I just watched the whole mess unfold from the sidelines. Zane's music scene and his ultra cool buddies? That wasn't my idea of a good time."

"Tell me about the money," I said.

"About a year ago, Alexander started having medical problems. It turned out that he needed surgery. Anabelle had insurance but it wasn't enough. She was pretty frantic. Her credit cards are maxed out. The loan officer at the bank just laughed at her. She needed money fast and she had no way to get it."

"Why didn't she contact her family and ask for help?"

"Her father had told her that she was dead to him." Taran's voice was hard. "She would have groveled for Alexander's sake, if that's what it took. But she didn't think it would do any good."

Would Claire's parents have turned their back on a grandchild in need? I wondered. The notion seemed almost incomprehensible to me. But then I couldn't imagine throwing a child out of the house in the first place.

"So I got this bright idea about borrowing the money from Nick. He was living in Connecticut and doing pretty well. His business was starting to take off."

"And Anabelle agreed to that?"

"No way. She told me absolutely not. She figured Nick was like the rest of her family. That he'd turn his back on her too."

"And yet he gave her the money she needed," I said.

"That's right," Taran told me. "But Anabelle didn't know that because I never told her where I got the money from. At least not at first, anyway. And I didn't tell Nick what I needed the loan for either."

"You're quite the manipulator," I said.

Taran shook his head. "You're missing the point. It wasn't about me. It was about making things work. So Alexander had his operation and everything went great. The only problem was, Anabelle didn't have the money to pay me back. Which meant that I couldn't repay Nick."

"What did you do when he started pressuring you?"

"I stalled for a while. What other choice did I have? Nick was pissed about it, but I just kept putting him off. He and I had been buddies for a long time, and this loan put a big strain on our friendship. Eventually I had to do something, so I confessed to Anabelle about where the money had come from."

"And when she found out, she called Nick," I said.

"Well, first she read me the riot act." Taran smiled ruefully. "And then she got all teary-eyed about the fact that the money to save Alexander had come from a brother she thought had forgotten all about her. But finally, after she pulled herself together, Anabelle said that it wasn't fair for me to be caught in the middle, especially since I'd only been trying to help. So she called Nick and told him where the money had gone."

"He must have been shocked to hear from her," I said.

"He was. But also—according to what Anabelle told me—really happy about it too. Nick was thrilled to find out that he had a nephew. He said that he was going to break the news to Claire, and then he wanted to make plans for all of them to get together."

I exhaled slowly. Hearing about their missed opportunity felt like a punch in the gut. "What a shame that Nick never got to go through with his plan."

"I know, right? Anabelle was heartbroken. She heard about his death on the news. What a way to find out. She'd finally managed to reconnect with her long-lost family and next thing she knew Nick was dead. It really put her into a tailspin."

"But she still has Claire," I said. "Claire is Anabelle's family too. And now that Nick is gone—"

"You don't get it," said Taran. "That's precisely the problem. Anabelle doesn't want to have anything to do with Claire."

"Why on earth not?"

"She's gotten this stupid idea in her head that she's bad luck. Nick helped her and now he's dead. She told me she couldn't stand it if something happened to Claire too. Anabelle thinks the best thing she could do for her little sister would be to disappear again."

Chapter 21

"That's crazy!" I said.

"I know." Taran frowned. "But Anabelle made me promise that I wouldn't tell Claire about her. She intends to stay as far away from her little sister as possible."

"But Anabelle wasn't responsible for Nick's death." I peered at Taran across the table. "Was she?"

"Of course not! But you told me the police are looking for her. So they must think she's a suspect."

"No," I said. "They just want to talk to her, because they know she was in touch Nick right before he died."

"If the police want to talk to Anabelle," said Taran, "they're going to have to find her themselves. I wouldn't wish that guy—what's his name, O'Malley?—on my worst enemy."

"So you've already met the detective?"

"Oh yeah." Taran lifted his near-empty mug and drained the dregs. "We had a long chat. Diana sicced him on me. She told him that I had a motive for wanting Nick dead and he agreed. It was just lucky for me that I had an ironclad alibi."

Taran reached across the table and slid the bowl of peanuts over in front of himself. There were as many empty shells as peanuts left in the bowl now. Idly he sifted through the remains.

"Look," he said. "Here's where I'm coming from. Anabelle never talks about her family but I know she still misses them. And with Zane out of the picture, she and Alexander are all alone. I promised Anabelle that I wouldn't contact Claire myself. But I didn't say anything about encouraging someone else to get them together."

"That's the message you spoke about earlier?"

"Could be." Taran held up his hands palms facing outward, and gazed at me innocently. "It didn't come from me. I just happen to think that somebody . . . you know, some *friend* . . . might want to do something to help."

I nodded.

"And one more thing."

Holy moley, there was *more?* I signaled to the waitress and beckoned her over. Taran's tab was definitely on me.

He waited until I had completed the arrangements and then said, "You know how I told you that Diana sent O'Malley after me? I'm thinking she did that to draw the detective's attention away from herself."

"How come?" I asked.

"I'll let her tell you that."

Taran stood up and headed for the door. I wasn't ready for our interview to end, but apparently Taran had decided that it was over. I grabbed my purse and hurried after him.

He opened the door and held it for me. We stepped out onto the sidewalk together.

"Ask Diana what she did when she found out that Nick was more involved with one of his clients than he'd let on," he said.

"Which client?" I called after him as he began to walk away. I had a pretty good guess but I wanted to hear him say the name.

Taran didn't oblige me. He just shrugged and kept on walking.

* * *

On the way home, I stopped at Post Pizza and picked up dinner. I figure that if you choose wisely, pizza gives you a shot at all the important food groups. So by the time I'd added a mixed salad and poured the kids a couple glasses of milk, I was feeling positively virtuous about the meal.

After dinner, Bob called to let me know that he and I had an appointment the following afternoon.

"Nice of you to check my schedule first," I said. "Where are we going?"

"New Canaan," Bob replied. "And hey, we're all busy. I figured you could find a way to fit this in, especially since you've left me to do all the detective work by myself."

For a moment, I was utterly stumped. I'd had so much on my mind lately, I had no idea what Bob was talking about. Then the light bulb went on.

"Oh," I said. "The diamond ring."

"Of course, the diamond ring. What else would I be calling about?"

"Don't ask."

"If you say so."

My ex-husband lives by the credo *Don't borrow trouble*. If I could only figure out a way to adopt the same attitude, it would simply my life enormously.

"You remember the Morrises, right?" he asked.

"Sure. But you said Emily Morris told you the ring wasn't hers."

"It's not. But today I found out that having seen it, she got interested in its provenance too. She went looking through their old records and made a few calls. Eventually she found her way to a couple in New Canaan named Jim and Susan Bell."

"And they fit into the story how?"

"The Morrises bought this house from an elderly couple who had lived here since the middle of the last century. Both of them have since passed on. Susan Bell is their granddaughter."

"It sounds like Emily Morris was the one doing all the detective work," I mentioned.

"Some of it, sure." Bob adopted a wounded tone. "But I followed up and convinced the Bells to meet with us."

"Well done," I told him.

Just like my Poodles, my ex responds well to positive reinforcement. I let him preen for a few minutes, then suggested that he pick me up after lunch on Sunday so that we could ride to New Canaan together. After we hung up it occurred to me to wonder whether Bob had taken my advice and stashed the ring at a bank—and if he'd done so, whether it had occurred to him that he wouldn't be able to retrieve the ring in the morning.

Not my problem, I thought. As it turned out, I needn't have worried. When Bob showed up, he had the ring with him.

Sam had taken the kids to a matinee so when Bob's dark green Explorer pulled in the driveway the following afternoon, I tucked Augie into his crate, gave the rest of the Poodles a good-bye pat, and ran outside to meet him. As I climbed into the SUV and got settled in the front seat beside him, Bob reached into his pocket, withdrew the small, velvet jewelry pouch, and tossed it onto my lap.

"Hold on to that, would you?"

"I'd be happy to."

I unknotted the drawstring and tipped the ring out of the bag into the palm of my hand. The diamonds sparkled and glinted in the sun as I rolled the piece from side to side. Unable to resist, I slid the ring on my little finger, then held up my hand to admire the look.

"If we don't find a home for this," I teased, "I could be convinced to take it off your hands."

"You'd have to get in line," Bob muttered. Head swiveled around to look behind us, he backed out of the driveway and onto the road.

"Behind whom?"

Bob waited until he'd straightened out before replying. "Remember that ghost problem I thought I was having?"

I nodded but didn't say a thing. My expression must have revealed what I was thinking, however, because Bob glanced my way and said, "Yeah, I know. You thought it was dumb."

"I didn't say that."

"You didn't have to. Even *I* knew that the idea was a little out there."

"A little?" I laughed.

"Okay, maybe way out. But I got this notion in my head that when I opened up the walls of the house, I was somehow reawakening its past. And yes, I know that sounds a little crazy in the light of day. But in my defense, I was trying to come up with an explanation for the noises I'd been hearing. And now I have. I'm pretty sure that it was James."

"James . . . ?" I said, then stopped. If you discarded the ghost theory—which I most emphatically did—I supposed that Bob's covetous next-door neighbor had to be the next most likely culprit. Except for one thing. Bob had started hearing noises *before* he found the diamond ring. "You'd better start at the beginning," I said.

"You know how close together the houses are in that neighborhood?"

"Of course." I nodded. I'd lived there too.

"Well, the other day James made some offhand comment about things that go bump in the night. I asked him what he meant and it turns out that a couple of times when I'd been working kind of late, he and Amber could hear me banging around when they were trying to sleep."

"If it bothered them, why didn't he call and tell you to stop?"

Bob shrugged. "I guess he didn't think that would be a neighborly thing to do."

"But thumping around outside your house *would?*" I asked incredulously.

"Don't ask me to justify it. I can't even begin to make sense of how James's mind works. He still keeps coming over and wanting to help me knock stuff down. He actually seems to believe that we're going to find more hidden jewels."

"And how exactly would that help him?" I asked.

"Finders keepers?"

"Possession is nine tenths of the law," I countered. "I hope you're keeping your doors locked now."

"Believe me, I am. This whole situation has me kind of creeped out. I used to think it was a good thing to be a trusting person. But not anymore. I'm thinking about changing the locks, too."

"You should," I agreed.

"When I do, I'll make sure that you and Davey get a new set of keys."

"Thanks. I'd appreciate that."

"And speaking of James," Bob said as he flipped on his blinker and turned the SUV up the ramp onto the parkway. "Here's something else. I told him he needs to go out and find himself a job. Any job. Even if it's not the kind of thing he did before. When I said that, he acted really oddly. Kind of furtive, I guess, but also excited at the same time. He told me he's already working on something, that there's the prospect of a big opportunity coming up."

"Oh really?" I swiveled in the seat to face my ex. "Let me guess. Is this the same get-rich-quick scheme that he wanted you to invest in before?"

"Apparently so. James offered me the chance again to join him and get in on the ground floor."

"What a great guy," I said with a laugh. "The ground floor of what? Did you manage to find out what his plan is this time?"

"Not exactly," Bob admitted. "But trust me, James isn't

nearly as subtle as he thinks he is. A couple of times recently he's sounded me out to see how I feel about the new medical marijuana laws. He's never come right out and said it but I'm guessing that his big opportunity has to do with growing pot."

"You're kidding."

"I wish I was. Somehow that doesn't sound like the kind of career move that's going to get James out of my hair."

"It doesn't sound like any career move at all to me," I said flatly. "The medical marijuana field is highly regulated. I'm pretty sure that Connecticut has all sorts of strict requirements and qualifications for growers. It's not just some cash crop that you can cultivate in a bin in your basement."

"I don't think James has a clue about all that."

"Well, he'd better get one fast. Otherwise what he's planning is illegal. You might try passing that news along."

"No way. I'm steering clear of the whole mess." Bob shook his head firmly as we exited the parkway at South Avenue and headed toward downtown New Canaan. "Whatever kind of idiocy James hopes to get himself involved in, I don't want any part of it. As far as I know, things are still in the planning stages. With luck, he'll come to his senses before it goes any further."

"I certainly hope so," I said. If not, one of us might need to go have a chat with Detective O'Malley about the neighbor's budding business.

Bob turned down a side street and slowed the car so that we could read the identifying numbers on the mailboxes. On either side of the road were beautifully maintained, classic, older homes on side-by-side half-acre lots. In New Canaan, this was considered a starter neighborhood.

The Bells' house was at the end of the road. A low fence circled the backyard, which contained a swing set and an elaborate bird feeder hanging from a large maple tree. Idly

I wondered if the Bells had a dog. That's just the way my mind works.

Susan Bell answered the door with a baby on her hip and a smile on her face. Her husband, Jim, was right behind her. Clearly they'd been anticipating our arrival.

"I can't wait to see Grandma's ring," Susan said as Bob and I walked inside. Then she stopped and laughed. "I'm sorry. That was horribly rude of me. I guess we should start with introductions."

So we did. Jim was tall and spare, with a direct gaze and a firm handshake. He worked in a corporate office in downtown Stamford. The baby's name was Franny and she was the Bells' first child. She gurgled and squealed, and when she made a grab for my hair, I laughed with her. Susan was in her early thirties, with sleek brown hair and a spray of freckles across her nose. She was, she confided, newly pregnant with their second child.

"You're lucky to be having two so close together," I said. Bob and I followed the couple into a living room that was bright with color, and appeared to have been decorated with a baby's needs in mind.

"How old are yours?" Susan got Franny settled in a baby bouncy seat, then sat down in a chair beside it.

"I have two boys," I told her. "Davey's eleven and Kevin is two. Bob is Davey's father. We're divorced."

"Oh." Susan sounded surprised. "I hadn't realized that. But you still live in the same house?"

"No, we don't." Once again, I was reminded that our living arrangements were more tangled than most. "Bob is the one who currently lives in the home that once belonged to your grandmother. He and I bought the house together when we got married twelve years ago. Since the divorce, one or the other of us has always lived there. But not both at the same time."

That was a highly simplified version of the moves that had taken place over the years, but hopefully I'd conveyed enough information to make sense. Susan nodded, and Bob picked up the story.

"When I moved back in, I started doing some updating," he said. "That's when I discovered the ring. Before we show it to you, could you tell me why you think it belonged to your grandmother, and how it ended up where I found it?"

"You're right to be cautious," said Jim. "I've never seen the ring myself but I've heard family stories about it. I understand that it's a valuable piece."

Susan leaned forward in her seat. She was almost bouncing with eagerness. "The ring's history in my family goes back four generations. My great-grandmother Ethel was a war bride. She met my great-grandfather in England during World War I. After the war she immigrated to the United States to be with him. That ring was purchased to mark the occasion of her arrival."

"The jeweler told me that the ring's design was Art Deco," Bob said. "That fits with the time period."

"I've been told that Ethel never removed the ring from her finger," Susan continued. "When she died, she left it to her oldest daughter, my grandmother, with the stipulation that it would always remain in the family, passed down in each succeeding generation to the eldest daughter."

"What a great story," I said. "I can see why you'd be anxious to get the ring back. Do you know how your grandmother lost it?"

"No, I don't. I was a very young child at the time. All I know is that Grandma was devastated when she discovered it was gone. She thought it must have slipped off her finger while she was doing housework. I remember hearing her say that she had looked everywhere for it, but none of us ever saw the ring again."

"It was upstairs, in the bathroom," I told her. "Bob was breaking down a wall when he came across it in the rubble."

Susan sighed happily. "Grandma would have been thrilled to know that it's finally been found. My mother too. She lives in Florida now. When she called to say that she'd heard from Emily Morris, she told me that when I was a toddler I used to take Grandma's ring, put it on, and dance around the room."

"It's the kind of ring that inspires dancing," I said with a smile.

"We have a picture," Jim said, rising from his seat. "Let me get it for you."

He left the room and returned a minute later with a black-and-white photograph in a scrolled silver frame. He handed the picture to Bob and I leaned over to have a look too. The image was of a woman seated on a sofa, holding a small child on her lap. Judging by their dress and hairstyles, I guessed the photograph had been taken in the 1950s.

Susan reached across the space between us and pointed. "The little girl is my mother. Look where her mother's hand curls around her waist to hold her steady. You can see the ring there."

Bob lifted the picture up to take a closer look. We both squinted at it. Susan Bell's grandmother did indeed appear to be wearing a ring on her finger. Whether or not it was the same ring as the one Bob had found in his bathroom, I couldn't begin to fathom.

"That picture is just for context," Jim said quickly. "Once we knew you were coming, I took the photograph out of the frame and scanned it. Then I enlarged the area in question. You can see the ring much more clearly here."

He handed me a sheet of paper. I held it between me and Bob so he could see too. The image on the paper was gray and grainy. Even so, I was able to make out enough of the ring's distinctive features to be convinced.

Bob looked at me and nodded. We were both in agreement. I reached down and withdrew the small pouch from my pocket.

Susan's eyes widened at the sight of it. She seemed to be holding her breath. When I held out my hand, she hesitated a moment before lifting the jewelry bag from my fingers.

"Go ahead and take it," I said. "It belongs to you."

Chapter 22

"After all these years . . ." Susan said on a slow, indrawn, breath. I can hardly believe it."

Her husband laughed and nudged her hand forward. "Take a look," he said. "The suspense is killing me."

Susan laughed with him then. Hesitation gone, she grabbed the pouch. Her fingers scrambled to undo the slender drawstring. When she pulled it loose, the ring tumbled out into her hand.

For a moment, she didn't even look at it. Instead she closed her fingers tightly over the piece of jewelry, encasing it in her fist, and simply reveling in its possession.

"It's the right ring," she said. "I feel it."

"You haven't even seen it yet," Jim pointed out.

"I don't need to. I just know."

Susan glanced over at me. I nodded. I'd been there.

Slowly she uncurled her fingers and revealed the family heirloom. Its diamonds flashed and sparkled in the light. Jim just stood and stared. Susan's lower lip began to quiver, then abruptly she burst into tears.

Bob looked taken aback. He glanced over at me. "That's good . . . right?"

I swallowed heavily. The emotion of the moment had gotten to me too. "That's very good," I told him.

"Don't mind me," Susan wailed between sobs. "It's just the pregnancy hormones."

Franny looked up from her padded seat. Seeing her mother's tears, she began to cry too. Jim strode over, unbuckled his young daughter, and picked her up. Automatically he began to bounce up and down in place.

"Your great-grandmother's ring," he said gently to his wife. "Home at last."

"Thank you!" Susan launched herself up out of her seat. She spread her arms wide and managed to hug both me and Bob at the same time. "You have no idea how much this means to me."

"I think I'm getting a clue," Bob said with a laugh.

Susan straightened and walked over to where her husband and daughter stood. "Look at the beautiful ring," she said, waving the bauble in Franny's face. "Someday it will be yours."

"And on another day far, far, in the future," Jim added, "it will belong to your daughter."

"But in the meantime," Susan said, tears still running down her face, "you can wear it anytime you want to dance around the room and pretend to be a princess."

"That's so great." I sighed.

Bob's expression clouded. It looked as though he was finally beginning to understand the impact of the ring's emotional heft. "Why don't we have any family heirlooms like that?" he asked me.

I reached over and patted his arm. "Bob, we don't even have a family together anymore."

"Oh yeah. Right." He shook his head. "For a moment there, I forgot."

We both stood up to go.

"You did a good thing today," I told him.

"I guess every so often I get something right."

"You do better than that," I said.

Jim and Susan were standing beside one another, with

Franny tucked in between them. The adults were engaged in a whispered conversation. I figured we should probably let ourselves out.

As we started for the door, Jim called us back. "Susan and I want to give you a reward," he said.

Bob and I looked at each other. Once again, we were in agreement.

"That's not necessary," I told Jim.

"But you deserve a reward," said Susan. "You could have kept the ring for yourselves. You could have decided it was too hard to track us down. We would never have known the difference. At the very least, let us repay you for your time and effort."

Bob stepped back to where the couple was standing and extended his hand. Susan reached out and grasped it in both of hers.

"Thank you," he said earnestly. "But Melanie and I already got all the reward we need."

Moments like that, I remember why I married that man.

Monday morning. Another work week, more stuff to do.

The first thing I did was call Diana Lee. Well, actually not the first thing. By the time I called Nick's girlfriend, I'd already made breakfast, washed the dishes, delivered Davey to camp, and taken the Poodles for a two mile walk. Diana didn't strike me as the early riser type. So I got around to her midmorning.

Good thing I'd exercised some restraint, because she sounded half-asleep when she picked up the phone. I offered to buy her a grande coffee and she agreed to meet me at the Starbucks on Greenwich Avenue in half an hour.

"Sorry," I said to Sam. "Kev's all yours again. Diana doesn't do children."

"Her loss," he said with a shrug.

"She doesn't do dogs either," I told him.

"Now I know I wouldn't like her."

"She has long blond hair and a perfect manicure," I mentioned. You know, just throwing it out there.

Sam laughed. He didn't take the bait. Instead, he leaned down, gave me a quick kiss, and said, "And you have an orange juice stain on the front of your shirt."

"Oh man." I groaned. "Seriously? I just got dressed."

So I clumped upstairs, changed my shirt, then drove over to Greenwich to meet Diana. Midmorning, the coffee bar was nearly empty. An elderly woman was reading a book at one table. At another, two teenagers were passing an iPad back and forth.

Apparently Diana had taken my offer of free coffee seriously because when I arrived I saw that she'd staked out a table by the window, but not yet purchased a drink. I took her request, went to the counter and ordered for both of us, then joined her at the table five minutes later.

Diana had been checking her e-mail on her phone. Now she tucked the device into her purse and said, "Where's the kid?"

"At home with his father."

I slid Diana's espresso macchiato across the table. The dark drink looked like a straight shot of caffeine. If I was lucky, she'd gulp it down and start to chatter like an organ grinder's monkey.

"Home?" She lifted one finely arched brow.

"Sure." I sipped my mocha latte and licked a stray bit of whipped cream off my lip. "What's the matter with that?"

"It's Monday. I would have expected your husband to be at work."

"He might be working," I told her. "Although Kevin can be a pretty strong deterrent to productivity when he wants to be. Sam works for himself. He designs computer software."

Diana lifted her glass and took a small sip. Maybe the beverage was still too hot for gulping. I continued to hold out hope.

"Is that a lucrative field?" Diana asked.

"If you're good." Just for good measure, I punctuated the comment with a Cheshire cat smile.

Stew on that, I thought. I wasn't about to mention that Sam was still collecting royalties from a wildly successful video game he'd designed while in business school. Diana would probably jump to the conclusion that I'd married Sam for his money.

Just like last time, it was difficult for me to imagine this woman as a long-term love interest for Nick Walden. Or heck, even a short-term one. Sure she was beautiful. But seriously, they had to have talked *sometime*, didn't they?

Yet another reason why men remain a mystery to the legions of smart, capable, worthy, but not drop-dead-gorgeous women of the world.

I gave my head a slight shake, putting my wayward thoughts back in order, and got down to business. "I spoke with Taran Black," I said.

Diana gazed at me over the rim of her cup. "Did he confess?"

I snorted under my breath. "No. And in fact, he has an alibi for the night that Nick was killed."

I didn't add *unlike you*, but the thought hung there in the air between us.

"Lucky," she murmured.

"Even better," I countered. "Not guilty. Taran told me to ask you what happened when you found out that Nick was fooling around with one of this clients."

"Of course he'd bring *that* up," she snapped.

I took another drink of my latte and waited for her to elaborate.

"Taran's the kind of guy who likes stirring up trouble," Diana said after a minute.

"For Nick?" I asked. "For you? Or just for people in general?"

Diana glanced at the slim gold watch on her wrist. "You ask the dumbest questions."

Sad to say, it's not the first time someone has said that.

"Feel free to point me in the direction of better ones," I told her.

"Why should I?"

"Because you want to see Nick's killer brought to justice." I paused, then added, "You do, don't you?"

"It doesn't matter what I want," Diana said with a shrug. "It's not up to me."

"Then there's no harm in discussing what happened. I'm guessing we're talking about Carol Luna?"

"Do you know her?"

"Not yet," I admitted.

"No great loss."

I was betting Carol Luna might have said the same thing about her.

"Tell me about her relationship with Nick," I invited.

"She has some little yappy dog. Maybe a Poodle." Diana looked up. "That's what you have, right?"

"Same breed. But mine are big and they don't yap."

"Well, Carol's dog never shuts up. That's why she hired Nick. Me, I'd have had the thing unbarked. You can do that. I read about it on the Internet."

I nodded and didn't correct her terminology. There was no point in allowing myself to get sidetracked when Diana was already feeling antsy.

"But instead she asked Nick to help her," I said.

"That's how they met. Or maybe I should say, that's how Carol got her clutches into him."

"Nick was a grown man," I mentioned. "He was capable of making his own decisions."

Diana shook her head. She didn't want to hear it.

"We were happy together," she told me. "He wouldn't have strayed if she hadn't gone after him. Carol seduced him; that's what happened."

Or that was what she wanted to believe.

"Even so—" I began.

"Any man is susceptible," Diana said loftily, "when a woman puts her mind to it."

Said the gorgeous woman who'd probably never heard the word *no* in her life. It's a good thing I'm an adult. Otherwise I'd have stuck out my tongue. Did she truly have no idea how the other half lived?

"And you found out," I said.

"Of course I found out. The woman had no shame. She called Nick. She *pursued* him. Only an idiot wouldn't have noticed that something was going on." Diana stared at me across the table. "And I am *not* an idiot."

"Surely not," I agreed.

"I know what infidelity looks like."

I wasn't about to ask how.

"Nick promised me it was over between them," Diana growled. "But still that woman wouldn't go away. And then I found out that he was still training her little yapper. How could it be over if he was still seeing her?"

"Did you ask Nick that?"

"I most certainly did. And he had the nerve to tell me that she was a good client. That things were strictly business between them now."

"But you didn't believe him?"

Diana shook her head. "Did you hear me *say* that I'm not an idiot?"

Point taken.

"I decided that something needed to be done to illustrate my unhappiness. Something that would make my feelings known. You know—in a way that even a *man* would notice."

"So what did you do?"

"I built a little fire in Nick's backyard," Diana said with satisfaction. "And I burned half his clothes."

I'd heard of women throwing hissy fits like that. But I'd

never actually met someone in person who'd done it. All the women I count as friends are entirely too practical to be so wasteful. Sitting there with Diana, I suddenly felt like an anthropologist who'd stumbled upon a new subspecies of female *homo sapiens*.

One that definitely demanded further study.

"Which half?" I asked curiously.

"What?"

"You said you burned half of Nick's clothing. I was wondering which half."

"Are you always this literal?"

"Usually," I admitted.

"It was a rhetorical question," Diana said curtly. "But since you asked, I didn't pick and choose. I just burned the ones that were in the front of his closet. I grabbed an armload and went to work."

I'm sure this wasn't Diana's intention, but here's what I took away from that story. One: she had a volatile and perhaps irrational temper. And two: Diana had had access to Nick's house when he wasn't there. Which meant that she could have let herself inside without Nick's knowledge on the night that he was killed.

"So you resorted to violence to get your point across," I said.

"Against *clothes*," Diana specified. "It's not like I actually hurt anyone."

"Do the police know about that?"

"Not unless somebody else told them. I certainly didn't."

"I can see why not," I said. "They might have found the fact you were angry enough at Nick to attack him in that way pretty suspicious."

"Let me repeat." Diana spoke slowly and emphasized each word as though I was stupid. "The only thing I attacked was Nick's *clothing*. It's not the same thing at all."

Or maybe she was making too fine a distinction.

"How long before Nick died did all this happen?" I asked.

"A while," Diana replied airily. "At least a couple of weeks. Nick and I had long since made up by then. Everything was copacetic between us."

"I'm glad to hear that."

Her eyes narrowed. "You don't believe me."

I regarded her across the table. "Does it matter what I believe?"

"It does if you're planning to go running to the police and tell on me."

"We're not in kindergarten, Diana. This is serious."

"I know that."

She reached up a hand and brushed back several strands of hair that had fallen forward over her face. Once upon a time, Veronica Lake had used the same gesture to great effect. Unfortunately its appeal was wasted on me.

"Which is precisely why I don't want to get any more involved than I already am," Diana said.

Her espresso was finished. She pushed her cup away, then unwound her purse from the back of her chair and looped it over her shoulder as she stood up. "I never should have come here today," she said. "Agreeing to meet with you again was a mistake."

"Why did you?" I asked.

"You're a woman. I thought you'd understand. Men think it's their world. That they can do whatever they want and get away with it. And that's just not right."

It sounded like a flimsy rationalization to me. "So by burning Nick's clothes you were striking a blow for *all* women?"

Diana glowered down at me. "I have nothing more to say to you. Don't ever call me again."

The mocha latte was too good to waste. I stayed and finished every drop before leaving. My car was parked on a side street three blocks away. I was almost there when my phone rang. The number was unfamiliar but it was a Greenwich exchange.

"Hello?" I said.

"Is this Melanie Travis?"

Great, I thought. A telemarketer. "Yes, it is."

"This is Fran Dolan. Do you remember me?"

It took me a few seconds to place the name. Then I said, "Sure I do. You're Barney's owner."

I could almost hear her smile. "That's right. I hope it's okay that I called you. Claire told me it would be."

"Claire?" I asked.

"You know, Nick Walden's sister? Something's the matter with Barney. Before, I would have asked Nick what to do. Now I couldn't think of who else to call so I got in touch with Claire. She sent me to you. I'm hoping you can help me."

"I can try," I said slowly. "What seems to be the problem?"

"It's the way Barney's behaving. He's acting all strange."

I thought of the low-slung Basset Hound who'd done nothing but sleep during my recent visit to the Dolan household and wondered how she could tell. Then I gave myself a mental kick for being mean. Fran Dolan lived just north of the parkway. I'd be headed in that direction just as soon as I got to my car. Stopping by and having a look at the Basset would take me only a few minutes out of my way.

I conveyed that news to Fran and told her I'd be there soon.

"You're an angel!" she said happily. "We'll be waiting for you."

I hoped she wasn't placing too much faith in my abilities. Nick had been the expert on canine behavior. So was Aunt Peg. I didn't have their knowledge or their experience. Compared to those two, I was nothing more than a concerned dog lover who also happened to be available.

Fran met me at the door to her house and hustled me quickly inside. "Barney's in the backyard," she said. "I had him in here with me, but he started having a little problem with his bladder, so I put him out."

"Is that normal for him?" I asked.

"No, not at all. Barney's been housebroken since he was a puppy. And he's always very good about minding his manners."

"So that's one problem," I said. "Are there others?"

Fran bobbed her head up and down several times. Her hands were clasped together at her waist, fingers twisting in agitation.

Rather than waiting for her to explain further, I started toward the back of the house. She could supply the details along the way.

"Let's go see how he's doing," I said.

While we hurried down the hallway, I got more background information. I asked what Fran and Barney been doing all day and whether anything unusual or unexpected had happened. I also wanted to know whether there had been any changes in their routine.

Fran paused to think before answering. I liked that. I wanted her to consider my questions carefully.

"No, there was nothing," she said after a minute. "Today was the same as always. I got up this morning and put Barney outside."

"He seemed okay to you then?"

"I think so."

"Good." I nodded encouragingly. "Go on."

"After that it was just morning stuff. I got the coffee started and took a shower. When I came downstairs again, I opened the back door. Barney was over by the shed. I called him and he came inside."

"Just like every other morning?" I asked.

Fran nodded. "Well . . . I had to stop and clean off his

front feet. They were covered with dirt. It looked like he'd been digging again."

"Again," I repeated. "So that would be something he's done before?"

"Oh yes. Barney enjoys digging. This time it looked like he was trying to tunnel his way into the shed. You know that nose of his. I thought maybe a rabbit had gotten inside there."

"Did you go and have a look?" I asked.

"No, there wouldn't have been any point. My son stores his stuff in there and he always keeps it locked. If there's a rabbit inside, he'll have to deal with it himself. I just brought the dog in the house, poured myself a cup of coffee, and started my day. Then about an hour later, I noticed that Barney didn't look right."

We had reached the kitchen and I could see Fran's backyard through the wide windows. The area was about half an acre in size, mostly lawn, studded here and there with mature trees. A border of densely packed trees marked its boundaries and provided plenty of shade. The shed, sitting off to one side, looked less neglected than the last time I'd seen it. Someone had started to work on making repairs.

I glanced around quickly but didn't see Barney anywhere. Then the Basset began to howl and I realized that he was standing in the shadow of the house, not far from the back door. The hound's eyes were closed and his muzzle was lifted high in the air. His full-bodied baying had the eerie quality of a keening wail.

Fran opened the door and we both slipped outside. At first Barney didn't react to our approach. He didn't seem to notice us at all.

"Shush!" Fran said sharply. "Stop that noise right now."

Barney lowered his nose and turned his head slowly in our direction. His eyes blinked open, but he didn't appear to be looking at us. I'm accustomed to Poodles who think and react faster than I do. By comparison, Barney seemed to be responding in slow motion.

I squatted down several feet in front of him and held out a hand. "Com'ere, boy. What's the matter? What's going on?" My voice was pitched low, and its tone was soothing. I kept up a steady patter of words. "Hey Barney, watcha up to? Come over here and talk to me."

The Basset opened his mouth and began to pant heavily. The day was warm, but it wasn't hot. And we were standing in the shade. An accumulation of saliva pooled in his flews, then spilled over the side. A thick strand of drool dangled toward the ground.

"See?" said Fran. "There's definitely something wrong with him. Barney's the friendliest dog you ever met. Usually he'd come right up to you. But now it's like he doesn't want to walk or something."

Fran sat down on the ground beside me, and Barney tried to take a step toward us then. He didn't walk so much as stagger. The Basset's body rolled unsteadily from side to side with the effort.

Abruptly I rose to my feet. I'd seen enough.

"Who's your vet?" I asked Fran.

"Dr. Cochrane at the Banksville Animal Hospital," she replied, looking worried.

"Call and tell him we're on our way."

Quickly I crossed to where the Basset was standing and leaned down to pick him up. The low-slung hound weighed a ton. It took two tries for me to get him up into my arms.

"I think Barney's been poisoned," I said.

Chapter 23

My car was already in the driveway. I drove while Fran cradled a woozy Barney on her lap. Ignoring the speed limit, we raced north into New York State.

Luckily the Dolan residence was less than ten minutes from the border. Almost as soon as we crossed into Banksville, Fran leaned over and pointed toward a white clapboard building approaching on the left. I saw the Animal Hospital sign; it was shaped like the intertwined silhouettes of a cat and a dog.

The Volvo's tires squealed as I braked and turned hard into the driveway. Holding Barney between us, we hurried into the building. Dr. Cochrane and his staff were waiting for us inside. Quickly we were shown into an examination room.

Dr. Cochrane plied Fran with questions, many of them similar to those that I'd asked earlier. A vet tech recorded Barney's vital signs, then the vet began his own examination. I stood back against the wall of the room and watched the professionals work, relieved that the Basset Hound's fate no longer rested in my hands.

"How long ago did Barney start acting like this?" Dr. Cochrane asked.

"More than an hour now," Fran told him. "Maybe ninety

minutes. At first I thought he was just goofing around. But then I began to get worried. So I called Melanie."

The vet, still occupied with the groggy Basset on the examining table, lifted his head and glanced my way.

"Nice to meet you," I said.

"You're the one who mentioned the possibility of poisoning?"

"That's right. The dog seemed disoriented. He was staggering. It was the first thing I thought of."

"Did you attempt to make him throw up?" he asked.

Fran and I both shook our heads. "We just came straight here," she said.

After a few minutes, Dr. Cochrane finished his exam. He conferred with the vet tech, then picked up the Basset and placed him carefully in her arms. Dog and girl disappeared through a door in the rear wall of the room.

"We're just going to take Barney in the back and run a few tests," he told us. "We want to draw blood and obtain a urine sample. There are several things that could be causing his symptoms and some are quite serious. But there's another option—perhaps the most likely one—that would be less critical with regard to Barney's long-term health."

"Then let's hope for that one," I said, and Fran nodded.

Dr. Cochrane looked back and forth between the two of us. "Is there any possibility this dog could have been exposed to marijuana?" he asked.

My eyes widened. I hadn't been expecting that.

Beside me, Fran cleared her throat. "Like . . . Barney *smoked* something?" She sounded incredulous.

Dr. Cochrane smiled. "More likely he ingested something. Marijuana cooked into food for example. Or he might have eaten the leaves and stems of a plant."

"I don't know." Fran looked puzzled. "Barney's been with me all day. How could something like that have happened?"

"Think about it," said the vet. He reached over and patted Fran's arm. "It happens more frequently than you might think, and fortunately most dogs recover uneventfully. At any rate, we'll run a urine test in our lab so we should have an answer before too long."

"If it is marijuana toxicity," I asked, "then what?"

"We'll put Barney on fluids. Give him charcoal to help absorb the drug and get it out of his system faster. He may be uncomfortable for a couple of days, but he should be just fine after that."

"So that would be good news," I said.

I expected Fran to agree, but instead she remained silent. Her arms were crossed over her chest, her shoulders had slumped inward. She still looked worried about her pet's prognosis.

"We'd like to keep Barney here overnight," Dr. Cochrane said. "But hopefully we'll have some answers for you later this afternoon. Is that all right?"

"That would be fine," Fran agreed.

We headed for the door and Dr. Cochrane saw us out.

"Thank you for your help," I said to him as we left the examining room.

"I'll be in touch," he told Fran.

I dropped Fran off at her house then continued on to Stamford. While I drove, I pondered the events that had just taken place. The last time I'd given any thought to marijuana and/or its effects was more than a decade earlier in college. Now the subject had come up twice in two days. Was that merely an odd coincidence? I wondered. Or could it be something more?

I might have devoted more time thinking that through, but when I arrived home not only were Sam and Kevin waiting for me, Claire Walden was there as well.

"I'm glad you're back," said Sam. "I expected you home a while ago. That's what I told Claire when she showed up. She's out on the deck with Kevin. She's been waiting an hour."

"Why didn't you call me?" I asked. Not that there was anything I could have done about my tardy arrival. But at least Sam would have been able to explain to Claire that I'd been held up.

My husband gave me that look. You know the one.

So I pulled my phone out of my purse and checked. I had two missed calls.

"Sorry," I said. "I've been busy. I'll bring you up to speed later."

"You'd better. Now go on outside and see what Claire wants."

I could probably guess the answer to that. Claire wanted to know what I'd been doing since we spoke on Friday. And while I'd actually accomplished a great deal, unfortunately the most pressing question still remained unanswered.

I did have some good news for Claire, however, because her visit would give me a chance to deliver Taran's message. Hopefully she would be elated by the prospect of a family reunion, even if it looked as though the meeting itself might require some luck and a bit of wrangling to bring about.

When I walked outside, I found Claire sitting on a chaise with Kevin in her lap. A stack of my son's books spilled off the lounger and onto the deck beneath. Claire was reading aloud from Dr. Seuss while Kev pointed at the pictures and turned the pages. Both had big smiles on their faces. Even the Poodles, who were sitting in attendance, seemed to be having a good time.

I detoured past Faith and brushed my hand over the top of her head. As I paused to scratch behind the Poodle's ears, Claire sensed my presence and paused in her reading. She and Kevin both looked up.

"Don't stop on my account," I said.

"Don't stop," Kevin echoed. He clapped his hands imperiously.

Claire laughed. "Let me just finish this book," she said.

"Sure. Take your time. But only if you want to. There's no reason that the Little Dictator"—I leveled a look in Kevin's direction—"needs to think that he's in charge of the world."

"I don't mind." Claire gave my son a gentle squeeze. "And Kevin's a sweetheart."

"When he wants to be," I agreed easily.

I pulled up a chair and sat down. Faith came over and rested her head on my lap. We all listened while Claire read aloud about many different fish of varying colors. Kevin especially liked the one with the little car.

"Again!" he cried when she was done.

"Sorry kiddo, not right now." I stood up and retrieved my son from my visitor's lap. A discreet sniff revealed that all was well in diaper-land. "Claire has entertained you long enough for one day. Why don't you go dig in your sandbox for a while?"

Kevin's brow puckered as he considered his options. "Augie dig too?" he asked.

I didn't even want to think about what all that sand could do to a show coat.

"Not Augie," I told him. I swung Kevin down off the low deck and set him on his feet in the grass. "But Tar can."

"Tar come," Kevin said, and the big male Poodle hopped up eagerly. The two of them set off across the yard.

"How cute is that." Claire sighed happily, watching as boy and dog strolled away. "I can't wait until I have kids of my own."

"That's how I felt before I had them," I said with a laugh.

Claire gathered up the books and set them aside as I sat back down. "I'm sorry I kept you waiting so long," I said.

"I didn't know you were here. I was in Greenwich with Fran Dolan. She said you were the one who told her to call me?"

"Yes. I hope that was all right?" Claire suddenly looked worried. "She seems like a nice lady and I know she was one of Nick's favorite clients. I wanted to help her but I didn't know how."

"Sure, it was fine. I was in Greenwich anyway when she called. Her Basset Hound, Barney, wasn't feeling well. We ended up dropping him off at the vet."

"Poor dog. Her son didn't do something to him, did he?"

"What do you mean?"

Claire shook her head. "Don't listen to me. I'm probably entirely off base. It was just that Nick mentioned something once about Mrs. Dolan having an adult son who didn't get along with the dog. Which, you know, made his job harder."

"In what way?" I asked curiously.

"I guess the guy used to follow Nick around when he was there and ask him what Barney was saying. Like he thought that the two of them were holding actual conversations. Nick explained that wasn't how it worked, but the son kept bugging him anyway."

"I hate to break it to you," I said with a smile. "But all of Nick's clients that I've spoken to believed that he knew exactly what their dogs were thinking. Every single one of them was in awe of his canine communication skills."

"I can understand why," said Claire. "Nick certainly had a better handle on Thor and Jojo than I'm ever going to be able to achieve."

"Problems?"

"Nothing I can't manage. But I didn't come here today to talk about dogs. I wanted to let you know that the police have located Anabelle."

"Actually," I told her. "So have I."

"You have?"

I nodded. "Remember your old buddy, Taran Black? I talked to him on Saturday. He's been in touch with her."

Claire looked shocked. "But how? Since when?"

"Apparently for a long time," I said gently. "Ever since he came up to New York for a job."

"But . . ." She shook her head in confusion. "He never said anything."

"Anabelle didn't want him to. She didn't feel like she was a part of your family anymore."

"I guess I can see that," Claire said slowly. "But that must mean that she's known where Nick and I were all along."

"I think so. I'm not really sure." I watched her process the unwelcome information.

"So she rejected us, just like our parents rejected her."

"I don't think you want to make that assumption without first hearing her side of things," I said.

Claire looked up. "Have you heard *her* side?"

"No. I only know what Taran told me. But it sounds to me as though none of you were treated fairly in this situation. So maybe you don't want to rush to judgment about what Anabelle's been through—"

"You mean like my father did?"

I shrugged but didn't reply.

Claire sat in silence for several minutes. Finally she said, "Since the last time we spoke I've been thinking about Anabelle a lot. When Detective O'Malley told me he'd located her, I got really excited. I couldn't believe that she was in New Rochelle. All this time, we've only been thirty miles apart! I thought about what it would be like to see her again. I pictured us having this great reunion." Claire stopped abruptly. When she started speaking again, she sounded stricken. "I guess that was silly of me."

"It wasn't," I said firmly.

"Except that now you're telling me Anabelle has known all along where to find me and Nick and that she just never bothered."

"I don't think that's the way she looked at it."

"Why do you keep telling me what my sister was thinking? How do you *know*?"

"I don't," I said. "I'm just hoping that you'll keep an open mind."

"My mind is wide open," Claire replied tightly. "It's also filled with questions."

"You should see your sister."

"That's what I thought before I came here today." Claire frowned. "Now I'm not so sure. How much did Taran tell you about her?"

"Quite a bit," I admitted.

"Did he know why Anabelle called Nick before he died?"

"He did."

"And?"

"There's something else I need to tell you," I said. "Anabelle has a son."

Claire had been looking at me intently. Now her features froze. "A son?" she repeated. "I have a nephew?"

"Yes. His name is Alexander."

"That was my grandfather's name," she said softly. "Is Anabelle still with Zane?"

"No, that's been over for a long time. Alexander had some medical bills last year and Anabelle wasn't able to pay them. Without her knowledge, Taran asked Nick for a loan. He didn't tell your brother what the money was for."

"Then why did Anabelle call him?"

"Afterward, neither Taran nor Anabelle had the money to pay back the loan. And that was causing a lot of friction between Nick and Taran. Eventually Taran had to confess to Anabelle what he'd done. At that point, she called Nick to tell him where the money had gone."

"Why didn't Nick tell me?" Claire's voice rose to a wail.

"I'm sorry," I said. "I don't know the answer to that."

"So Nick and Anabelle reconnected after ten years apart and three days later he was dead."

I nodded.

"But those two events had nothing to do with one another."

"I don't believe so. No."

"Then maybe you should tell me what you *do* believe happened." Claire was growing angry now. "Because I thought you were supposed to be helping. Or detecting. Or doing *something* useful. But all I keep hearing about is the answers you *don't* have."

"I'm trying," I said. Even to my own ears that sounded pretty weak.

"So are the police," she said, rising to her feet. "But none of you seem to be getting anywhere."

"I'm sorry," I said again.

"Me too," Claire snapped.

She stepped down off the deck and strode around the side of the house. As I watched, she let herself out through the gate and was gone.

"That looked ugly," Sam said, coming up behind me.

"Tell me about it. Am I really as useless as Claire just made me feel?"

"Not all the time," Sam replied.

Unfortunately it wasn't even as though I could disagree. Claire's disgruntled response had been just about what I deserved.

Chapter 24

Claire's unhappy exit forced me to stop and think about what I was doing. Unfortunately things not going the way I'd hoped was beginning to seem like a trend in my life. Maybe I needed to take a step back, I realized. Perhaps rather than pursuing more information, I should work on making sense of the facts I already had.

From experience, I knew that the best way to make that happen was to keep myself busy with other things while ideas felt free to bounce around my subconscious unimpeded. With that in mind, I spent the next day and a half doing the Mom thing. I cooked, I cleaned, I bathed and blew dry Poodles. I bought Kevin new shoes, made entries for Augie's next show, and renewed Davey's subscription to *National Geographic*.

To my great relief, nobody stopped by unexpectedly, or contacted me, or asked my opinion about anything. I didn't hear from Claire, or Bob, or even Aunt Peg. All of which felt enormously liberating.

Briefly I debated getting in touch with Detective O'Malley, but I couldn't imagine that he'd be amenable to comparing notes. And as for my sharing what I had learned, all I appeared to have was a jumbled assortment of information that refused to fall into place.

That, and a coincidence that continued to nag at me.

In the end, that became the impetus for my midweek call to Fran Dolan. I started the conversation by asking her how Barney was doing.

"He's just fine," she told me happily. "I went and picked him up this morning. I can't thank you enough for your quick thinking."

"I was lucky to be in the right place at the right time," I said. "I'm glad everything turned out well."

"That dog'll eat anything he can get his mouth onto," she said fondly. "It's probably a wonder it took him this long to get into trouble. But marijuana? I never saw that coming."

"So the tests confirmed Dr. Cochrane's suspicions?"

"That's right. It was a good thing he knew what to look for, and how to treat it. Because Barney's right as rain now."

Good thing indeed, I thought. But where had the Basset gotten the marijuana from? I wondered if Fran knew the answer to that. And if not, whether she'd given the matter some serious thought.

Something about the sequence of recent events continued to irk me. One vital piece of the puzzle was still missing. If I could just figure out what that was, I was pretty sure that everything else would fall into place.

First, before I did anything else, I needed to find out how much Fran knew, I realized. It wouldn't be an easy conversation. And it wasn't one that I wanted to have over the phone.

"Fran, would it be okay if I stopped by this afternoon?" I asked. "I'd love to see how Barney's doing now that he's home and feeling better."

"Sure, come on over. He and I will be here. And that will give me a chance to say thank you in person."

When I told Sam where I was going, he just nodded. He was sitting at his desk, staring at his two computer screens, and frowning in concentration. I got Kevin settled in the corner of Sam's office with a box of juice and a tin of Lincoln Logs. Eventually Sam would look up and realize that he was in charge. Either that or the Poodles would take it upon themselves to clue him in.

Unlike my two previous visits to Fran's home, this time Barney answered the door with his mistress. The Basset looked bright and alert, a gratifying change from the last time I'd seen him. As I walked inside the house, he padded over to me. Nose snuffling, he inspected every inch of my blue-jean-clad legs that he could reach.

"Barney, cut that out." Fran took hold of the hound's collar and tried to haul him away. "Don't be rude to Melanie."

"Don't worry about it." I leaned down and patted the Basset's smooth skull. "He probably smells my dogs. When I get home, they'll just repeat the process at that end."

I followed Fran and Barney back to the sunroom. Once there, my gaze was immediately drawn to the windows. In the far corner of the backyard, I could see the shed where Barney had been digging just before he'd gotten sick. I wondered whether Fran had ever speculated about what her son was storing out there. Maybe since Barney's illness, she'd put two and two together. If not, now might be the time to start.

A shiny metal padlock looked incongruous on the faded wooden door. I wondered why I hadn't noticed it before.

Fran took a seat in one of the wicker chairs and Barney flopped down onto the cool tile floor beside her feet. She slipped one foot out of its sandal and began to rub the Basset's side with her toes. I sat in a chair opposite the pair.

"I think Barney scared himself the other day," Fran said. "He hasn't left my side for longer than a minute or two since I brought him home."

"It had to have been a terrifying experience for him," I agreed. "Being disoriented like that and having no idea why. Have you figured out how he was exposed to the drug?"

Fran shrugged. "No, but I wish I knew. I guess I'll just have to make sure that I keep a closer eye on him in the future."

"On Monday when I got here, you told me that Barney had been digging near the shed."

"Did I?" Fran's gaze skittered away. "I don't remember. I was pretty upset at the time."

"With good reason," I said mildly. "Barney was very ill."

"That whole day is just like a blur to me now. I'd rather just concentrate on the happy ending."

Because asking the questions that needed to be asked was clearly making her uncomfortable, I thought. "If you don't figure out how Barney got sick, how will you prevent it from happening again?"

"Like I said, I'll have to keep him with me."

"Or maybe keep him away from the shed?"

Fran looked out the window, then back at me. "What are you saying?"

"You mentioned the other day that your son stored things out there."

"That's right."

"What kinds of things?"

She appeared surprised by the question. "I don't know. I've never looked."

"Aren't you curious?"

"Not particularly. My son's an adult. He's entitled to his privacy. What kind of a mother would I be if I went around checking up on him behind his back?"

The normal kind, I thought. Especially since by my reckoning, Fran's son had given her reason enough to be suspicious about what the shed might contain.

"So you don't even want to have a look?"

"A look at what?" a voice asked from behind me.

I swiveled in my seat to see who had posed the question. Abruptly my heart gave a small jolt. James's friend, Phil, was standing in the doorway. Hands jammed in his pockets, wire-rimmed glasses perched halfway down his nose, Phil stared in my direction. He looked just as surprised to see me as I was to see him.

Fran hopped to her feet and crossed the room. "Melanie," she said. "This is my son, Phil." She took her son's arm and gave it a squeeze. "Phil, this is my friend, Melanie. We were just talking about you, dear."

Her son, Phil?

And suddenly there it was. The last piece of the puzzle slipped effortlessly into place. This was the man whom Nick had complained to Claire about—the one who'd followed him around and who hadn't liked his mother's dog. He was also the same man who had felt the need to secure his belongings behind a thick metal lock.

I could see why, I thought. Fran's son definitely looked like he had something to hide.

Previously, when envisioning what the shed might contain, I'd pictured someone's small, personal stash. Now I was forced to realign my thinking. No wonder James had believed that his get-rich-quick scheme was such a great opportunity. I was willing to bet that his good buddy, Phil, had already shown him how someone could make good money cultivating the lucrative cash crop.

All at once I felt vulnerable, sitting below them in my seat. As I rose to my feet, I said to Fran, "Phil and I have already met."

"You have?" she asked. "What a nice surprise." She gazed up at her son. "Melanie was just telling me she thought she and I should have a look inside the old shed."

"Really?" Phil's tone was flat. His expression gave nothing away. "Why would you want to do that?"

"In case what's there had something to do with why Barney got sick."

Hearing his name, the Basset lifted his head and opened his eyes. He peered at Fran, thumped his tail on the floor twice, then heaved a sigh and went back to sleep.

"Dog looks fine to me now," Phil said with a shrug. "I can't imagine how my old stuff could have had anything to do with his problems."

"I'm sure you must be right," I said quickly.

Earlier I had been hoping that Fran would put two and two together. Now I prayed with greater fervor that her son would not. Everything I hadn't understood before suddenly seemed much clearer. And before Phil figured out how much I knew, I wanted to be back in my car and on my way to Detective O'Malley. It was definitely time for me to take my leave.

When I started for the door, however, Phil casually edged his body sideways. Now he was blocking the exit. The hair on the back of my neck began to tingle. So much for hoping for an easy escape.

"There's nothing out there but some old dorm furniture," Phil said. "Boxes of books, maybe some tools. I'd be happy to give you a look if you like."

"That won't be necessary," I told him. "I really should be heading home."

"I insist." Phil smiled crookedly. "I'd hate for you to think that I have anything to hide."

"Thanks for offering," I told him. "But I'm afraid I don't have time."

I strode toward the door. Fran moved out of the way. Phil did not. Instead he reached out and grabbed my upper arm, pulling me to an abrupt stop.

"Don't worry," he said. "This won't take long."

Fran frowned at her son. "Phil, what's gotten into you? If Melanie needs to leave, she can see that old shed some other time."

"Of course, you're right, Mama." Phil's fingers uncurled slowly. Even as his hand fell away, I could still feel the imprint of its rigid grasp. "It's just that I was hoping to have the chance to talk to Melanie alone."

"About what?" Fran asked, perplexed.

"Her son Davey."

As he said the name, Phil smiled again. There was no humor in his expression, however. Instead, I saw the self-satisfied smile of a cat toying with a mouse.

"What about Davey?" I asked.

"He spends quite a bit of time with a friend of mine, and I'm not sure that's a safe environment for him. It would be terrible if something bad happened to him, don't you think?"

I heard the menace in Phil's tone. I saw the malice in his eyes. A vein in the side of my head began to throb. Suddenly I couldn't seem to breathe.

Standing to one side, Fran was happily oblivious to the undercurrents swirling around us. She beamed at Phil and said, "That's my boy, always looking out for other people." Then she settled her hand between my shoulder blades and gave me a gentle nudge. "Go ahead. If it's about your son, you should probably hear what Phil has to say."

Before I could protest, Phil quickly herded me across the kitchen and out the back door. Once outside, he grabbed my arm again. Secured firmly within his fisted hand, I found myself being marched in the direction of the shed.

"You wanted to see," he snarled. "Let's go see."

I didn't bother to answer. There didn't appear to be any point. Phil had enough to say for both of us.

"I want to know what Nick told you," he demanded. "And what James told your boyfriend."

"Boyfriend?" I stumbled and my shoulder wrenched. I was hauled painfully upright again. "What boyfriend?"

"Bob," Phil snarled. "The neighbor."

Oh.

"Bob's my ex-husband," I said through gritted teeth. "And he doesn't know anything. If he did, I'd still be married to him."

"Well, somebody's been talking to somebody, because

here you are, itching to go snooping around in my business. Bob said you were good at solving mysteries. I thought he was kidding, but I guess not."

"I don't know what you're talking about," I said.

Phil didn't waste time arguing. Instead he gave my arm another yank. "You were friends with the dog trainer. And that stupid hound told him everything. I should have shot the dog, too, when I had the chance."

I gasped out loud, horrified by his callous tone. Phil didn't even notice. He was too busy steering me across the yard.

Seconds later, we arrived at the shed. Its door was in a side wall, visible from the house but angled away. As Phil fumbled in his pocket for the key to the padlock, I looked around, measuring the distance of open lawn I'd have to cross before reaching the cover of the woods.

If Phil gave me any chance to run for it, I was going to be gone.

"Don't even think it," he said sharply. "I've got a gun, remember?"

Hard to forget, under the circumstances. But if Phil had the gun on him now, it had to be a very small one. He was attired much the same way I was: jeans, T-shirt, sneakers. There didn't seem to be any place on his person that he could be concealing a weapon.

As things turned out, it didn't matter. Phil never released me, even for a second. He unlocked the door one-handed, then shoved it open with his shoulder. Pushing me inside the shed, he slammed the door shut behind us.

Immediately my sense of smell was overwhelmed by a sweet, earthy aroma. It took a few moments for my eyes to adjust to the lack of light within but even before they did, I already knew what I would see. The shed contained pot, lots and lots of it.

A dozen airtight containers were stacked in the back half of the small building. Smaller packages, wrapped in plastic, were piled haphazardly on top of them. Several had spilled over the side and landed on the ground. Phil didn't appear to be the most careful custodian. No wonder Barney had been able to help himself.

Simply inhaling in the small, enclosed, space was a heady experience. As I'd suspected, this was no user's secret stash of weed. These were the hidden assets of a booming business. On the street, this much marijuana had to be worth thousands of dollars.

The rest of the shed was filled with a haphazard pile of junk. I saw cardboard boxes, a broken lawn mower, and a dented garbage can. Pushed against one wall was a threadbare upholstered chair. A small rickety table sat beside it. The tabletop held only two items: an ashtray and a roach clip.

"See?" Phil said with a snicker, following the direction of my gaze. "What did I tell you? Dorm furniture." He shoved me that way. "Have a seat. I need time to think."

Given no choice in the matter, I did as I was told. I tried to perch on the edge of the shabby seat but the chair's springs were shot. Its cushion was flat, stuffing half- disintegrated by years of use. No matter which way I shifted my weight, I felt as though I was being sucked downward into the seat's upholstered depths.

Nobody could make a quick getaway out of that chair. Which was probably just what Phil had intended.

"You can't keep me here," I said, struggling to sit upright. False bravado wasn't much, but I figured it was better than nothing.

"Nice try." Phil laughed. He leaned back against the door. "Lady, I can do whatever I want. I just have to take a few minutes and figure out what that is. Just like that dog trainer, you already know too much."

"What did Nick do to you?" I asked. "Why were you so threatened by him?"

Phil straightened and strode to the opposite corner. He knelt down on the shed's dirt floor and began to rummage through a jumbled assortment of clutter. It was too dark for me to see what he was looking for, but when he stood up again, he was holding a metal toolbox.

"It was Barney," he said. "That was the problem."

"What problem?"

"He and that dog trainer were like long lost brothers. The damn dog told him everything."

"Barney talks?" I said. Hopefully he'd realize how silly that sounded.

No such luck. Phil, busy pawing through the open tool chest, took my question at face value. Without glancing up, he said, "He did to that guy. That was Nick's whole shtick. He was like one of those animal communicator people. He understood what dogs were saying. And they told him stuff. All kinds of stuff. Even things that were none of his business."

I thought of Fran's lavish praise of Nick's empathetic skills and sighed. "Did Fran tell you that?"

"Yeah, at first. But then I saw it for myself too. And right away I knew I had a problem."

"How come?"

"Because Barney's a hound, all right? Nick told my mother that they're called scent hounds because of their noses. Do you know what scent hounds are trained to do?"

I did, but I shook my head anyway.

"They sniff things out of hidden places. Like at airports."

"They detect bombs," I said.

"And drugs," Phil added flatly. "None of which ever mattered before. I mean, Barney's a dog, who's he gonna tell? I thought that was pretty funny until Nick came along. Then all of a sudden the joke was on me and it began to seem pretty damn serious."

"So you killed him because you thought he knew your secret," I said.

Phil set down the toolbox and turned around. He had a coil of rope in one hand and a roll of duct tape in the other. Even though it was warm inside the shed, I felt myself start to shiver.

"I killed him because I had to protect what was mine," Phil said emphatically. "Nick thought he was so smart, talking to animals and finding out people's secrets. Well, who looks smart now? Because I'm still here, and I'm still in charge. And thanks to me that dog trainer won't ever be talking to anybody again."

Chapter 25

The words themselves were chilling enough. But their effect was heightened by Phil's triumphant tone. He wasn't even sorry about what he'd done.

There was still one more thing I wanted to know. "What about Thor?" I asked. "How did you get past him?"

"Who?"

"Nick's Rottweiler. When you were at Nick's house that night, how come he didn't come after you?"

"Because that dog trainer was a fool," Phil said with a smirk. "That's why. He made the big dog lie down and be quiet when I got there. Nick told him that I was a friend. And by the time he knew differently, it was too late."

I swallowed heavily. If anything, Phil's explanation had made me feel worse. When he started toward me, I sank back into the chair's depths. "You don't want to do this," I told him.

Phil just laughed. "Says who? You? You don't have a clue what I want or don't want. Not that it matters now. I don't have a choice anymore."

"Of course you do," I said quickly. "There are always choices."

"Like what?"

"You could let me walk out of here. Things will go better for you if you do."

Phil shook his head. "Sorry. That's not going to happen."

"Think about it. Isn't your mother going to wonder what happened if I don't come back? If I just disappear?"

I probably shouldn't have encouraged him to give the matter some thought. Because now Phil appeared to do exactly that.

"After I'm done here, I'll go move your car down the road somewhere," he said after a minute. "My mother won't even notice. I'll tell her you left in a hurry because you were worried about Davey."

After I'm done here. I didn't even want to think about what that might entail.

"She won't believe you," I said.

"Sure she will. She believes everything I tell her. You'll wait here until it gets dark," Phil informed me. "And then I'll move you too."

Not if I could help it, I thought.

He stopped in front of the chair. "Stand up."

"Why?"

"Because I said so." Phil leaned down, grabbed my arm, and pulled me to my feet. "Give me your phone."

"I don't have it with me."

Phil shook his head. He looked annoyed. "You want me to go looking for it?"

I reached around and slipped the phone out of a back pocket. The damn thing was always ringing when I didn't want to be disturbed. Now when I desperately needed a connection to the outside world, not even a peep. Reluctantly I handed it over.

"Now your car keys." Phil beckoned with his fingers.

I dug them out of another pocket and dropped them into his palm.

"Where's your purse?"

"In my car."

"You really don't want to mess with me," Phil warned.

Or what? I wondered. How could things possibly be any worse?

"Go look for yourself," I told him. "I didn't need it for anything so I left it in the car. I *thought* this was a safe neighborhood."

"Your mistake." He chuckled under his breath. It wasn't a pretty sound. "Hold out your hands."

"What are you going to do?"

Phil uncoiled the rope. "What do you think?"

As long as we were talking, I still had a chance. Once Phil tied me up, I'd be completely under his control. I'd lose all possibility of escape. I couldn't allow that to happen.

I tried to back up but the chair was right behind me. To my right was a stack of plastic containers. Left, toward the door, was where Phil stood. Wildly I looked around for a weapon.

I wanted something big and heavy. Something that would make me look formidable, fierce. And everywhere I looked I saw . . . nothing. I was surrounded by junk and none of it was even remotely useful.

As my gaze swung back toward Phil, it skimmed past the roach clip. Then stopped and returned. If I couldn't find big and heavy, something small and sharp would have to do. I reached down and snatched it up.

"What are you going to do with that thing?" Phil asked incredulously. "Poke me?"

"If I have to."

"Yeah, I'm scared now."

He dropped the coil of rope to the floor at his feet. Then Phil looked up and took a step forward. His hand lifted and curled into a fist. I tried to duck to one side but I wasn't nearly fast enough.

His fist flew toward me and connected with my jaw. My head snapped back. Pain exploded in a burst of light behind my eyes. It was white hot and all encompassing.

I fell backward into oblivion.

* * *

When I came to, I was half-sitting, half-lying, on the shed's dirt floor. My back was propped against the wall and my hands, bound tightly together, rested in my lap. A length of rope connected them to my feet, which extended out in front of me and were tied as well. A wide strip of duct tape covered my mouth.

That realization immediately caused my muscles to clench in panic. All at once I felt as though I couldn't breathe. Eyes wide and terrified, I inhaled sharply through my nose.

Even that sudden burst of oxygen wasn't reassurance enough. On the edge of panic I began to struggle against the ropes. They tore at my skin but the knots that held the bonds in place didn't budge. Rope burns formed quickly and that fresh throbbing finally halted my fruitless, frantic, endeavors. It brought me to my senses and made me stop and think.

But when I leaned my head back against the wall to consider my next move, a spasm of pain radiated up the side of my jaw. Reflex made me twist my head and jerk away. Helpless, unable to cradle the area with my hand, I could do nothing but clench my teeth and endure.

My eyes began to water. Then my nose started to run. I shook my head to try and clear it. That was a huge mistake. My agonized gasp was swallowed by the tape that pulled at my lips. Once again I felt skin begin to tear.

Stop it! I told myself angrily. *Stop and breathe and calm down. You have to do better than this.*

Once again—this time gingerly—I leaned back and let the wall support my weight. I needed a good idea. I needed a plan of escape. Phil had said that he'd be back for me after dark. Through the narrow slits of space between the shed's warped boards, I could still see light outside. Hopefully that meant I had time to maneuver.

First I had to get free. I looked around, scanning the

shed's interior. All I needed was a sharp edge, something keen enough to fray the thick rope so that I could pull the knots apart.

The tool chest was shoved back into the far corner, and I could see that its lid was tightly latched. Earlier, Phil had found a length of rope and a roll of duct tape inside the box. I wondered what other kind of resources it might contain.

Pushing myself away from the wall I began to move, inchworm-style, across the ground. Progress was slow and painful. Twice I unbalanced and tipped sideways, my head and shoulder smacking down hard onto the earthen floor. Each time, I lost precious minutes struggling to right myself again.

Halfway there I paused, breathing heavily from the exertion. My chest felt tight. Blood pounded in my ears. I lifted my head and shoulders and stretched them back, aching for relief.

The movement lifted my gaze. Was it my imagination, I wondered, or was the light outside growing dimmer? Could the sun already be dropping in the sky? I had no idea how much time I might have lost while unconscious.

Sam was probably already looking for me, I realized. But there'd be no way for him to track me here. No doubt he'd try my cell phone first. He would be annoyed, but not alarmed when I didn't pick up. No one was going to come riding to my rescue. And I had only myself to blame.

I sighed and started across the floor once again. My progress was still slow, but it was steady. Goal in sight and coming closer, I stopped thinking and just kept moving.

Ten long minutes later, I reached the toolbox. I twisted around, angling my body sideways so that my hands could reach the latch. My fingers fumbled briefly then popped the clasp open. The box's lid lifted, then fell backward, revealing a cluttered upper tray. A Phillips head screwdriver, a pair of pliers, a small hammer, and an assortment of loose nails and screws were crammed in beside the roll of duct tape.

Nothing useful there.

Bracing both hands together, I slid my fingers under the handle, lifted the tray, and slid it sideways. My aim was awkward and off-kilter. The tray caught on the edge of the metal box and began to tip. Unable to move quickly, I couldn't right it in time. Instead I could only watch as the tools slid off the lowered side and clattered into the dirt. The damage was already done, so I let the tray slip from my fingers too. It landed on top of the discarded gear.

Turning back to the tool chest, I had another look inside. In the semi-darkness, it took me a moment to realize what I was seeing. Then my eyes opened wide. My nose pinched inward as I sucked in a startled breath.

Gun.

Tucked away in the bottom of the box, the weapon was half-covered by an oily rag. Its barrel jutted out of one side. The butt of the handle was visible on the other. Just looking at it, I felt a frisson of fear snake its way down my spine.

I've got a gun, Phil had told me earlier. And here it was.

Let's be clear about something. Everything I know about guns I learned from watching crime dramas on TV. Which is to say that I'm the last person in the world that should be ever handling one. I wanted no part of that thing.

Even so, I couldn't help but stare. I was half-fascinated, half-afraid. The rational part of my brain knew that the gun couldn't move—much less shoot—without human intervention, but it still seemed unwise to take my eyes off it. As if I thought there was a chance that the weapon might leap up of its own accord and fire.

It was a silly reaction on my part; I knew that even then. And it made me wonder if that punch to the jaw had addled my brain more than I'd realized. Annoyed by the possibility, I wrenched my gaze away and had a look at the rest of the container's contents.

It was then, finally, that my luck began to change.

Nestled in beside a vise grip, a tape measure, and another hammer, was a box cutter. A ray of hope lent new energy to my movements as I reached inside the metal chest and pulled the tool out. The implement's blade was retracted into its handle. Fingers scrambling, I found the catch and released it. There was a soft snick and a razor-sharp edge appeared.

After several false starts, I figured out how to angle the blade so that I could maneuver it back and forth for maximum effect. The knife edge sliced through the rope with swift, clean, efficiency. As soon as the first coil binding my wrists split and fell away, I was able to start wriggling one hand loose. With the first one free, the other soon followed.

Immediately I reached up and I peeled away one corner of the duct tape. Bracing myself, I gave the strip a sharp yank. A searing wash of pain brought fresh tears to my eyes as the tape tore free. The discomfort was well worth it, however, when I was finally able to open my mouth wide and draw in a deep, restorative, gulp of oxygen.

After that I made short work of the shackles around my ankles. Within minutes I was able to kick the ropes away. My legs ached as I straightened them and stood up, but it felt wonderful to be on my feet again—almost as if I was once more in control of my own destiny.

Carefully I retracted the blade and tucked the box cutter into my pocket. If the need for a weapon arose again, I had no intention of being caught empty-handed a second time. Then that decision led to another realization: I needed to do something with the gun.

Even unarmed, Phil was bigger and stronger than I was.

And if he had the weapon in his hand, I'd have no means of defense at all. I had to make sure that he couldn't find it quickly.

Once again, I surveyed my surroundings. My gaze went to the shabby upholstered chair with its ragged cushion. I strode over and lifted the seat pillow, looking for a seam in the back. Better yet, there was a zipper. When I slid it open, bits of decayed and crumbled foam rubber came tumbling out. Perfect.

Using just the tips of my forefinger and thumb, I pinched the rag around the gun. Then I lifted it out of the toolbox, carried it across the shed, and dropped it inside the cushion. With a smooth whir, the zipper closed the opening. Carefully I maneuvered the big pillow back down into place. When I was finished, the chair looked as though it had never been disturbed.

Quickly I gathered up the remaining tools and packed them back in the box. Then I shoved the chest itself back in the dark corner. One problem solved. Now I just had to figure out how to get myself out of the shed without being seen.

A discreet rattle of the shed's door confirmed what I'd already suspected: the padlock was back in place. I was locked in.

Considering the shed's state of disrepair, I could probably kick loose a couple of boards, then pry them apart to create an opening. But that seemed like entirely too noisy a proposition. I had no idea where Phil might be, and the last thing I wanted to do was alert him to the fact that I was not only awake, I was also untied.

Time was passing much too quickly. The sun was dropping lower in the sky. Pressing my eye to a narrow opening between boards, I saw that dusk's long shadows were beginning to fall across the yard. The oncoming darkness would help hide my escape, but it also meant that Phil might return at any time. My window of opportunity was starting to close.

I looked around the shed once more, hoping for inspiration. I felt like I was overlooking something important, something that should have been obvious. I stared at the containers piled in the rear of the shed and frowned thoughtfully. Then all at once, it hit me. I knew what I'd been missing.

I'd forgotten about Barney, the dog who would eat anything. Two days earlier before we'd taken him to the vet, Barney had been digging around the shed. Basset Hounds are expert and enthusiastic tunnelers. If Barney had created an entry to get himself into the shed, then there was a way for me to get out. All I had to do was find it.

I strode over to the stacks of containers and began shoving them aside to reveal the base of the wall. At first I saw nothing. The packed earth floor I exposed looked as though it hadn't been disturbed in years. I moved a second stack, and then a third. Aching, sweating profusely, I was beginning to question the wisdom of my idea when I lifted a container to set it aside, and finally found what I was looking for.

Loose dirt scattered across the floor drew my eyes to a Basset Hound sized hole that was just visible beneath the lower edge of the wall. Quickly I stooped down for a closer look. Bending low over the opening, I dipped my head into the opening and twisted around to look out. I could see the tops of trees and the darkening sky above them.

I could see freedom.

Luckily for me, Barney was a chunky dog. The tunnel he'd created for his own use was already pretty sizeable. Nevertheless, I dug at the crumbling edges and clawed at the loose dirt with my fingers to enlarge the hole's rounded perimeter.

Within minutes, I had a space that looked like it might be big enough for me to fit through. I spun around, lay on my back, and shoved myself down into the opening head-first. Pushing with my feet, pulling with my hands, I inched beneath the wooden boards.

Dirt tangled in my hair. A jagged rock tore at my shirt. My shoulders were too wide; they caught at the base of the hole. With a sharp jerk, I twisted them free and kept going. Back aching, feet scrambling on the loose debris, I shimmied and swiveled and maneuvered my way through the narrow tunnel.

Head tipped upward, all I could see was sky. That was more than enough to keep me moving.

By the time my hips reached the bottom of the passage, my arms and shoulders had cleared its upper edge on the outside. I leaned back and braced my elbows on the ground behind me, then gritted my teeth and pulled hard. With one last painful wrench, I dragged my legs through the opening. Their final release sent me sprawling backward.

Breathing heavily, covered in dirt, I collapsed in a heap on the grass. I'd gained my freedom but I felt utterly drained by my efforts. And I wasn't in the clear yet. Not by a long shot.

Lying on the ground, partially hidden by the shed, I hoped I wasn't visible from the back of the house. But I couldn't afford to relax. I needed to gather my strength quickly. I had to be gone before Phil discovered that I was missing. And without knowing where he was, any direction I chose to run was going to be a calculated gamble.

With a quick look around, I opted for the route that offered the shortest distance from the shed to the sheltering woods at the perimeter of the yard. The span of open lawn I would have to cross was about twenty feet. I could sprint that far in a matter of seconds. Once I reached the woods, it wouldn't be hard to hike to a neighboring house or out to the road. If I could just get to that dense band of trees, I'd have a chance—as long as Phil didn't see me and come racing in pursuit.

It was now or never, I thought. I didn't feel ready, but it didn't matter. I still had to go. It was time to take my chances.

Slowly I levered myself up. Crouching, I hugged the side of the shed, hoping that its dark shadows would swallow me. Once I was out in the open, I would need to be moving fast. I was gathering my resources, getting ready to make a run for it, when the back door to the house flew open. It banged against the wall and as Phil came racing out.

"Hey!" he shouted.

That was all the impetus I needed. A burst of adrenaline shot through me. I pushed away from the shed and began to run. Knees pumping, feet pounding, I sucked air into my lungs and dashed across the lawn.

I could hear Phil coming, somewhere behind me. The shed was positioned toward the back of the yard. That gave me a good head start. Even so, I knew Phil had to be gaining on me. I didn't dare look around to find out.

Then all at once, over the pounding in my ears, I heard another sound. It was the elated, full-bodied howl of a hound on the hunt. Barney burst out of the house through the open door.

Now I did glance back and what I saw caused my heart to leap. The Basset must have thought that he and Phil were playing a game, because Barney was racing after his quarry as fast as his short, stubby, legs could carry him. Phil, meanwhile, was totally oblivious to his pursuer. Intent on catching me, he wasn't even looking at the dog.

So when Barney cut across the yard to catch up, then launched himself into the air, Phil never knew what hit him.

The Basset's bulk knocked Phil's legs right out from

under him. His arms flailed briefly as he lost his balance and stumbled forward. I watched as he tried, then failed, to right himself.

Barney's howl turned into a yelp of surprise as Phil somersaulted down on top of him. Momentum sent the two of them rolling end-over-end together. I hoped that Barney wasn't hurt but I didn't stop to find out.

Instead I just kept running. Moments later I reached the trees and disappeared into their embrace. It was a relief to be enveloped by the cool, sheltering, darkness.

Chapter 26

Four-acre zoning, I thought. Back country Greenwich was known for its beautiful estates and its spacious, private lots.

Ridiculous, the things that go through your mind when fear and exhaustion have wiped everything else clean and all you can think about is continuing to put one foot in front of the other. That, and not stopping for anything. Hands held up and out in front of me, eyes straining to see in the darkness, I scrambled through the underbrush and dodged between the trees.

Right, left. Right, left.

Concentrating on the steady rhythm kept me going me through the wide band of forest that separated Fran's house from the neighboring property. One minute I was surrounded by thick foliage, looking downward as I ran, and trying desperately not to step in a hole or trip over a fallen branch. And in the next I had quite suddenly broken through the verge of the arboreal boundary and stumbled onto another manicured lawn.

A house, big and brick, with wide front steps and massive white columns rose up before me like a mirage in the desert, glittering with the promise of salvation. Amber lights glowed softly on either side of the front door. Spotlights, situated up below the eaves, illuminated the approach.

Almost safe, I thought. I exhaled an unsteady breath and refused to even consider the fact that someone might not be home. I had seen Phil go down, but he could have gotten up again. Even now, he might still be following me. I couldn't afford to let my guard down yet.

Holding my side, gasping for air to fill my burning lungs, I navigated the wide expanse of lawn and staggered up the steps. I didn't mean to lean against the doorbell, but it happened anyway. Even so, several minutes passed—and my fleeting sense of relief began to edge once more toward alarm—before someone opened the door.

By the time that happened I was sitting down. Actually I had crumpled into an exhausted heap on the ornate doormat. So I had to turn and look way up to see the face of my would-be rescuer.

He was a man in his sixties, with a fringe of white hair and a thick pair of reading glasses. A gnarled hand, dropped to his side, was holding a book. One look at the startled expression on his face reminded of what a bedraggled mess I was. I was muddy and bruised. My clothing was ripped, my hair snarled. No wonder his first reaction was to take a step back.

I braced my hands on the prickly mat and pushed myself wearily to my feet. "Please," I said. "Could you call the police? Ask for Detective O'Malley. Tell him it's an emergency."

"I should hope so," the man replied. He was frowning. "Wait there."

As if I had a choice. The door snicked shut in my face. Another several minutes passed.

I hoped the man was doing as I'd asked. If not, I would have no choice but to keep going until I came to someone who might be willing to help. At that depressing thought, my legs simply gave out. I sat down on the mat again and concentrated on conserving what little strength I had left.

Then the door reopened. The man was back. Now he was holding a telephone.

"The police are on their way," he said. "Do you require an ambulance?"

I shook my head.

The poor man stared down at me, looking utterly perplexed by this unexpected event that had intruded upon his orderly life. He hadn't the slightest idea what to do with me. I could hardly blame him for that.

"A drink of water perhaps?" he offered.

"That would be great," I said.

He turned around and disappeared again. This time he left the door to the house open. Maybe he'd decided to trust me. Either that, or he'd realized that in my exhausted state I was in no condition to pose a threat.

The first squad car arrived ten minutes later. By that time, Mr. Fowler and I had introduced ourselves and I had drunk two tall glasses of cold water. Then I'd used Mr. Fowler's phone to make a quick call to Sam to outline my situation. I had even begun to feel somewhat restored.

That was a good thing because when Detective O'Malley—who came up the driveway right behind the squad car—heard what I had to say, he was not happy. I had hoped the bruise on my jaw might earn me a more sympathetic reception, but apparently not. Nevertheless, O'Malley listened to everything I told him and followed up by asking all the right questions.

"And you can connect this guy not just to Nick Walden, but to his murder?" he said.

"Phil still has the gun," I told him. "And I hid it before I left. If he doesn't know where it is, he can't get rid of it."

That revelation led to an immediate flurry of activity. The two officers already on hand were quickly dispatched to Fran's house. Then O'Malley placed a call to the station and requested backup.

"Stay available," the detective told me before heading next door himself. "We may have more questions."

"I will," I promised.

As O'Malley left, another pair of headlights, vehicle moving faster than was strictly prudent, came flying up the driveway. When it drew near, I recognized my husband's SUV and saw Sam behind the wheel.

He hopped out, came over, and put his arms around me. Supported by my husband's strength, I felt the tension and anxiety of the last several hours finally begin to ebb away. Wearily I relaxed into Sam's embrace.

Together he and I thanked Mr. Fowler profusely for his help. Then, moving slowly and carefully, Sam helped me to the car and fastened me securely into my seat. I meant to close my eyes for only a minute but the next time I opened them, I was already right where I wanted to be.

Home.

Once the police had Phil's gun in their possession, anything further I might have told them became superfluous. Which was totally fine by me. I spent the next several weeks reading updates about the case in the newspaper and online like everybody else. I also went over all the new developments with Aunt Peg, who was seriously miffed to have missed out on all the action.

According to Peg's always impeccable sources, once Phil was in custody he began to sing like the proverbial canary. Looking to make a deal any way he could, Phil was revealing everything he knew about anyone he'd ever done business with. The information he supplied would be enough to keep Fairfield County police departments busy for a very long time.

Fortunately for Bob's neighbor James, his involvement in Phil's marijuana enterprise had still been in the planning stages. Nevertheless, a For Sale sign appeared in the Fines' front yard shortly after Phil was indicted on a wide range of charges. Apparently James and Amber had come to the correct conclusion that nobody in that family neighborhood would ever again regard them with the same degree of goodwill that they'd previously enjoyed. They packed up their belongings and moved out, opting to make a fresh start somewhere else.

With a little prodding from me and Bob, Claire put aside her ambivalence about meeting with her sister, and she and Anabelle got together for a family reunion a few weeks later. Claire said that the high point of the meeting was having the opportunity to make the acquaintance of her eight-year-old nephew, Alexander. She and Anabelle are in contact regularly now and I heard from Bob that Claire will be planning Alexander's next birthday party.

Speaking of Bob, when I asked him which part of his house he intended to tear down and rebuild next, I received an unexpected answer. Bob told me that he intended to leave that decision up to Claire since he's planning to propose just as soon as he gets up his nerve.

Having blurted out that information without thinking, my ex-husband's next move was to swiftly swear me to secrecy. I told him he didn't have to worry, I'm good with other people's secrets. Still, the suspense of waiting for him to do the deed is killing me.

I'm really hoping that Claire says yes. I'd love to be able to welcome her to the family and I know she'll fit right in. No doubt the adjustment will be tougher for Thor and Jojo, not to mention Bosco the Siamese. That cat will throw a hissy fit when he finds out that he's going to be adding two dogs to his domain.

But I'm not going to worry about that now. One way or another, the whole crew will manage to blend itself together. If there's one thing I've learned, it's that the best things in life never come easy. But the effort is always well worth it in the end.